Hoodie

A LOVE STORY. IN BLACK AND WHITE.

S. WALDEN

Penny Press

Hoodie

Copyright © 2012, S. Walden

Penny Press Publishing

This work and all rights of the author S. Walden to this work are protected under U.S. copyright law, Title 17 of the United States Code. All rights reserved. No part of this publication may be reproduced, stored in a retrieval system, copied in any form or by any means electronic or mechanical, photocopied, recorded or otherwise transmitted without written permission from the publisher. This book is licensed for your personal enjoyment only. Thank you for respecting the hard work of the author.

ISBN-13: 978-1481005203
ISBN-10: 1481005200

CreateSpace paperback printing November 2012

Cover art by Alfred Porter
alfredporter@gmail.com

This is a work of fiction. Any similarities to real persons, places, or events are entirely coincidental.

To Marsha—who openly wept for my characters in public, the only validation I really wanted. Your support and love for my book are the reasons for its publication.

CHAPTER 1
WEDNESDAY, APRIL 15

Emma observed her partner from the opposite side of the classroom. He slouched in his seat, long legs spread on either side of the desk in front of him, arms folded over his chest defensively. He looked like he had an attitude, and she wondered if she should speak to him at all.

She was already annoyed. Apparently he cared very little about the project, and while she felt her irritation growing exponentially, she decided against voicing it. After all, she didn't want to be responsible for an uncomfortable, rocky start to their working relationship. So she forced a smile, walked over to him, and took a seat in the empty desk in front of his only after he moved his leg aside for her. She tried her best to appear friendly, but her body language betrayed her. He noticed her rigid posture, how she sat stiff and straight with her legs crossed tightly. She was uncomfortable near him, he realized, and it pissed him off.

"I'm Emma," she said working hard to maintain the smile painfully plastered on her face.

"I know who you are," Anton replied. He studied

her. There seemed to be an air of haughtiness about her—an attitude of superiority—though perhaps he was imagining it.

Emma didn't know how to respond. Anton said nothing as he reached in his book bag for his cell phone.

"What's yo' number?" he asked indifferently.

"Here," she said, handing him a small piece of paper with her full name, address, home and cell phone numbers, and the best times to reach her written in a neat, slanted cursive.

Anton laughed. "You that student," he observed, shaking his head as he glanced over her information. "But I knew that already. Got it all together. Always on point. Axin' all kinda questions in class all the time. Makin' comments. Tryin' to impress us with yo' literary insights."

"Excuse me?" she replied. The smile vanished.

"Literary insights," he repeated. "Oh, I see. You thought I wouldn't know words like 'literary' and 'insights' 'cause I'm black."

Emma stared at him, mouth slightly agape, only closing it when he indelicately informed her that it was hanging open.

He moved his eyes over her then, taking in the long auburn curls that framed her face, her light blue eyes with just the right amount of eye liner and mascara, soft peachy cheeks and glossy lips, her shirt that hugged her breasts perfectly. She was meticulously manicured, he thought, like an airbrushed picture on the front of a magazine. No, more like a porcelain statue than a real person, he decided. He was afraid if he touched her she would shatter.

He opened the notebook on his desk and scrawled his information. He ripped out the sheet and held it out to her watching her face. She looked put out, and he liked it. She snatched the paper from his hand, and he watched as she read to herself: *Anton Jamal Robinson. The Projects. Cell: 919-555-4621. Call for availability*. She looked up at him and saw a slight grin on his face. She stuffed the paper in her binder and left the room before the bell rang.

She couldn't concentrate in Sociology. She couldn't concentrate on anything since English class. She could think of nothing all day but the assignment and her partner whom she already disliked—a partner whom appeared to dislike her. She was confused and angry. What had she done to deserve such a reception from him? He was rude without cause, and she bristled at the idea of spending six weeks working with him. She wondered why her teacher paired them together. She could hear his voice booming in the tiny classroom, and scowled.

"Sit down and shut up!" Dr. Thompson bellowed from behind his desk, pushing his crooked glasses farther up his nose.

A low grumble throughout the room replaced the rowdiness as students reluctantly shuffled to their seats. Dr. Thompson waited for absolute silence before continuing.

"Okay. So you've gotten your acceptance letters," he said. "Well, probably most of you. And good for you. We're all very impressed that you'll be taking the next step in your academic careers by going to college." His tone dripped with sarcasm.

"You're comfortable and happy and could care less about the next six weeks of your lives here at school," he continued. "So where does that leave me as your educator?"

He scanned the room of half-interested to completely indifferent faces and rolled his eyes.

"That leaves me in the unfortunate position of having to teach a bunch of self-absorbed students who don't give a shit when I'd rather be playing golf."

Some students perked up at that.

"Dr. Thompson, are you allowed to talk to us like that?" came a girl's voice from the middle of the room. She often asked this question because Dr. Thompson often talked to them like that, but he never answered her once the entire school year. He did, however, have to answer to the principal on a few occasions when her parents complained about his lack of professionalism.

"So after extensive arguing with the other English teachers and most of the administration at this school, I finally succeeded in getting approval for my end-of-year project for this class."

There was an audible groan throughout the room, and Dr. Thompson patiently awaited silence once more.

"You won't have a final," he said, and the groans immediately turned to cheers. "What you will have is a term paper due to me on the day the final is scheduled," and the cheers died away.

"The term paper will count for sixty percent of your grade. So if you do a lousy job, chances are you'll receive a failing grade on the paper and flunk the class. If you don't pass my class, you won't graduate. So bye-bye carefree summer and hello summer school.

"You will work with a partner to explore each of your cultural backgrounds using what you've learned to analyze our most recent book. Think about it like this: How would you interpret the plot, characters, and themes in our novel based on your culture?" he asked.

Most students stared blankly. A few scribbled notes furiously, Emma being one of them.

"Dr. Thompson, man, this sound like some college-level crap," offered a student from the back of the classroom.

"Well, lucky for you, Mr. Robinson, and take that hood off your head, I have my Ph.D., so I'm more than qualified to teach you on the college level."

A few students laughed.

"People," Dr. Thompson continued, "you act like this is the first time you've ever studied a novel. You've been doing it all year."

"Yeah, but not like this. What does our culture have to do with this book?" whined a student from the front of the room.

And then the questions and comments poured forth as though a dam suddenly broke.

"I don't even know what a culture is."

"Why you havin' us do this? Can't we just take a test?"

"We've gotta work on a paper this big with someone we don't know?"

"That's not right, Dr. Thompson. What if the other person does nothing?"

Dr. Thompson listened patiently to the comments and concerns, running a hand through his graying hair.

"Dr. Thompson, why was it a big deal getting this assignment approved?"

He decided to address the last question.

"Because most of the teachers and staff at this school think you're too immature to handle such an assignment. They don't think you can deal with hanging around a person who's totally different from you and then write a paper together on top of that."

He paused for a moment as though considering something. "They think it's too hard," he admitted and heard a murmur of agreement throughout the classroom. "I look at it as a learning experience, a chance for you to try and break free from the high school mold."

"What's the high school mold?" asked a tall boy in the back row.

"I'll strive for elegance here, Mr. Andrews. Cliques. Cliques that create within young people minds so narrow that they haven't the ability to look beyond themselves to the world around them. They hide within the safety of their own kind, afraid to venture out and attempt to understand something new. Does that answer your question?"

"See, Dr. Thompson, I take great offense to that. Just 'cause we hang with our own kind don't make us narrow-minded. It's in our nature to wanna be with people like us."

It was the boy Dr. Thompson called Mr. Robinson who spoke. He received several nods of approval and grunts of appreciation.

"Then perhaps it's time to call into question your nature, Mr. Robinson," Dr. Thompson replied.

Many of the students turned to look at the boy called Mr. Robinson in anticipation of his reply. But he had none, so Dr. Thompson continued.

"I'm giving you a handout that explains this assignment in detail. Read it over to yourselves. You're seniors. You can do that."

He walked across the front of the room handing stacks of papers to the students in front of the rows to pass back.

"Now listen carefully for the name of your partner," he said. "I'm giving you class time today to meet and exchange contact information. Talk over the assignment together as well. Don't come to me. Try to get a sense of what's being asked of you on your own. Again, you're seniors. You can do that."

"But what if there's something we really don't understand?" Emma asked.

"You can ask me all the questions you want tomorrow, Ms. Chapman. We'll have a discussion day for the assignment then."

The announcement of partners was more tedious and time consuming than Dr. Thompson thought. He prepared himself for a few grumbles and protests, but instead he got utter confusion. As he called names, students wandered around the classroom aimlessly. It occurred to him that no one knew each other. How was that possible, he wondered, that students who had spent an entire academic year together in his classroom had no idea who their classmates were?

Emma sat patiently waiting for Anton to approach her and exchange information, but he never came. She turned around to see him lounging in his seat, staring straight ahead, apparently indifferent to Dr. Thompson's instructions. Her heart dropped. She instantly considered the possibility of being stuck with a bad partner, one who would do very little to no work at all leaving her to write the entire term paper alone for which he would receive equal credit. She hated collaborative work, and feeling her face tighten, she got up from her seat to go to him.

"Jackass," Emma muttered as she thought of Anton. A few students sitting close by turned in her direction.

"Who's a jackass?" whispered a boy to her left.

Emma jerked up from her notebook and looked at the boy who addressed her. She smiled at him sheepishly as the final bell rang. He returned a grin and hopped up from his desk to join the other students exiting the classroom. She followed behind him navigating the crowded hallway to Dr. Thompson's class. She had a few concerns she needed to voice.

—

Dr. Thompson listened patiently as Emma finished. He was hoping to leave work right after the final bell and had just locked his desk when she came into the classroom. She spent ten minutes listing reasons why she felt it appropriate to be assigned a different partner for the term paper. He tried twice to interrupt her, but she appeared to have memorized her speech, rattling off arguments without pausing to even breathe. It was a flawless presentation; her intonations and voice fluctuations were spot on, and he was tempted to ask her when she found time during the school day to write, edit, and practice her speech.

When he was certain she was finished, noting a look of premature victory on her face, he replied, "I'm sorry Emma. It's not going to happen. The partners stay as is. And anyway, it's just the first day. How could you already have such issues with Anton?"

Before Emma could reply, she heard the door to the classroom open.

"Forget something, Mr. Robinson?" Dr. Thompson asked, peering around Emma's body.

She tensed up immediately.

"Maybe," he said.

"Listen, do you have a minute?" Dr. Thompson asked.

"I guess," he replied, sauntering up to the teacher's desk.

He stood close to Emma, his arm brushing hers, knowing full well that it made her terribly uneasy.

"Let's get this figured out now," Dr. Thompson continued. "Emma is concerned about doing this paper with you."

Emma didn't know where to look. She couldn't look at Dr. Thompson. She wanted to fly across the desk and claw his eyes out. She didn't dare look at Anton. She could only imagine the thoughts going through his head, calling her any number of unmentionable names.

Anton looked at Emma with an expression of mock surprise.

"You told me you couldn't wait to get started! You said you was so happy we was partners, that you was secretly prayin' Dr. Thompson'd pair us up. You said you had a crush on me! Now I'm hearin' this? Dr. Thompson, I don't even know what to think right now. My feelin's is so hurt."

"Give it a rest, Anton," Dr. Thompson said. "Now, Emma is concerned that you have no plans to take this assignment seriously, and quite frankly, I'm starting to understand why. This isn't a joke, son. This is sixty percent of your grade. So stop clowning around and figure out how the two of you are going to work together for the next six weeks. I will not change the partners. You've got to learn to work with people you might not necessarily want to. That's life."

Anton nodded while Emma didn't move.

"And as for you, Emma," Dr. Thompson continued. "You're a senior. Know what I mean? It's time to grow up and deal with it. And when I say 'it' I mean, well, everything."

Emma felt the heat of humiliation on her face. There was nothing left to say. She turned to leave the room wanting to follow behind Anton, but he waited for her to go first, opening the classroom door like a perfect gentleman.

Once they were in the deserted hallway, she finally forced herself to look at him. She opened her mouth to speak, but the words failed her.

He looked her up and down and snorted. "You nothin' but an uptight white bitch who's mad she gotta work with a nigga."

The words stung, and she stood speechless as she watched him walk away.

—

"He called me a bitch," Emma said into the phone.

"Well, you've got to tell Dr. Thompson. Isn't that,

like, harassment or something?" Morgan asked on the other end.

Emma sat on her bed studying the ends of her hair. She snipped the strands with a pair of scissors when she found splits in the follicles. She had her best friend on speaker phone.

"No, I can't tell him. Didn't you hear what I told you he said to me?" Emma replied irritated. "Apparently I need to grow up and deal with it."

"Then go to the principal about him. He's a teacher. He can't talk to you like that. He's supposed to be helping us," Morgan answered.

"I am so not doing that, Morgan," Emma replied. She found another split end and snipped.

"Well, what are you going to do then?" Morgan asked.

"Deal with it, I guess. But how am I going to work with someone who called me a bitch?" she asked. "I'm not a bitch, am I?"

"Girl, you are so far from a bitch. Now Alyssa, she's a bitch. Beth? Total bitch and ugly too. But you? You're an angel from heaven," Morgan said sweetly.

Emma grinned. "Thank you."

"So anyways, I gotta run. It's family game night. Isn't that the dumbest thing you've ever heard?"

"I don't know. I think it sounds kind of nice," Emma responded whose family never had game night.

"Of course you do. Although you don't have little brothers or sisters. If you did, you'd think differently."

Emma grunted.

"Okay, I'll see you tomorrow. Bye!" And Morgan hung up.

Emma turned off her phone then lay back on her bed. She stared up at the ceiling replaying the events over in her head. Why was he so rude to her? What had she done? She thought hard trying to remember anything in her behavior or words that might have been offensive, but she was at a loss. She was polite, at least up until the moment he insulted her for no reason, making fun of the way she acted in class. Since when was it a bad thing to participate, she thought bitterly? He participated in class all of the time, and not just to be argumentative. He made observations about the books they read. So why did he make fun of her for doing the same?

And then it occurred to her, a realization that panicked her, that maybe it had nothing to do with her personally. Perhaps he didn't like white people in general. Narrow-minded indeed, she thought, remembering Dr. Thompson's words to the class. She knew she could allow the panic to win over and create in her a fear of him. It was easy, and she was tempted. She cringed at the thought of the following day—having to see him and talk to him. The panic rose, and she entertained it, imagining how he would treat her for the next six weeks. The things he would say. The way he would look at her.

With great effort, she focused on replacing her fear with anger. She recalled him calling her a bitch. She let that replay over and over in her head until the sinking in her heart was supplanted by a steady glowing hate. She lay on her bed and nurtured it, letting it glow brighter, build up in her until she resolved to say something to him. What, she did not know, but she had to say something.

CHAPTER 2
THURSDAY, APRIL 16

She was unwavering in her decision even as she felt the beads of sweat pop up under her arms. She took a deep breath and walked towards him. He was at his locker pulling books.

"I'm not a bitch," she said once she was close to him.

He looked at her skeptically. His friends were standing around him, and they laughed. When he said nothing, her anger exploded.

"I'm not a fucking bitch!" she yelled, turning a few heads.

"I didn't call you a fuckin' bitch. I called you an uptight white bitch. Is that the same thing?" he asked, closing his locker softly.

"You can't talk to me like that! I . . . I don't deserve that. You don't even know me!"

"I know you uptight," he responded.

His friends looked her up and down—she could sense it—though she kept her eyes on him.

"I am *not* uptight," she said, stamping her foot in frustration.

He laughed and reached for her necklace.

"Yeah you are," he said tugging gently on the pearls.

"Don't touch me!" she screamed, slapping his hand away. She heard his friends say, "Aw, no!" and "She scrappy!"

"Relax," he replied. "Me touchin' you won't turn you black."

"I . . . that's not—" she began.

The tardy bell rang, and he turned to leave. Instinctively she grabbed his arm and pulled him. He pretended to trip, and he fell into her, dropping his books, pushing her back against the lockers and pinning himself on her. He was tall: the top of her head didn't reach his collarbone. He smelled of something she couldn't pinpoint, but it wasn't unpleasant. She had the fleeting, horrifying thought that she liked the way he smelled. He stayed pinned against her for a half moment before apologizing into her ear for being clumsy. She felt the brush of his lips.

He was far down the hallway before she understood what happened. She looked at him laughing with his friends. They were laughing at her tough girl act, and she was humiliated for it. She felt the tears brimming, and she cursed her sensitivity. He turned around to see if she was still there. He caught sight of her walking swiftly to the bathroom, head down. He stopped laughing even though the laughter around him was ripe and loud.

—

Dr. Thompson gave the students the last twenty minutes of the period to meet and discuss their projects. He noticed that Emma stayed in her seat pretending to write things in her notebook. He was tempted to call her to his desk and ask how things were going with her partner, but he refrained. They could work it out, he decided. They would have to.

Anton watched her. He thought the right thing to do

would be to approach her and apologize. It also helped that his friends weren't around to give him shit about it. Her hair hung down shielding most of her face, but he could still see her eye. He watched her staring at the page. She wasn't writing. Her eye would be moving if she were writing.

He licked his lips in contemplation. He wanted to apologize. He didn't talk to women like that. His mama would smack the shit out of him if she knew he called a girl a bitch. He was raised to be respectful. But he was just so angry. She decided to dislike him before even getting to know him. He could sense it in her body language when she walked over to his desk yesterday. She was arrogant. He was certain of it, ignoring the possibility that he completely misread her.

The truth was that he was uncomfortable around her. He thought she was beautiful, and he didn't like that. She wasn't from his world as evident by the address on the piece of paper she gave him. He snorted slightly. Five-sixty Avondale Drive, he thought. Rich ass girl. And not black. He didn't want to be attracted to her. He knew he could never date her or else he'd have to explain that to his friends, his mama. Maybe Mama wouldn't care, but his friends would. And it pissed him off that he couldn't control his attraction. There were plenty of fine black girls at school, but he only wanted to look at her. When did that happen? It was last year. He could see the moment clearly though he wasn't sure if it happened earlier or later in the year. She said something clever in class, and everyone laughed. He watched her shrug her shoulders and smirk, and since then, all he wanted to do was keep looking at her.

Maybe he was completely to blame for creating the animosity between them. But then, she did go to their teacher like a little whiny brat. Perhaps that was his fault, though. After all, he did act like he didn't care. And he couldn't understand that. Was he trying to look cool in front of her? Did he think that would make her like him? He shook his head.

He thought he would never get the chance to speak to her, but the opportunity finally presented itself. He couldn't believe his luck at being paired with her. He got his chance, but he played it all wrong, and then to top it off he called her a bitch. How could he ever recover from that? And then she asked for an apology. Well, in her own way. She was trying to be a tough girl. He laughed at her act because he knew it wasn't her. But he should have apologized. He would have apologized if not for his stupid friends. Why did he care so much about what they thought?

He shouldn't have pinned her to those lockers. He knew it was wrong. He wanted to humiliate her. He didn't know why he wanted to do that when it would probably make her cry. He didn't want to make her cry.

"Anton? Get out of my classroom." Dr. Thompson was standing over him. "I've got another class coming in."

He didn't say a word but left in a hurry. When did the bell ring?

He walked down the hall searching for her. He resolved to apologize and try to start things over regardless of what his friends thought. She wasn't at her locker. He knew she had calculus next; he'd seen her walk into Mrs. Hartsford's classroom across from Dr. Thompson's room. He peeked inside the room and spotted her sitting near the window. He inhaled deeply and went inside. Just then the bell rang and Mrs. Hartsford stood up behind her desk. She noticed Anton walking towards the windows.

"Um, excuse me, sir? You aren't in this class," she said, watching him walk over to Emma.

"I know. This'll only take a second," Anton replied.

"Um, no. You'll leave my class now, please," Mrs.

Hartsford said.

"Look, I need to talk to her for a minute, okay?" he said pointing at Emma.

"That's why there's time in between classes. Now, I'll ask you again to please leave."

Anton ignored her and turned to Emma.

"I'm sorry. Okay? I shouldn't of called you a bitch. You ain't a bitch. At least I don't know. Maybe you a bitch. Maybe you not. How do I know? I mean, I don't even know you. How am I gonna call you a bitch when I don't even know you?"

Emma stared wide-eyed, mouth drawn tight.

"So we cool?" Anton asked.

"Uh, yeah," Emma whispered. "Now leave."

"I can't tell if you really accept my apology. Look, we got six weeks of work, know what I'm sayin'? I can't be dealin' with all this hostility. You forgive me?" he asked.

He was squatting beside her staring up at her imploringly. Mrs. Hartsford was on the phone asking for the assistance of office personnel to escort a boy out of her room who didn't belong there and wouldn't leave.

"Can we discuss this later? You're already in trouble," Emma whispered though she didn't know why. The class was completely silent watching the scene. They heard every word.

"Okay, okay. You forgive me though?"

"Yes," she replied, and she saw a wave of relief wash over his face.

"Okay, so you meet me after school?"

"Yes," she said uneasily.

"Anton!" It was the vice principal. His voice sounded tired, defeated, as though he had been dealing with unruly students all day and hadn't the energy anymore to care. He looked nothing like a disciplinarian standing in the doorway watching Anton leave.

"Can't you just be where you're supposed to be?"

Emma heard as the door slowly closed.

"It was important, Mr. McCullum. I ain't tryin' to be bad. You know that."

The hallway was clearing out as she watched him load his book bag with textbooks and binders. Did he really do any work when he got home, she thought? He didn't seem like the studious type. Anton threw his bag over his shoulder and walked towards her. She grew nervous, knowing it would manifest itself on her face in the form of bright red cheeks.

When he reached her, he dropped his bag and looked down at her. He said nothing, clearly inviting her to speak first.

"You pushed me up against the lockers on purpose," Emma said suddenly. She didn't mean to open the conversation with that.

"I know," he said shaking his head. "I don't know why I did that. I was just tryin' to show off in front of my friends."

"It was humiliating," Emma replied, her voice shaking slightly.

"I meant it to be," Anton said.

She wasn't prepared for that response.

"Why would you want to do that? Why would you want to hurt me?" Emma asked, her tempering rising.

"I was tryin' to put you in yo' place."

"I don't even know what that means," she replied.

"You stuck up. You think you better than me," Anton explained.

"You're so off base with that," Emma said. She shook her head in disbelief.

"Oh yeah? I saw the way you was lookin' at me in class. You looked at me like I was a big waste of yo' time."

"I was irritated with you. You acted like you didn't care at all about this project, slouching in your desk like you were too good for—"

"Why you dislike me so much?" Anton interrupted. "You don't know me any more than I know you."

"I don't dislike you," Emma replied. "You didn't give me a chance to even be nice to you. You acted like a jerk in class when we were supposed to be getting to know each other. You mocked me."

"Mocked you?" he asked.

"Don't pretend you weren't making fun of me when you wrote down your contact information for me," Emma said.

Anton snorted. "Oh that. I was just messin' around. You take shit too personal."

"Yeah, I take being made fun of personally. Most people do," Emma snapped.

Anton looked at the floor while shuffling his feet.

"You right. I shouldn't of done that before gettin' to know you. I just clown around. It was supposed to be playful," he said still looking at the floor.

Emma said nothing. She turned instinctively when she heard the doors at the end of the hallway open. The last of the remaining students were leaving, and when the doors closed again, the hallway felt uncomfortably quiet.

"I do care," Anton said.

She turned to look at him. "Huh?"

"The project. I do care," he said.

"Then why did you act like you didn't?" Emma asked.

"Man, I don't know," Anton replied, scratching the back of his head. He paused for a moment before adding quietly, "I'm uncomfortable around you."

"Why?"

"I don't know," he replied lamely.

The truth was that he did know. Even now as he

stood before her forcing himself to appear relaxed, even a bit aloof, his insides twisted excitedly at the thought of her body being so close to his.

"Well, I can't help that," Emma said. "But you have to be nice to me. We have to work together."

"You talkin' about me not bein' nice, not givin' you a chance. You didn't give me no chance either. Why'd you go runnin' to Dr. Thompson about me?" Anton asked. "That was weak."

"Yes, and incredibly embarrassing. And I'm sorry. But I think you paid me back when you called me an uptight bitch."

"An uptight *white* bitch," he corrected with a smirk. She thought alarmingly that his smile was cute.

"Well, I guess I am a little uptight," she admitted. "And white."

"But not a bitch. And I'm sorry I said that. If my mama knew I said that, she'd whoop me so bad," he said.

"Hmm, maybe I'll just have to tell her," Emma said. "That would be really funny to watch."

She laughed then, and it surprised him.

"Oh, you think that's funny, huh? Imaginin' my mama whoopin' me?"

She nodded her head giggling. He was grateful for it, and not wanting the friendly moment to end, he searched for something else to say that would keep her laughing.

"Okay, so remember when you was younger and yo' mama or daddy come after you to spank you, and you be runnin' holdin' yo' ass and pushing yo' hips as far out in front of you as you could lookin' like a retard?"

He demonstrated by running down the hall yelling, "Mama don't!" and holding his bottom.

Emma doubled over with laughter. She heard the classroom door open and tried to regain her composure.

"What the hell is going on out here?" It was Dr. Thompson peering out into the hallway with his usual disheveled hair and glasses askew. He spotted Anton then looked at Emma. She shrugged.

"We sorry, Dr. Thompson," Anton said, walking back towards Emma. "I was just showin' my girl here how I used to—"

"Save it. And go home. I don't know why you people hang around school when you don't have to," Dr. Thompson said. He tried to sound annoyed, but there was a clear sense of relief in his words. They were finally getting along. Now maybe he wouldn't have to hear from Emma's unbearable parents.

"Sorry," Emma offered, picking up her bag. Anton did the same, and they started down the hallway.

"Now you gotta show me how you tried to sideswipe those whoopin's," he said.

"Yeah right," Emma replied.

"Now it's only fair. I showed you," he said. And before she could reply, she felt a playful pop on her bottom. He couldn't believe he did it! They had only just become friendly with one another. But it felt so easy and natural. He was certain she wouldn't object.

"Anton!" she squealed, instinctively covering her bottom with her hands.

"You betta run, girl. That's all I can say," he said, grinning. His eyes twinkled with mischief.

And she did. She ran for the exit feeling him close behind her, knowing he could take her in two strides. She burst through the doors and turned on him suddenly, her bag falling off her shoulder. He stopped short, this time running into her without meaning to. She stumbled backwards, but he caught her around her waist.

"Thank you," she said, while he still held her.

"You welcome," he said, smacking her bottom again. He was careful to watch her reaction.

She grinned, pushing him away playfully while feigning outrage.

"You can't do that to me, Anton," she said, and he felt he'd get on the ground and kiss her feet to hear her say his name again.

"Relax. I'm just playin' with you," he said casually.

She felt she broke the magic and cursed herself for saying anything. But she hadn't. The magic was coursing through him, and he knew he needed to get on his bike and get far away from her or the magic might burst. He didn't want to be responsible for what would happen when the magic burst.

"Want a ride home?" she asked.

"What? Oh, I see. I live in the projects and can't afford no car."

"I didn't mean to insinuate that," Emma said. She felt embarrassed.

"Nah, it's a'ight. You right anyway. I ain't got no car," he said, trying to sound indifferent. "But what I do got is this snazzy bike."

He pointed to the bike rack, but there was no bike.

"Okay, well I did have a muthafuckin' bike," he said.

Emma was unsure how to respond.

"How somebody gonna steal someone else's bike?" he asked. "It wasn't even a good bike neither. Piece of shit."

Emma was on the verge of laughter, and she felt mortified. She tried to hold it in. It was no laughing matter. His property had been stolen. She didn't want to seem callous, and she certainly didn't want to come off looking like a snotty, spoiled little girl. But it was the way he reacted—like fake surprise, she thought. Like he expected it and was only just putting on a show about it because she was standing there. She tried, but the laughter broke through.

"What? How you gonna be laughin' that somebody stole my bike?" Anton asked, his face filled with mock incredulity.

"I'm so sorry," Emma said between giggles.

"That little punk finally took it back," Anton said to himself as the realization dawned.

"What?" Emma asked.

Anton shook his head, then hung it shamefully.

"I stole that thing. It wasn't even mine to begin with."

"You stole someone's bike?" Emma asked.

"It's not like it was even a good bike. If you'd of seen it, you'd understand."

"Is this something you do a lot? Steal people's things?"

"Take it easy. It was some punkass bitch who was talkin' shit about me and my friends and how we was losers for not havin' no ride. Like he had a ride. Shit. Rollin' around on that piece of shit, fallin' apart, handles broken, chain-draggin'-on-the-ground bike. So I took him out then took his bike. That shut him up."

Emma looked nonplussed. "Why did you steal it if it's so bad?"

"To make a point." Anton continued to look in the direction of the bike rack. He was afraid to look at Emma. He had no idea why he revealed that incident to her. Now he was afraid that the hard won politeness and even mild flirtation between them would completely disappear and never return.

He finally turned to look at her. She was walking towards the parking lot.

"Hey!" he called after her. "Where you goin'? Can I get a ride?"

"I don't think so," she called back, and he saw the hint of a smile on her face.

"Oh, okay. I see how it is. You gonna teach me some lesson about consequences or some shit. Yeah, okay. Well, it ain't even a big deal. I just live right around the corner. Five-minute walk tops. Yeah, go on and get in yo' car.

Ignore what I'm sayin'."

He watched her wave to him as she pulled out of the parking lot and thought for a split second that he'd like to pin her up against the lockers again. He shook his head and started his six-mile walk home.

CHAPTER 3
SATURDAY, APRIL 17

"Hey, you busy?" Anton said into the phone, lying sprawled out on his bed. It was eleven on Saturday morning, and he had just woken up.

"Who's this?" came a voice on the other end of the line.

"Girl, you know who this is. It's Anton."

"I'm sorry, I don't know an Anton," was the reply.

Confused, Anton pulled the phone away from his ear and looked at the screen. He cross-referenced the number he dialed to the number on the piece of paper Emma had given him. The numbers matched. It was then that he heard a stifled giggle.

"Oh, you funny," he said, his heartbeat quickening.

"I'm just messin'," Emma said. "What are you up to?"

"I'm callin' to ax you about gettin' together today," Anton replied. "You busy?"

"Not at all," she said. She, too, was in bed but not because she had just woken up. She had gone for a long run in the early morning hours, had come home to shower, then crawled back into bed once the deliciously languid feeling of complete exhaustion overtook her body.

"So how you wanna do this?" Anton asked.

"Well, that's a good question. I guess the first thing is learning about each other's cultures," Emma said. "But how do we do that?"

"I don't know. I guess maybe we gotta hang around each other?" Anton offered.

"Hmm. I guess," Emma said thoughtfully.

"Well don't sound too excited about it," Anton replied, laughing.

"Sorry. I was just thinking," Emma said. "Do you want to meet at the library?"

"For what?"

"To work."

"How we gonna learn about each other at a library?" Anton asked.

"Yeah, I suppose you're right," Emma said. "You wanna come over here?"

"To yo' house? Please. I'd get arrested."

Emma laughed.

"You come over here," Anton decided. He was unsure, but he figured that eventually she would see where he lived anyway.

"To your house?" Emma asked doubtfully.

"Don't worry. Ain't nobody gonna try to sell you drugs or nothin'. Least I don't think so."

"I'm not sure," Emma said.

"What you mean? You offered me a ride home the other day?" Anton reminded her.

"Yeah. I was just being polite," Emma admitted.

"Girl, you killin' me. Look, we gonna do this thing or not? Sixty percent of our grade, remember?"

"I know."

There was a brief pause.

"My mama gonna be here. Do that make you feel better?" he asked.

He waited, imagining that he could hear the thoughts

running wildly about in her head. She was scared, he knew, and he didn't know what bothered him more: the fact that she was scared of where he lived or the fact that he was scared of actually showing her where he lived. He constantly felt trapped between feelings of loyalty to his neighborhood and feelings of embarrassment. He wondered if other black people felt the same way, and if that was just a condition of living in the ghetto. He was jolted out of his contemplation by the sound of her voice.

"What's your address?"

—

He sat out on his front stoop watching for her. He thought that she should have been there by now and wondered if she changed her mind. He looked at his surroundings and snorted. She had no idea what she was about to learn, he thought.

After hanging up with her earlier, he went outside to clean up the trash littered about his duplex. It wasn't his or his mama's. She always complained about the trash, but they lived beside the worst tenants imaginable, and nothing was ever done about it. Beer bottles, burger wrappers and napkins from fast food restaurants, even used condoms were strewn everywhere. He wouldn't touch the condoms, but he still wanted them out of sight. It was embarrassing enough having her see the actual buildings of his housing project without them being decorated with used contraceptives. Well, at least they're practicing safe sex, he thought amused.

He found latex gloves in the house and armed himself for the work ahead. His mother watched him from the living room window walking about slowly and methodically, picking up trash, collecting it in a plastic bag. He kicked at the ground to push dirt and leaves over the condoms. She smiled to herself even as her heart tightened. I'm getting us outta here, baby, she thought. And she was. She was going to school to be a nurse and was a few months away from graduation. She worked constantly—often the night shifts at the local hospital—and when she wasn't working she was studying. It took her many years to get to where she was, but she did it, and she was almost finished. They were almost out.

He came in after awhile and saw his mother at the sink. She was washing dishes. She turned to him and smiled.

"I dusted a little," she said. "You wanna run that vacuum through right quick?"

"Yeah."

"You make your bed? Put your clothes away? I'm always yellin' at you 'bout them clothes," she said. She placed the remaining dishes in the draining rack and scrubbed down the counter tops.

"Yeah, Mama."

They finished the chores in silence, then Anton went back outside to wait for Emma.

She was already fifteen minutes late. He didn't know if he felt angry that she wasn't there or relieved. When he saw her pull up, his heart dropped. He wished for a moment that she had never come. But it was too late now. He stood up and walked towards her car, trying for casualness even as his nerves jumped.

"I'm so sorry," Emma said exiting her car. She looked frazzled. "I got lost."

She slammed the car door in frustration and looked at him.

"Freakin' GPS, right? I'm all over No Man's Land. It's taking me down roads that don't exist! What the hell?"

All of the tension he felt vanished immediately. He expected her to get out of her car with a frightened look on her face. He expected her to look at his house and then look at him with pity in her eyes. He expected that she would try too hard to act like she wasn't feeling awkward being in a neighborhood so clearly foreign to her. But she did none of those things. In that moment, he was glad her GPS malfunctioned.

"Come on. My mama inside. She wanna meet you before she gotta go to class," Anton said.

Emma followed him up the stairs to his apartment and was greeted by a short, stout woman. She wore her hair cropped and accessorized her earlobes with large oval hoops. When she smiled, the tops of her cheeks nearly hid her eyes, eyes that sparkled with friendliness.

"I'm Ms. Robinson," she said, extending her hand.

"Nice to meet you. I'm Emma, Anton's classmate," Emma replied politely, shaking Ms. Robinson's hand. She was expecting someone much taller, tall like Anton, but apparently he inherited his height from his father.

"I'm so sorry I'm late," Emma continued. "I'm never late for anything."

"That's alright," Ms. Robinson said. "Would you like something to drink? Iced tea?"

"Yes, thank you," Emma replied.

She looked around the living room. It was clean and orderly with yellow slip-covered furniture and an old boxy Magnavox television. She had never seen a television like that in someone's house. On old T.V. shows, yes, but not in someone's house. She thought of her own flat screen television opposite her bed and blushed. She hoped Anton didn't see.

The kitchen was just off the living room, large enough for a small table and chairs. There was no dining room, she noticed. A short hallway led to what she thought were two bedrooms and a bathroom. The whole apartment couldn't have been more than 900 square feet. That was the size of her garage, she thought shamefully.

"You wanna sit down?" Anton asked, noticing her looking around. He didn't want to know what she was thinking. He already had a pretty good idea anyway.

"Yeah, thanks," she answered, making her way to the couch. She sat down next to an end table overflowing with framed pictures. She picked one up.

"Is this little Anton?" she asked grinning at him.

"Girl, put that down. Mama, why you gotta have those pictures out all the time? They embarrassin'!" he called to his mother who was in the kitchen pouring three glasses of iced tea.

"Oh hush," she called back. "You were a cute baby."

"You were," Emma agreed, studying the rest of the pictures.

Anton blushed as he sat down in a chair across from her.

"So what happened?" she asked playfully.

"Oh, you funny." He turned to look at his mother in the kitchen. She was getting something out of the refrigerator and probably wouldn't hear if he spoke softly.

"Please girl, you know I'm fly. I can't help you wanna stare at me all the time."

Now Emma blushed. She fingered the picture frames for something to do until his mother returned to the living room with a tray of sandwiches and iced tea. She placed the tray on the coffee table and sat down next to Emma on the couch.

"I don't know how long you'll be here today, Emma," she said handing her a glass of tea. "So I made some sandwiches for you and Anton. If you anything like me, you get hungry doing school work."

"I do," Emma replied. "And thank you."

"Mama goin' to school to be a nurse," Anton said. There was a note of pride in his voice. "She almost finished, right?"

"Yep," his mother replied. "And thank goodness. I'm so tired of working all the time and goin' to school. It wear me out."

"Speakin' of workin'," Anton said. "I got a job."

"You did? Where?" his mother asked. And then she added more excitedly, "You get that UPS job?"

"You know it," he replied. He flashed a huge smile and did a little upper body dance with his head and shoulders. "I'll be loadin' them boxes all day long."

"Baby, I'm so proud of you," Ms. Robinson said. "But I don't want you workin' too much. You still got school, even after you graduate."

"I know, Mama," Anton said.

"Do you have a job, Emma?" Ms. Robinson asked.

"I lifeguard during the summer," Emma replied. "My parents won't let me work during the school year."

"Well, they want you to focus on your grades," Ms. Robinson said. "And that's the most important thing when you in school."

Emma smiled and took a sip of her iced tea. It was deliciously sweet. She fell into an easy conversation with his mother, Anton interjecting with comments here and there, all the while stealing glances in his direction from time to time. She wanted to judge for herself how "fly" he thought he was. And she realized he wasn't joking.

He was tall—at least six feet four inches, she judged—with long legs and large hands. She thought he could fold her hand in his completely, making it disappear from sight. He was lean and muscular and had the silkiest, most perfect dark skin she had ever seen. It surprised her. Shouldn't he be suffering from acne like every other senior at their school? Perhaps he had gotten over that earlier in his life.

She couldn't help but notice his lips. They were plump with a faint pinkish hue—very kissable, she thought, then quickly disregarded it. His lips were fascinating, but his eyes were captivating. She had never seen eyes that color and didn't quite know how to describe them. They looked like honey—a dark, rich honey near his pupils and a lighter amber color around the edges. She was scared to let him look at her with those eyes believing he could draw out her secrets with them against her will.

Ms. Robinson was commenting on Anton's shorts when Emma redirected her attention.

"Baby, I told you time and again to pull up those shorts. I don't understand why you boys walk around all the time lookin' like you gotta load in your pants."

Anton had taken his empty glass to the kitchen.

"Mama, what you want me to tell you? It's the style," he said.

"Whose style?" she asked.

Anton ignored her.

"Emma, it was so good to meet you, and I do wish I could stay longer, but I've got class," Ms. Robinson said.

"No, I understand. It was nice meeting you, too," Emma replied. And she meant it. She wasn't sure what to expect before meeting Anton's mother, but she found that she liked her immediately. Ms. Robinson was warm and funny and comfortable.

Anton's mother collected her bags at the front door and kissed her son goodbye. She turned to Emma once more and said, "I'm sure I'll be seein' you again."

When she left, Emma looked at Anton who was still standing in the kitchen.

"Your mother is so nice," she said.

"I know it," he replied. "My mama's the best in the world."

"You know, I think you may be right about that," Emma said in all sincerity, and he found it a peculiar statement.

"So tell me what you really think of this place," he said.

"What do you mean?"

"Girl, please. I know where you live. This apartment

prolly the size of yo' bedroom," he said.

"What do you want me to say?"

"Nothing. Forget it. I ain't tryin' to make you feel uncomfortable. Come on. I'll give you the grand tour."

She followed him down the hallway and poked her head inside when he pointed out his mother's room. She noticed a lot of lavender. Directly across from his mother's room was his bedroom, and he opened the door for her to go in. She hesitated at the threshold.

"What? Nothin' gonna jump out and bite you," he said.

When she still didn't move, he asked, "You never been in a boy's room before?"

"Actually no, I haven't," she replied.

"You think you 'bout to do somethin' wrong walkin' into my bedroom, huh? Yo' mama and daddy teach you never to go in a boy's room, didn't they?" He looked down at her shiny hair and knew he was absolutely right.

She ignored him, raising her head in defiance, and walked inside. It looked like a typical boy's room. Several posters of rap artists decorated the wall. She thought she recognized one of them. A dark blue duvet cover lay crooked on a clumsily-made bed. She could see a hint of plaid sheets underneath. There was no headboard and footboard. She didn't know why she thought that was odd. A desk beside the bed held stacks of CDs and books along with disorganized papers and a few pictures. A chest of drawers opposite the desk was piled high with paraphernalia as well. She was curious to go through it.

"Well, this is it," he said.

She stood in the middle of the room looking around. It was then that she noticed several piles of books stacked in the corner—so many books, in fact, that it put her small collection to shame. She wasn't prepared to see something like that in his bedroom and heard herself address him a bit snobbishly.

"Don't tell me you've actually read all those," she said, pointing to the teetering piles.

"Why you think I haven't?" he asked. "You think I can't read or somethin'?"

"I didn't say you couldn't read," she replied. She walked over to the books and picked up a worn copy of *Huckleberry Finn*. She laughed and showed Anton.

"Why you think that's so funny? Ain't nothin' wrong with bein' well read," he argued. "And anyway, that shit is good."

Emma replaced the book and picked up another. "*Fear and Loathing in Las Vegas*?" she asked.

"Girl, just read that book and you ain't never wanna do no hard drugs ever," Anton replied. "You can borrow it."

Emma nodded and searched for another book.

"You think cause I'm black I don't read. Or maybe you think I only read black shit like *A Raisin in the Sun*. Girl, I've out-read you a hundred times over. I read everything. Like *Frankenstein*," Anton said pointing to the book in Emma's hand.

"We had to read this for school," Emma reminded him.

"Man, I read that thing years before we was supposed to," he replied.

Emma was dumbfounded. "Why?" she asked turning to face him.

"'Cause I like to read."

"Why?"

"You seen where I live? You standin' right in it. What else I'm supposed to do?"

Emma turned back to the mountain of books to hide her face. She needed the moment to compose herself. The concept was a foreign one to her—that some people read to imagine away their brutal realities. She never considered the idea of reading as an escape from a hard, unforgiving existence. She never had to.

She turned around to see Anton staring at her. It made her uncomfortable, and she searched for something to say.

"You listen to Tupac?" she asked after a time, pointing to one of the posters on his wall.

"You know who he is?" Anton said amazed.

"Doesn't everyone?" she asked.

"Just surprised is all," he said. "You ever listen to his stuff?"

"No."

"Nah, I guess you wouldn't. His music's older. He died in '96. We was babies then," Anton replied. He thought for a moment. "You want to?"

"Want to what?" Emma looked uncertain.

Anton thought better. "Well, I was gonna see if you wanted to listen to some of his stuff, but nah. You ain't ready for all that yet. I forgot you only just got here. I don't wanna be overwhelmin' you with all my blackness."

"I've listened to rap music before," Emma pointed out.

"That shit on the radio?" Anton asked. "Girl, that ain't no rap music. There ain't been no good rap music since the '90s. Well, in my opinion anyway."

"The '90s, huh? So you listened to rap music as an infant?" Emma asked sarcastically.

"Why you think I don't know older people who introduced me to that music? It ain't just young people who live in the ghetto," Anton replied.

He plopped down on his bed, leaving her standing in the center of the room. She was unsure what to do.

"Girl, sit down," he said, and then mumbled, "Lookin' like a fish outta water."

He leaned over and pulled the chair out from underneath his desk offering it to her. She sat down tentatively across from him, their knees almost touching.

Suddenly she was nervous. She hadn't felt that way when she was talking to his mother. But now, being in his room and surrounded by his things—just the intimacy of seeing his personal belongings—made her anxious.

"You so funny," he said, watching her smooth her skirt on her thighs.

"Why do you say that?" she asked.

"You all nervous and shit. It ain't no big deal bein' in my room. If anyone should feel nervous, it's me."

"Why?"

"I can't imagine what's goin' through yo' mind right now. I'm sure you think this house a dump. You prolly countin' down the minutes 'til you get outta here," he said. He couldn't believe his honesty and was not even embarrassed by it.

Emma, however, was extremely embarrassed. She shifted in her seat. "I don't think that at all."

"Sure," he said, unconvinced.

"What can I say to that?" she asked. "What do you want me to say? I told you I don't care, and you don't believe me. Do you want me to feel uncomfortable being here? Will that make you feel better?"

Now Anton shifted uncomfortably. He shouldn't have said those things to her. It wasn't fair. It was a barrier he tried to erect to protect his heart from what he thought were her impressions of his house. He wanted her to be okay with it. He wanted her to feel comfortable. But he was also realistic.

"You hungry?" he asked, deciding to change the subject.

She realized then that she was. He didn't wait for a reply and went into the living room to get the tray of sandwiches his mother made. He stood over the coffee table for a moment looking down at them. He noticed how his mother put them together carefully, slicing them in triangles and placing them on the tray in a perfect fan.

He smiled thinking he really did have the best mama in the world.

He heard the sounds of a song coming from his bedroom and abandoned all thoughts of his wonderful mother. He walked swiftly to his room and discovered Emma hunched over listening to his CD player. He had the sudden urge to ask her where she learned to work a CD player—a device no doubt extinct in her world—but decided against it. She had found a Tupac CD, and he only just realized she was listening to "Hit 'Em Up." He hurried over to the stereo and turned it off. He was mortified. He wanted to look a certain way to her. He only wanted her to see certain things. What would she think of him after that?

"Excuse me?" she asked irritably.

"I don't think you need to be listenin' to that," he said.

He suddenly felt the urge to shield her from certain aspects of his world. He looked wildly about for other things that might be controversial, might betray his wicked nature, reveal him to be a person she could never like. The artists in his posters were giving him the finger. Why didn't he think to take them down before she came?

"I'm not a little kid," she argued. "I was listening to that."

"Yeah, I know. But we ain't gonna go there yet," he said.

"You asked me if I wanted to listen to some of his stuff!" she said, exasperated.

"Yeah, well, I wasn't gonna play you that," he said, laughing lightly.

"Oh I see. You were going to show me one side of him. You were going to show me one side of you," she replied. And then after a moment added cynically, "You probably never make your bed."

He laughed genuinely. "You right. I only make it

when my mama yell at me."

She couldn't help but smile.

"Okay, fine. We listen to it. But lemme explain first," he said.

She grabbed a sandwich and started eating.

"Okay, so Tupac had beef with this other rapper, Biggie Smalls." Anton pointed to another poster hanging on his closet door. "That's Biggie. So anyway, it started after he thought Biggie Smalls and his crew had something to do with him gettin' shot. Well, shot the first time anyway. The second time he got shot, he died. But anyway, the first time he got shot five times and survived it. After that, a rivalry broke out between East and West."

Emma looked confused.

"Rappers on the East Coast and rappers on the West Coast," he clarified.

She nodded.

"Well, that's the more popular version of it. The rivalry actually started before Pac and Biggie and didn't have nothin' to do with them. But I guess you can say it intensified when Tupac claimed that Biggie tried to kill him. You followin' this?" Anton asked.

Emma nodded thinking how tasty her sandwich was.

"Anyway, it was a big deal in the 90s," Anton continued. "Basically everybody got shot. Lots of rappers died. But after Tupac and Biggie died, people started thinkin' that maybe they shouldn't be goin' around and killin' each other. So you don't have all that goin' on in the hip hop world no more."

Emma was intrigued.

"So anyway, this song basically Tupac being all pissed and talkin' shit to Biggie and his crew. It's really explicit and I still don't think you should listen to it."

"What are you? My dad?" Emma asked.

Anton rolled his eyes and pressed PLAY. They sat in silence listening to Tupac explain how he was a "self-made millionaire" and a "Bad Boy killa" all the while eating sandwiches and drinking iced tea. Anton watched Emma's face for the duration of the song. It stayed screwed up in concentration as though she were taking mental notes. He imagined she would have a lot of questions. When the song ended, she turned off the CD player and looked at Anton.

"What's a glock?" she asked.

"A type of gun," he replied.

"What's a fo fo?"

"Oh, well it's four-four. He just pronounce it fo-fo 'cause he black," Anton replied. "It's another type of gun."

"Hmm. Apparently he likes guns," Emma said.

She was quiet for a moment. Anton chewed his lip for something to do.

"Do you listen to this a lot?" she asked.

"No, mostly when I'm pissed or somethin'," he said.

"I can't imagine it puts you in a better mood," she observed.

"I don't want it to."

"Oh."

"Not all his music like that," Anton explained. "Some is playful. A lot of it about social issues. Growin' up poor in the ghetto and stuff. He write about his mama. That stuff is real powerful."

"But his music is so old," she said looking at the back of the CD jewel case. She pointed out the copyright date.

"It don't matter," Anton replied taking the jewel case from her hand. "Some music eternal, you know? It just go on and on. It always be relevant, always make a point."

Emma sat quietly, thinking. She had a hard time understanding how the woman she just met allowed her son to listen to such music. Then again, perhaps she didn't know, but Emma shook her head at that. Their rooms were directly across from one another, and she was sure that in a house like this, the doors and walls weren't well insulated. She scanned his desk and noticed a Bible.

"Do you go to church?" Emma asked.

"'Course I do," Anton replied. "What kinda question is that?"

"I'm confused. You listen to that and then you go to church?" she asked, holding up his Bible.

"What's yo' point?" Anton asked.

Emma placed the Bible back on his desk and smiled.

"You're strange," she said.

"Well, then. I guess we got somethin' in common."

CHAPTER 4
MONDAY, APRIL 19

Anton stood at the bathroom mirror surveying himself. He actually woke up early this morning for school, something he never did, and took his time getting ready. It was important to him that he looked good. He made a new friend over the weekend and wanted to impress her. He wanted her to find him attractive. He wanted to be more than friends, he thought. He smiled in the mirror examining his teeth, relishing the feel of the glowing ball of excitement deep inside his belly.

"Man, I got nice teeth," he said to his reflection. "How she not gonna like that?"

He looked at the baseball cap on his head. It was sky blue with the UNC Tar Heels emblem.

"And I look so good in hats. How she not gonna like me in a hat?"

He chewed his lower lip as he continued his examination. He flexed his right arm and whistled low.

"Damn nigga, you got some guns. How she gonna keep her hands off yo' guns?"

He chuckled.

"It can't happen. It just can't," he decided.

He inhaled deeply.

"And you smell so good," he went on. "She gonna be crawlin' all over you 'cause you smell so good. What girl don't like a guy to wear some cologne?"

He decided to wear cologne today. It was an expensive designer brand his mother bought him last year for Christmas when she started making more money. It was a good Christmas, he thought, remembering how happy she was that she was beginning to see all of her hard work materializing. And he had been careful with that cologne ever since he got it, only using it on special occasions. He thought today was one of them.

He lifted his blue polo shirt and studied his stomach.

"Maybe if she lucky, I'll let her put her hands on these rock hard abs," he said, and then heard an angry knock on the bathroom door.

"Anton! Get yo' butt outta that bathroom!" his mother yelled. "You been in there forever! What are you doin'?"

Anton opened the door to find his mother standing in the hallway wrapped in a bathrobe, an expression of intense irritation plastered on her face.

"I'm sorry Mama," he said, kissing the top of her head.

"What were you doin' in there? And why are you even up?" she asked. "You never get up this early for school."

"Sure I do," he said, then told her he was off to catch the early bus.

His mother stood perplexed staring after him.

—

He waited by his locker. He was impatient and annoyed that he had gotten to school so early. What was he thinking? This was when all the nerds arrived so they could have more time to study before a test or go visit with teachers because they were complete losers, he thought. Suddenly he wondered if she would think he was a loser. He'd have to lie when she would ask and say he had just arrived.

He walked down the hallway to the soda machine and purchased a Coke. He was running out of things to do and felt anxious. Just then she appeared, and his heart leapt into his throat. She wore her hair in a ponytail today he observed first. And he liked it. He liked the way it swung from side to side as she walked. Her ears sported diamond studs—real, he figured—and she wore a pale pink collar shirt with brown khaki shorts.

Her shorts were the perfect length, he decided. Not too short like some of the other girls wore. He thought those girls were nothing but hos letting their asses hang out, leaving nothing to the imagination. He liked to imagine; that was part of the fun. But her shorts weren't too long either, so she didn't look like that other type of girl at school: the clueless dork. A thin pink belt hugged her waist, and he felt jealous of it, wishing he could wrap his arms around her in place of it. Her sandals sparkled with sequins and jewels. They were pretty and dainty like her, he thought.

He watched as she walked to her locker and put her books up. She was completely unaware of his presence, and he liked being able to observe her in secret. She bent down to scratch her knee. She checked her face in her locker mirror, touching a spot under her eye and frowning. She fixed her ponytail. He thought now was a good time to go and say hello. His friends weren't at school yet, so he knew it would be safe. He walked towards her looking around for any of her friends. No one was in sight.

"Hey," he said, approaching her locker.

"Oh hi," she said. He thought he saw her face brighten. "What are you doing here already?"

"Oh, I just got here," he said casually. He leaned against the lockers to appear more relaxed though his heart was racing.

"I had fun on Saturday," she said, closing her locker. "Thanks for inviting me."

"You welcome," he said. He wanted to tell her he had a fun time too, but he wanted to play it cool.

"You ever been to that park on Gordon Street?" he asked.

"Lots of times. I love that park," she replied.

He wished she would ask him if he'd like to go today after school. That's what he wanted to do, but he didn't want to appear too eager to hang out with her.

"Maybe we could go there sometime to work," she offered.

"Yeah, that sounds good," he said, rejoicing inside. Now all she had to do was ask if he wanted to go today.

"What do you think about this afternoon? I'm free," she said.

God, he loved this girl. She was making it so easy for him.

"Yeah, I think that'll work," he said.

"You look nice in a hat," she observed, lightly smacking the bill.

"Hey now, watch it!" he said, and heard a familiar voice at the other end of the hall.

"Emma!" Morgan shouted, walking towards her friend.

"I've gotta go," Emma replied. "I'll meet you after school at my car, okay?"

"Okay," he said, and his heart tensed with jealousy.

He was there first. How could her stupid friend come in and steal her away just like that? He knew he'd get no other opportunity to talk with her that day unless Dr. Thompson gave them class time to work on their papers. And he had a feeling that wasn't going to happen. He walked to the other side of the hallway back to his locker. It was not far from hers; in fact, it was very close, and so he contented himself with at least being able to look at her in between classes. And he knew he would have her all to himself that afternoon. Suddenly, he didn't care that Emma's friend stole her away. She was his in seven hours.

—

"You keep a blanket in yo' car?" he asked, helping her get it out of the trunk. It was large and bulky.

"I told you I come to the park a lot," she replied.

"And how you carry this thing by yo'self?" he asked. "It look heavier than you."

Emma rolled her eyes.

"Here, I'll take it," he said, balling it up as best he could. It weighed nothing to him, but it was cumbersome.

Emma offered to carry his bag for him, and he laughed.

"Nah, I can manage. In fact, why don't you give me yo' bag," he said, and before she could refuse, he took it off her shoulder.

They walked to a shady spot under a large oak tree near the edge of the park lake. Her arms were empty while Anton carried both book bags and the unwieldy blanket. She looked at him and grinned. Just like a boy, she thought. They have to be the heroes. She helped him spread the blanket then took her shoes off before sitting down. He reluctantly removed his shoes but left his socks on. Exposing his feet felt too vulnerable.

"I love doing work outside," she said. "Well, I love doing anything outside, really."

He watched her pull a binder from her book bag and open it to a page filled with notes about their paper.

"You got nice handwriting," he said. "You write in cursive all the time?" he asked, remembering the piece of paper she gave him with her contact information.

"Yeah, don't you?"

"Girl, I don't know how to write in no cursive," he said.

"You never learned?" she asked, bewildered.

"Well, sure. I mean I remember doin' some of that in fourth grade. I never picked it up though. It easier to write in print."

"Actually once you learn cursive, it's easier and faster to write that way," she said.

"Yeah, I guess you right. You always be scribblin' so fast in class takin' them notes," he observed. "You prolly write down every single word Mr. Cantinori says."

She looked at him oddly, and suddenly he felt self-conscious. How could he slip up like that? Now she knew he looked at her, watched her when she was completely oblivious to it. He prayed silently that she wouldn't say it out loud, wouldn't ask him why he was looking at her in class.

"Do you want me to teach you how to write your name?" she offered after a moment.

He was beyond grateful. He almost thought he could kiss her for not saying anything.

"Uh, okay."

She scooted closer to him, and he watched as she spelled "Anton" on the page in a neat, slanted script. He studied his name, the way she made it appear on the page, and decided that he liked it. He liked it very much. He wanted her to write his name again. And again.

"Okay, did you watch me form the letters?" she asked.

"Yeah."

"Okay, now you try," she said, and offered him her pen.

"But you left-handed. I'm a righty. Won't it be different for me?" he asked.

Emma thought for a moment.

"Well, the letters look the same, but you're right. Your hand is going to move differently. I didn't think about that," she said, mostly to herself.

Anton held the pen poised over the paper. He was unsure what to do and felt mildly ridiculous like he was back in kindergarten learning how to write for the first time.

Emma looked as though she were deciding something.

"Well, I guess I can try," she said to herself, and then placed her right hand over his.

His heart jumped at the feel of her hand. It was so small and warm, covering only a portion of his. She began guiding his hand to form the loops of his name. She giggled when they finished. It looked like chicken scratch.

"Okay, I so cannot write with my right hand," she said, scrutinizing the name they had both written.

She didn't notice that her hand was still covering his. She was so intent on studying the name. But he noticed, and he said nothing. She could keep her hand there as long as she wanted.

"Let's try one more time," she said, determined.

He let her guide him once more, forming the uncertain loops of his name, feeling the softness of her hand as she tried for control. She withdrew her hand suddenly and stared at the page.

"I give up," she said. "Someone else will have to show you how to write in cursive. Someone right-handed."

But Anton thought that he didn't want a right-handed person, and he almost voiced it aloud.

"It ain't no big deal," he said casually, trying to hide the disappointment he felt that her hand was gone.

He noticed that she didn't scoot back to where she was originally sitting. She stayed close beside him. He was sure that she simply wasn't aware that she stayed put, but he felt excited anyway. He could imagine that she stayed close to him on purpose, and it made him giddy.

"You smell nice," she said after a moment.

He thought he would die. She kept noticing everything. The hat earlier. Now his cologne. He was tempted to flex his arm and show her his muscles. Maybe that would put her on her back for him. He shook his head. Get yo' head outta the gutter, he thought frustrated.

"Thanks," he managed.

She immediately delved into their project, asking him questions about certain chapters in the book, contemplating the characters, making connections with what they had learned already about each other's lives. His heart dropped. He could not understand her. How in one minute she could tell him he smelled nice and then in the next breath ask him his thoughts on Carrie Meeber. He didn't give a shit about no gold diggin' ho, he thought. Why didn't she just put her hand on his again and try for a third time with his name?

He pretended to care. That's how he could keep her there with him. If he listened to her and answered her questions with even the slightest bit of thoughtfulness, he could keep her on the blanket all afternoon. Maybe even until the sun set. Maybe until the stars came out. Maybe forever. He watched her bite her lower lip in concentration. Every now and then she absent-mindedly touched the stud in her earlobe, fingering it and spinning it slowly.

They worked for an hour before she closed her binder. He was afraid she wanted to leave. They had not been there that long, he thought. How could he make her stay? But she did not want to leave; she was just tired of writing and needed a break.

"There's a guy at the park entrance who sells bread," she said. "To feed the ducks. He charges way too much, but he's convenient. And we could feed the ducks. If you want."

He agreed, and they left their blanket under the tree. She took her bag and binder, and he thought it funny that she entertained the notion that someone might steal their English paper notes.

"You never know," she said, smacking his arm as he laughed at her.

She was right. The old loaves of bread were overpriced, but she paid for one anyway and walked with him back down to the water's edge, dropping her bag and binder on the blanket as they went. The ducks could sense the food, swimming hurriedly to the edge of the lake then waddling as quickly as they could towards her. There were more ducks than usual, she noticed, huddling around them and quacking demands. The ones closest to Emma and Anton poked them impatiently with their bills. Emma could sense Anton's growing unease. He couldn't possibly be afraid of ducks, she thought. Grinning, she tossed the loaf to him, and he instinctively ran.

The ducks chased him down the lake's edge as he tore off pieces of the loaf and threw them behind him. She noted the expression on his face when he turned back to see if they were still at his heels. He looked like a cartoon character, she thought laughing aloud, his eyes wide with fright, arms flailing as he hoofed it down the bank.

For awhile he was out of sight until she saw him running back, still followed by a few ducks that had gotten none of the bread. He tossed the remainder of the loaf to Emma and hid behind her. He listened as she scolded the ducks for being mean then gave them the last of the loaf. When they discovered that Emma and Anton had nothing else for them, they waddled back to the water and continued their lazy swim.

"You did that on purpose," Anton said, still

breathing heavily from his run.

"I would never do such a thing," she said, affecting shock at his accusation.

"You knew exactly what you was doin'," he went on. "I can't even believe how scared I was over them ducks."

Emma laughed heartily then screamed when Anton picked her up and cradled her like a baby. She smelled the mixture of light perspiration and cologne on him, and she liked it.

"You think you funny," he said, making his way down to the edge of the lake.

"Oh my God, don't!" she squealed, clinging to his shoulders.

He ignored her. "But how funny you think it'd be if I tossed you in that water?"

"Anton, don't you dare," she warned. She couldn't help but laugh.

"Well, I think it's only fair. You had those ferocious ducks chasing me. Now you need to go in the water," he said, feeling her squeeze him hard and bury her face in his shoulder.

He would never throw her in. He could not bear to feel her leave him. He wanted her arms around him forever, her face nuzzled into his neck for eternity. No, he would not throw her in. But he would tease her. He walked closer until he was inches away from the water.

"How 'bout just a little?" he asked. "I won't put you in all the way."

He tossed her lightly and she screamed.

"We could call it even then?" he went on, feeling her clutch at him in desperation.

He began lowering her towards the water.

"Stop!" she cried in between laughter. "I'm begging!"

"Well, if I don't put you in this water then we ain't even. What am I supposed to do with you?" he asked.

"I don't know," she said frantically. "I'll think of

something."

He grinned at her and turned back to their blanket. He could have set her on her feet then, but he wanted to prolong the ecstasy of holding her, so he carried her back to the blanket before setting her down gently. It was difficult for him to let go of her not knowing when he would be able to touch her next. He only did it when the opportunity presented itself. It was never forced. He would never touch her without feeling like it was safe.

Anton sat down beside her and watched her reopen her notebook. He willed himself to focus, but all he could think about was the feel of her tiny arms around his neck, squeezing him until he was sure he would have to kiss her. They resumed their work, and he affected interest in it though his mind was very far away.

CHAPTER 5
TUESDAY, APRIL 20

"I cannot believe you have to work with him," Morgan said, scowling as she watched Anton change out books in his locker. "He's such a thug."

"He's not a thug, Morgan," Emma replied, amused.

She checked her face in the mirror attached to the inside of her locker door, and deciding she needed a touch up, dug out lip gloss from inside her purse. She glided the applicator gently over her lips, pressed them together, then studied herself again.

"Oh my God. He's watching you," Morgan observed.

Emma looked in Anton's direction, and he quickly turned his face away when their eyes met.

"No he wasn't," she said. Her heart gave a small jolt.

"Yes he was. I'm so grossed out right now," Morgan replied.

Emma watched Anton joke with his friends. There were four of them. He said something and they laughed, one of them smacking him in the back of his head. He retaliated with a light punch to the arm. She watched them walk down the hallway, turning the corner until they were out of sight.

"Are you listening to me?" Morgan asked.

"Yeah. You said you have to go to the dentist this afternoon," Emma said. She grinned at her best friend.

"No, actually I didn't say that at all," Morgan replied. "Listen to me, Emma!"

"Okay, okay. I'm sorry," Emma said, closing her locker and falling in step with Morgan as they walked down the corridor.

"What am I gonna do about Brian?" Morgan asked. "He's starting to act all jealous about me, like he doesn't want me going anywhere without him."

"You want my honest opinion?" Emma asked. She didn't wait for a reply. "I think he's a loser."

"Hey! That's my boyfriend you're talking about!"

"Morgan, you said yourself he was a loser," Emma pointed out.

"Well, I know," she said thoughtfully. "God, he's such a freakin' loser."

Emma chuckled. "You know, we all just put up with him because we love you."

"What, Aubrey and Sarah think he's a loser, too?" Morgan asked.

"Um, yeah," Emma said, bewildered. How could she not know that? "Listen, you're so pretty and smart and funny. Why are you with him?"

"I don't know," Morgan said, shrugging. "Because he's there?"

Emma laughed as they made their way into history class, the only other class she shared with Anton. She was careful to avoid looking at him. He shared this class with two of his friends, and while in the past she had never given any of them a single thought, she now felt slightly nervous being in a room with them. She had even decided to avoid speaking up in class so as not to draw attention to herself or give his friends reason to snicker at her. The laughter that ensued after her confrontation with Anton a few days back was still fresh in her mind.

She walked past them and heard one of them ask teasingly, "How yo' project goin', Anton?"

"It's fine," Anton replied. He knew she could hear them.

"She bein' nice to you?" the other asked.

"Man, everything fine. She fine," Anton said. He shifted nervously in his seat at the back of the class.

"You makin' her do all the work? Shit, I'd make her do all the work. She so fuckin' smart and all."

"Will you shut up, man?" Anton said.

His friends moved on to another topic of conversation as he watched Emma take her seat on the opposite side of the classroom. She was engaged in a conversation with her friend, and Anton realized that her friend was really the uptight bitch. He caught her giving him dirty looks on occasion in the hallway between classes, and he tried to understand that it was her way of being protective of Emma. Still, it pissed him off thinking of all the things she was saying to Emma about him—feeding her mind with hateful prejudices. He scowled watching her play with her long blonde hair while she listened to Emma talk. How could Emma be friends with her, he wondered?

The bell finally rang, and he settled himself for a fifty minute mind-numbing lecture on U.S. law. He stole glances in Emma's direction, watching her take notes. She was always so diligent in class. He was amazed by her fervor. She acted like she genuinely cared about school. He only worked as hard as he had to. He knew what grades he needed to get into a community college. He realized he'd have to start there and not at a four-year university. He screwed up those chances in ninth grade. Once he recognized that he needed to get his act together, it was too late. But he figured there was nothing wrong with community college. He knew a lot of other students starting there before going off to a big university.

He caught sight of Emma looking his way. She smiled at him, and he didn't know what to do. He turned away, sensing that her face fell with disappointment. Why didn't he just smile back? He couldn't risk his friends seeing. They'd want to know why he was smiling at her, if he liked her, and then they would give him unimaginable hell over it. No, he was right to look away. If she got her feelings hurt over that, then she was way too sensitive.

The bell rang. Another fifty minutes of his life wasted. He wondered how high school could be so unimportant, how four years of his life could be so dull and inconsequential. He felt like he was in a prison and was sure many other students felt the same, shuffling like zombies from one room to the other at the sound of a bell. What the hell *was* that?

Emma brushed by him on her way out of the room. She did not look at him, and he was certain she was mad. Over a smile, he thought, and chuckled. He followed her lazily down the hallway to his locker. His friends had disappeared leaving him alone to stare at her all he wanted unnoticed, unbothered. Her friend wasn't with her, and he plucked up the courage to go and talk to her. It was safe, he thought.

He approached her locker as she was shutting it.

"Hey," he said.

"Hi," she answered, aloof.

"When you wanna get together again?" he asked.

"I don't know. I'm kind of busy this week," she replied.

"You mad at me about somethin'?" Better to just confront it, he thought.

"Why would I be mad at you?" she replied.

"I don't know."

He hated when girls did that. And they were so good at doing that—affecting indifference when they were really pissed off. Why didn't they just say what they felt? It would make life for men so much easier.

They stared at one another. She seemed to be making up her mind about something.

"I guess we can meet somewhere tomorrow after school," she said finally.

So she was going to let it go, he thought relieved.

"You wanna come over to my house?" Anton asked.

"What? So you can get a ride home?" She grinned at him.

"Well, that too," he admitted. "You don't know what it's like ridin' that bus home. It's awful."

"You're right. I wouldn't know. I've never ridden a bus to school," she said.

"Imagine that," he said sarcastically, and she playfully punched his arm.

"You're such a butthead," she said.

Anton laughed hard.

"What?" she asked, grinning.

"Nothin'. I don't know. You the first person ever call me a butthead," he said still chuckling.

"I'm sure I won't be the last," she offered.

He looked down at her and smiled. His friends were right. She *was* scrappy. A scrappy munchkin, he thought. She didn't know what went through his mind as he looked at her, but she knew that she liked him looking at her that way.

"I guess I could come over today, too," she said. "I mean, that's if you're not busy. I know you've got that new job."

"I don't start 'til next week," he said.

A thought occurred to her. "How will you get to work? I mean, since you don't have a car."

Anton laughed. "Girl, you ever hear of public transportation? Man, what am I sayin'? 'Course you haven't. The bus line don't go anywhere near yo' house."

"Whatever," she replied, trying to brush him off.

How could she ask such a stupid question?

"I'm just playin' with you. You know that."

"Do you want me to come over today or not?" she asked.

"Sure. I mean, whatever. If you want," he said, trying to sound casual.

Emma placed her hands on her hips and looked up at him. Her eyebrow was raised in a question, and he knew she wouldn't be satisfied until she heard him say it.

"Yes, Emma, I want you to come over today," he said.

She turned to leave, and he followed after her.

"You gonna give me a ride home, right?"

"Yeah, yeah," she replied, picking up her speed to beat the tardy bell.

Anton stopped following her and watched her disappear into a classroom at the end of the hall. Just then the bell rang, and he couldn't remember what class he was supposed to be in.

—

They had been working for nearly an hour sharing childhood stories and trying to decide if anything was worth including in their paper when a knock sounded at the front door. Anton excused himself and left the room.

Emma went back to her work, hearing the low murmur of voices in the living room. Suddenly a head appeared in the bedroom doorway.

"Oh, you wasn't jokin'," a boy said. He wore a red bandana around his head and sported a small gold stud in his left nostril.

Anton pushed past him into the room.

"Emma, this is Nate," he said, sitting back down on the floor. Nate remained in the doorway.

"Hi," Emma said, placing the novel on the floor.

"Hey," Nate replied, disinterested. He looked over the papers and binders surrounding Anton and Emma. "So you ain't comin' then?" He directed the question to Anton.

"Man, I told you I can't," Anton replied. "And anyway, it's a school night."

Nate burst out laughing. "So when that make a difference?"

"Look, I ain't even tryin' to screw anything up right now. I'm about to graduate, man. And so are you, by the way," Anton said.

"You so dumb, Anton. There gonna be college girls there!" Nate said. "And liquor. Free liquor. And if we lucky, maybe some weed."

"I don't care. I got work to do."

"Man, fuck you. How you gonna be worryin' about school so much? You turnin' into a damn goody-goody," Nate replied glancing at Emma.

"Don't give me shit, Nate. Nobody tellin' you you can't go. Go. You don't need me there," Anton said.

He picked up his book and started reading. It was a clear message that the conversation was over.

"Fine man. Whateva," Nate said, and trudged out of the room.

Anton waited for the front door to close before he spoke.

"Sorry 'bout that," he said, shaking his head slightly.

"Do you want to wrap this up? I mean, if you want to go to the party or whatever it is," Emma offered.

"Girl, you crazy. We just got started. And no, I don't wanna go to some lame ass party. I know where this party is and I know who throwin' it, and lemme tell you somethin': there ain't gonna be one college girl there or any weed neither. And the only liquor gonna be some cheap ass shit that make you sick after one swallow. I kept tryin' to tell him that, but he don't listen. Dumb nigga."

Emma was taken aback. It was the only other time she heard him use that word. The first time he said it he was referring to himself and was terribly angry. Now he said it with nonchalance.

He looked at her. "What?"

"What? Nothing."

There was a moment of silence in which they both pretended to read. Anton used the time to figure out how best to broach the touchy subject of the "n" word with Emma.

"Look, I'm black if you hadn't noticed," he said finally.

"Where did that come from?" Emma asked.

"You gotta stop makin' them big eyes every time you hear me say things like 'nigga.' You be lookin' like a deer in headlights all the time."

"I'm sorry. It's just hard to hear. It makes me uncomfortable."

"Why? You ain't the one bein' called a nigga," Anton pointed out.

Emma cringed.

"See! There you go again," he said.

"I'm uncomfortable because I'm not sure how I'm supposed to react to it. I mean, I don't get it. It was used as a derogatory remark. I don't understand why you call each other something that racist white people used to call you," she said, and then after a thought added, "Actually, some still call you that."

Anton considered her remarks.

"Well, it's like this. We could either keep lettin' racist white people use it in a mean way, or we could take the word away from 'em. So we took it and turned it into somethin' different. Now we use it to show solidarity."

Emma's eyebrows shot up.

"Oh, you think 'cause I'm poor and black I don't know words like 'solidarity'?" Anton asked teasingly.

"I didn't think that. I thought you as Anton wouldn't know words like 'solidarity'," she replied. She smiled at her cleverness.

"Oh, you funny," he said, running his forefinger up the sole of her naked foot. She had taken her flip flops off at the front door when she arrived and was now sitting Indian style on his bedroom floor. She jerked her foot away.

"Don't you dare," she warned.

"Oh, you ticklish?" he asked, putting his novel down and moving towards her.

She drew her knees up to her chest planting her feet firmly on the floor.

"It won't be my fault if you get hurt," Emma said. "I'm serious. Don't tickle me."

He ignored her, wrapping his large hand around her right calf and tugging gently on her leg. She remained stiff, using all her might to keep her foot planted.

"So you like to joke," Anton said. "But you don't like when the joke's on you."

"That's not true," she argued.

He gave up pulling on her leg and instead put one arm under her knees and the other around her back picking her up swiftly and neatly depositing her on his bed. He trapped her feet in the crook of his arm and watched her squirm wildly. Her toenails were painted a bright cherry red, he observed, and her feet were soft and callus free.

"How you have such pretty feet? You not do nothin' like exercise or run or play no sports?"

"I just got a pedicure," she said, still trying to free herself from his grasp.

"Of course you did. Why didn't I think of that," he said amused.

He flashed her a devilish grin.

"Please, I'll do anything. Do not tickle my feet. I'll

die. I will die," she pleaded.

"You'll do anything?" Anton asked, unable to hide the sexual excitement in his voice. He had her trapped on his bed, vulnerable to him, and he knew the game was becoming a little too dangerous.

"Anything," she said, not noticing the lust in his tone. "Just please don't."

He ran his fingers softly over her sole and listened with delight as she screamed.

"I want you to say I'm fine," he said. "That I'm the flyest brotha you ever seen."

"I'm not saying that!" she said, and then squealed when he assaulted her foot once more. "Okay, okay! You're the flyest guy I've ever seen!"

"See now, I don't believe you," he teased. "I want you to look at my face and tell me that."

"Okay," she said defeated. She looked him in the eyes. "Anton, you are the flyest guy I've ever seen."

He smiled at her, feeling the rush of something warm and electric in his heart, and released her feet. She punched his stomach with one, and he doubled over.

"Shit, girl! That hurt!"

"Serves you right, you butthead," she snapped, getting out of his bed and returning to the floor.

"You right, you right."

He rubbed his stomach while watching her resume her work.

"Butthead," he mumbled chuckling, and went to sit beside her.

They worked for several hours before she left. He never thought he could have so much fun doing a school assignment. He had given no thought to the time, his friends, what he would be doing had she not been there. It was as if the world outside of his bedroom disappeared. Nothing was important apart from sitting on the floor with her, talking about a novel, getting to know each other, teasing her.

He couldn't believe with what ease he was beginning to open up to her, sharing everything about himself—everything from his favorite music to his spirituality. She found his beliefs surprisingly incongruous with the way he acted. He described his diet to her; most of the foods she'd never tasted. He couldn't believe she'd never had fried okra. He would have to remedy that. She would stay for dinner one night, and he'd get his mama to make it. He was sure she'd never want to eat another thing in her life after tasting his mama's fried okra.

The sun was setting, and he was reluctant to see her out. He wondered what kind of bedroom she went home to. He imagined that it was very large. He was sure she probably had her own T.V. and computer. That was a given. He wondered if she kept it organized, or if she just tossed her panties wherever. He shook his head to rid the thought, but once the image entered his mind, he could think of nothing else. He watched her pull out of the parking space thinking all the while of the panties she wore and where she would take them off and toss them when she got home. He went back to his bedroom and closed the door.

CHAPTER 6
THURSDAY, APRIL 22

Anton watched her during history. He had given up caring about that class months ago. She appeared to be listening. She wrote things in her notebook. Did she really care about this shit, he thought? His friend leaned over and whispered something to him. He stifled a laugh, and it drew her attention. She looked at him and then his friend. They both smiled at her—enormous grins—and she was uncertain if the joke was on her. She smoothed her hair and looked down to make sure none of her shirt buttons had come undone. She wiped at her face thinking that perhaps she had something on it.

They laughed again, and this time the teacher spoke.

"I had no idea that the judicial system was so funny, boys," Mr. Cantinori said. "Do share. We all want to be in on the joke."

"Sorry Mr. Cantinori. It ain't about the class," Anton's friend replied. "We was reminiscin' about the old days, you know? Being seniors and all, we just realize how much we gonna miss this place."

Emma couldn't help but think how full of shit he was.

"Well, Kareem, you haven't graduated yet," Mr.

Cantinori pointed out.

"You right, you right. I feel what you sayin'."

"Do you?" Mr. Cantinori replied. "Then be quiet." And he resumed his lecture.

Kareem closed his mouth and sunk down in his seat. He didn't appear phased by being corrected in front of the entire class, but then he was usually reprimanded that way.

Emma grinned, her face buried in her notebook, but Anton saw. He wondered how she got to be such a good girl. She probably never got in trouble once in her life, at least not at school. He imagined what she would do if a teacher scolded her in front of the whole class, and concluded that she would probably melt into the floor from sheer embarrassment and disappear forever. He smiled to himself. To be that good, he thought.

Class ended and he walked with Kareem to his locker. It was lunch time, and the students moved slowly throughout the hallway, taking their time at their lockers. He wanted to ask Emma if they were still on for Friday afternoon, but just as he was about to approach her, he noticed a boy conversing with her. His heart went tight with jealousy. It was instant and unsettling, and he tried to ignore it. But he couldn't, and he stood watching the boy look at Emma as though he knew something secretive about her that no one else did. Who was this guy? Emma never mentioned him.

He thought it absurd that he expected to know everything about her in less than a week. Regardless of the amount of time they had already spent together and the amount she had shared with him about her life, he still knew very little. Evidently she had a boyfriend, and he felt like an idiot. What did he actually think would happen between them? She was nice to him, even played along with his flirting, because she knew she had to work with him. She was just being nice, he thought bitterly. There was never anything more and could never be anything more.

The misery pervaded his body, and he thought how easy it would be to walk up to the boy and punch him in the face. A nice, strong right jab, he thought. Break a tooth in his fucking mouth. Take him to the floor and make him bleed. Make him swear to never talk to Emma again or he would kill him. The thoughts pacified him, and he felt the anger within him dissipate.

"Ugh, he gets on my nerves," he heard Emma say after the boy walked away. She was talking to her friend with the long blonde hair.

"That's mean, Emma," Morgan replied.

"I know, and I feel awful for feeling that way. How can you date someone in the past and feel like you loved them, and then you break up and you don't want to be anywhere near them? Like they disgust you? It's a horrible feeling to have, and I feel like a horrible person," Emma said.

Anton's heart sprouted wings.

"Well, I guess you shouldn't have let him go up your shirt," replied Morgan matter-of-factly.

Anton scowled.

"Thanks, Morgan. You're helpful."

He smiled at Emma's sarcasm. He could imagine her face to match.

"You know he wants to get back together with you. He's dying to," Morgan pointed out.

Anton curled his hands into fists.

"So not happening. As mean as this sounds, he just doesn't do it for me," Emma replied.

I can do it for you, Anton thought.

"Really? You aren't attracted to him anymore in the slightest?" Morgan asked.

What was this girl trying to do, he thought? Ruin his chances?

"No, I'm really not. It was tenth grade. It's over. I'm

done with it," Emma said.

That's right, girl, move on. Right on over to me, Anton thought.

"So who are you attracted to?" Morgan asked. "Anyone? You haven't mentioned a guy in a long time."

He knew she would never say it, but he stood there hoping she would.

"I don't know," Emma replied. "I'm not sure I want to get attached to anyone before starting college."

His heart splintered into a million pieces.

"That wasn't my question. I asked if you thought anyone around here was cute," Morgan said.

Say it Emma. Say it, he thought desperately.

"I don't know," Emma said blushing.

"Oh my God, you like someone! Spill it!" Morgan squealed.

Anton began tentatively piecing his heart back together.

"I never said that, Morgan," Emma replied, but her flushed face betrayed her.

"Well, I think I know someone who likes you," Morgan said.

His heart fell to pieces all over again.

"Who?" Emma asked.

"Your partner," Morgan said boldly, and he could feel her eyes on him.

He shoved his face deeper into his locker.

"What are you talking about?" Emma asked quietly, looking in Anton's direction.

"That guy you're working with on that stupid English paper. I think he likes you. I've been watching him for the past few days. He's always looking at you," Morgan said.

Somebody push me into this locker and close the door, Anton thought. And never let me out again.

"You're crazy," Emma said.

No she isn't, he thought sullenly.

"No, you're crazy. Or you would be if you did anything with him," Morgan said. Her tone held a note of warning.

Fuckin' bitch, Anton thought. Shut your fuckin' mouth.

"Morgan, there is nothing between us like that. I don't even think we're friends. You see we don't talk at school," Emma argued.

Anton's body went rigid. His heart had already died, so he wondered how he could still feel it ache.

"Good," Morgan replied. "Are we going to lunch?"

"Yes," Emma said quietly.

She glanced in Anton's direction once more. His head was hidden behind his locker door. She entertained the idea for only a moment that he actually liked her. It was ludicrous, she thought. He flirted with her, yes, but she had come to discover that he was a flirty guy by nature. She knew not to read too much into it. But she couldn't deny how it made her feel when he teased her and looked at her in certain ways—like she was the only person on the planet, the only person in his world. Like he built his world around her, and she was the golden statue in the center of it that he worshipped every day.

She wondered how some people had the ability to do that, to make others feel like they were the only ones. Sanguines, she thought smiling, remembering learning about the four temperaments in psychology. Sanguines had the special gift. And then her heart stiffened. She remembered something else about Sanguines. When they're through with you, they're through.

She followed her friend to the cafeteria.

—

He was waiting to board the bus home when she approached him. She made sure his friends weren't around; otherwise, she would not have extended the invitation.

"Wanna ride home?" she offered, approaching him as he sat on a metal bench.

"We didn't plan on working on our project today, did we?" he asked.

"No."

"So then why you wanna give me a ride home?"

"To be friendly," she said. She moved her school bag to the other shoulder. "Are you coming or not?"

She started walking towards the parking lot, and as much as he didn't want to follow her, he knew he had no choice. It bothered him that he would do anything to spend just a little bit of time with her, even if that meant riding in her car for a mere five minutes.

Emma chatted happily as they made their way to West Highland Park. He wanted to be in a sullen mood; after eavesdropping on her conversation with Morgan he felt utterly hopeless about any romantic future with her. But her cheerfulness affected him despite his resolve to stay glum.

"What are we listenin' to?" he asked after a time.

"Hey now. I listened to your music," Emma replied, glancing at his face. It was screwed up as though he had just eaten something sour.

"I know you did. I ain't sayin' nothin' bad about it," he replied.

"Well, you look like you hate it."

"How you gonna know what I look like? You starin' at me? You need to be watchin' the road."

Emma ignored him and turned the volume up on the stereo. The mournful melody filled the car.

"This gonna make me cry. We gotta change it," he said, reaching for the dial on the stereo.

"Don't touch it," she commanded.

"Why you listenin' to something so sad?"

"I like it. It helps me think about things," she replied.

"What things you need to be thinkin' about with a song like this? Nothin' good, I imagine."

Emma ignored him.

"And anyway," he went on, "you been runnin' yo' mouth ever since we got in this car. You ain't even listenin' to it."

"Good God," she said, and turned the stereo off. "Happy?"

She pulled into the familiar spot in front of his house and put the car in park.

"You can come in if you want," Anton said, opening his door. His tone was casual, but his heart was pleading.

"Okay. I can only stay for a bit, though. I have ballet tonight," she said, and walked with him into the house.

He was going to kiss her today, he resolved. He remembered her conversation with Morgan and decided that he didn't care. If she rejected him, then he would simply never look at her or talk to her again. They could work on their respective parts of the term paper separately, and he'd let her find a way to blend it all together. He'd mail her his section; she could do the rest.

He watched her walk about his room, fingering items on his dresser and desk. He liked her touching his things. She seemed interested in what she saw, and that made him hopeful.

"So that why you always standin' up straight all the time," he said.

"What?"

"You said you had ballet tonight. That why you have such good posture," he replied.

"Oh. Yeah, I suppose."

"Do you like it?" he asked, sitting on his bed. He wanted to invite her to join him, but the words stuck in his throat. It was so easy yesterday, he thought, when he picked her up and tossed her on the duvet cover to tickle her feet.

"Yeah, I do," she said thoughtfully. "It's the only thing my mother and I share."

Emma did not know why she voiced that. Her impersonal relationship with her mother was certainly none of his business. And why should he care? But she felt like she could tell him and he would not look at her like she was some poor little rich girl whose parents ignored her but gave her expensive things. That wasn't the case anyway. She was very close to her father.

Anton wasn't sure how he should reply. Did she mean to say that out loud, he wondered?

"You wanna sit down?" he asked.

She looked around the room, noticing a large pile of clutter on his desk chair, and made her way to his bed. She sat down tentatively and as far away from him as she could.

"Not everybody got good relationships with they parents," he said at last.

"I guess not," she replied. "It's weird though, because it's not like this out-and-out hostility between us. And I'm only talking about my mom here. My dad and I have a very good relationship. But my mom. She just expects so much. I have to be perfect all the time, and it's exhausting."

He listened.

"She put me in ballet. I was going to do it whether I liked it or not. So I learned to like it. And now I genuinely do. But just being forced. And I raised hell about the piano. My piano teacher told my mom that she was wasting her money. I never practiced. I didn't care. So I got out of that one."

Anton nodded.

It was pouring out of her and she couldn't stop it. Once the gates opened, she felt like she could talk for hours, get everything out of her heart and onto him. Let him deal with it, carry the weight of it, because she was too tired.

"It's just so stupid and typical, I guess. Being wealthy and unhappy. I mean, I shouldn't say I'm unhappy. I'm not unhappy. Just lonely, I guess. I just wish I had a sister or brother," Emma said.

She sat quietly thinking how her mood could change so suddenly. She was fine in the car earlier, happy even. Anton was thinking the same thing and decided he knew what she needed.

"Come on," he said, and grabbed her hand.

"Where are we going?"

"You'll see," he said, and led her out of his house to a building on the opposite side of his complex.

They climbed the stairs to another apartment, and Anton knocked on the door. A large woman answered. Her hair was wrapped in a mustard yellow scarf, and she wore a house dress.

"Anton, baby!" she cried and wrapped him in a tight hug.

"Hey Mrs. Williams," Anton replied.

"Where you been? These babies be drivin' me crazy!" she said releasing him.

"I just been busy with school. I'm workin' on this big school assignment. This my partner, Emma," he said, and moved aside to introduce her.

Mrs. Williams smiled at Emma and invited them inside. No sooner had Anton walked into the living room then three small children dashed towards him wrapping their arms around his legs. They squealed his name over and over, jumping up and down all the while clinging to his knees and thighs.

He laughed and picked one up, tossing him in the air and flipping him upside down making him scream with delight.

"My turn!" shouted another, and Anton did the same

with her.

"What about me?!" It was the voice of another little boy—he looked identical to the first one—and Anton threw him in the air as though he weighed as little as a bird.

Once they had all been tossed, he lined them up in a row, made them stand up straight, and bent down to address them like a drill sergeant.

"You listenin' to yo' mama?" he asked.

They nodded.

"You bein' good at school?"

They nodded.

"You ain't gettin' into no fights with other kids over toys or nothin' are you?"

They started to nod, but then shook their heads vigorously. Emma smiled.

"Good, because I brought a friend over to play today. And if I heard you was actin' out, then she wasn't gonna play."

Anton looked up at Emma and waved her over.

"This my friend, Emma," he said. "Now show her yo' manners."

"Hi Emma," said the little girl, and walked over to give her a hug.

Emma squatted and let the child wrap her skinny arms around her neck. She smelled like the outside, that wonderful child smell of dirt and grass and hours of nothing but fun.

The boys said hello, but they were shy and uncertain. They hung back, feeling safer being closer to Anton.

"Emma, this is Aesha, TaShawn, and LaMarcus," Anton said. "I'm sure you can tell these boys are twins."

Mrs. Williams walked over to LaMarcus and wiped at a smudge on his face.

"It's nice to meet all of you," Emma said sweetly.

"Anton, baby, how long you think you be here?"

Mrs. Williams asked. "I got to clean that bathroom and take a load of laundry downstairs."

"It's fine, Mrs. Williams. Go on and do what you need. We watch 'em," Anton replied, tickling TaShawn who fought ferociously to escape his grip.

"Thank you, honey," she said, the relief evident in her tone. She grabbed a laundry basket spilling over with clothes and disappeared out the door.

"Okay, so what are we playin'?" Anton asked. He was answered by the names of dozens of different games.

"Hold up!" he said. "Where our manners? We got us a guest here. Why don't we let her pick?"

The children hesitated for only a moment before agreeing. They looked at Emma and waited. She felt instantly nervous. She didn't know the make-believe games children played. She couldn't remember when she stopped playing them, but she thought that she was very young.

Anton walked over to stand near her.

"They really into Hide and Seek right now," he whispered in her ear.

She gave him a look of gratitude.

"I think I have the perfect game," she said excitedly. Their faces lit up, eyes sparkling, and they grinned wide with anticipation. "How about we play Hide and Seek?"

The children squealed and darted around the room, searching for their hiding spots before they had even decided on a seeker. Apparently Emma would be the seeker.

She stood in the corner of the living room and began counting aloud. All the while she counted she heard the gleeful screams of the children as they raced around the apartment searching for the perfect hiding spot. It was just like children to give themselves away without knowing, she thought. When did she start to know? What age was she when the knowledge came in to snuff out the magic?

"Here I come!" she yelled after counting to thirty. She turned around and spotted two of them immediately. They were grinning and nudging each other to be quiet, hiding under a table in the opposite corner of the room.

She pretended not to see them.

"Where, oh where could they be?" she said aloud, and they giggled more.

She crept around the living room and then disappeared down the hallway. She sensed them behind her. They were following her to see what she would do. They wanted her to catch them, she thought, and she wondered if she should scoop them up like Anton did and hug them close when she caught them.

She peered inside a bedroom and spotted the other. He was hiding under the bed. She raced towards him and fell to her knees by the edge of the bed. He squirmed to get out from the other side, but she grabbed his hand.

"Gotcha!" she yelled, and he squealed.

She wasted no time wheeling around to face the others who were close behind her. They screamed and started running for another room, but she was too quick. She caught their arms and pulled them to her sides.

"You're on my side now," she said addressing all three. "So let's work together to find Anton."

They agreed and discussed which directions they should take to find him. They split up and sneaked around the apartment. Her back was to the closet door when it opened, and she let out a stifled cry when she felt a large arm snake around her waist and a hand go to her mouth. He pulled her into the closet, closing the door. He held her still feeling her stomach rising and falling beneath his arm.

He could do it, he thought. Right now. Before the children came to find her. They must have heard her muffled cry. He could kiss her now if he wanted. She couldn't fight him. She was too small. He squeezed her tightly against him feeling her hands tugging on his arm. It wouldn't budge, so she tried tugging at the hand that covered her mouth. He could do it. He could move his hand and press his lips to hers in a mere second.

But his courage failed. He put his lips instead to her ear and felt her tremble.

"Don't say a word," he whispered.

He felt her smile beneath his hand.

"I got yo' princess!" he shouted. "What you gonna do?"

It was a challenge, and no sooner had he yelled it then the closet door flew open and six determined eyes stared him down. The game had changed that fast, she thought.

"Give us our princess!" screamed Aesha.

She ran towards Anton and the boys followed. They rained blows on his legs and back, their little fists flying and legs kicking in all earnestness. Anton pretended to be wounded, releasing Emma to them and falling to the floor. Aesha took Emma's hand and led her to the other side of the room.

"Hurry, Princess Emma!" she cried, and pointed to a spot on the floor where Emma would be safe. "Stay here," she ordered, and Emma obeyed.

The boys continued their attack on Anton, jumping on him and peppering him with soft blows from their fists. He winked at Emma before feigning a slow, tortuous death. His head rolled from side to side, and he let his tongue hang out of the corner of his mouth.

The children jumped up and down yelling in triumph, and Emma was shocked when the boys ran to her and gave her a hug. Just as quickly, they released her and ran back to Anton.

"Get up, Anton!" they shouted. "Let's play again!"

And they did. They played all afternoon, and Emma

completely forgot about her ballet lesson.

CHAPTER 7
FRIDAY, APRIL 23

She placed her hands on the ball, fingers turned inward, and chucked it as hard as she could towards the basket.

"Oh my God, you're killin' me," Anton said, watching the ball ricochet off the rim of the basket. He was quick enough to retrieve it before it rolled down the hill.

"What? Do I look like I know how to shoot a basketball?" Emma asked.

"Hell no," he answered. "But I'm gonna show you."

It was Friday afternoon, and they were at the park. Anton had rejected his friends' request to hang out in favor of spending time with Emma. He explained that he had to work on his project, and they made fun of him for being a goody-goody. He took the playful insults in stride, focusing instead on the butterfly feelings in his stomach at the thought of being with her all afternoon.

"I think I'd rather just get to work on our paper," Emma said.

"We are," Anton replied. "Basketball is a part of my culture, see? So now I'm gonna teach you 'bout it."

Emma looked uncertain. "I think a couple of white

guys invented the game, actually."

"So? Who the best at it now?" he argued.

"I don't know. I don't watch basketball," she answered.

Anton looked deeply offended.

"Are you for real? Wait, so you gonna tell me white guys invented the game, but you don't even watch it? First, how you know white guys invented the game if you don't know nothin' 'bout basketball?"

"I don't know. I guess I heard it somewhere."

"You don't watch any? No college tournaments, March Madness, nothin'?"

"I know. It's sinful," Emma said patiently.

"Girl, it is," Anton replied. "First I'm'll teach you the game. Then I'm'll take you to church to let you repent of yo' sins for not lovin' the game."

"I'm a white girl," she explained.

"Absolutely no excuse," Anton said.

"Jeez," Emma replied, rolling her eyes. "And by the way, I don't do church."

At this statement, Anton clutched at his chest feigning a massive heart attack.

"No church!" he said. "Girl, I don't even know what to make of yo' culture yet. But I can't be dealin' with that right now. I gotta just take it one step at a time with you. So I'm'll try to ignore the fact that you a heathen, and I'm'll focus on teaching you this game. We take care of Jesus later."

Emma just stared at him.

"Come 'ere," he said.

Sighing loudly, she walked over to him as slowly as she could.

"Yeah, drag yo' feet about it," he mumbled.

She placed one hand on her hip and the other out to him for the ball.

"No see, it ain't even gonna be like that. Don't come

over here with yo' attitude. You got to respect the ball. Respect the game. Now change that look on yo' face."

"You're bossy," Emma said.

"I'm bein' bossy cause this some serious stuff we doin'," Anton explained.

Emma did not understand how she was going to respect a basketball, but she felt it necessary to try. The look on his face told her that she needed to try.

"Okay then," she said, standing straight and removing her hand from her hip. "How do I do this?"

Anton's face brightened at the question, and he walked over to her and gave her the ball.

"Okay, first you gotta know how to hold the ball," he said. As he spoke, he placed her left hand toward the bottom of the ball and her right hand in the middle then paused.

"Hold up. You a lefty," he said.

She nodded.

"We gotta switch it up." And with that he moved her left hand to the center of the ball with her right hand on the side underneath.

Anton stood behind her and placed his own hands over hers. She tensed slightly at the closeness of his body, his arms around her holding her hands on the ball.

"Man, this feel weird to me," he said.

"Me too," she said, though she didn't think it was because of the way she was holding the basketball.

"Girl, how you know what feel weird to you? You ain't never shot a basketball right in yo' life."

"Okay, whatever," Emma said. "Just tell me what to do."

"No, I'm'll show you," he said.

"Fine."

"Okay, so a good shot is all about good form. You gotta have the form. Without it, you nothin'. You got to have the hands right, the arms right, the feet right. It all gotta be just right. So now, you gonna stand with your feet square shoulder-width apart."

Anton tapped the insides of her feet with his indicating that she needed to spread them farther apart. He watched as she positioned herself with her feet slightly turned out.

"Girl, square up them feet. Don't be turnin' them out like that. That look retarded," he said.

Emma repositioned her feet making sure to point her toes forward until Anton gave a grunt of satisfaction.

"Okay, we come back to the legs in a minute. So your left hand is gonna push the basketball. Your right hand is there for stability. You know, like to help you guide it. You gonna push, not chuck it like you did earlier. And you gonna use yo' legs to push. That's really important. That's how you get the range. See, a good shot come up through the legs to the hands. Not just from the hands. So go on now, bend yo' legs. Let's just practice going up and down."

Emma felt silly, bending up and down, up and down, with Anton behind her doing the same.

"Good. Now let's practice some arm action. We gonna do it all together at the same time," he said.

"You know, I'm a dancer," Emma said. She couldn't see his face, but she imagined he looked confused.

"I know that," he replied.

"What I mean is I've been a ballet dancer for eleven years now. I have a teacher who sits at the front of the studio and tells us what he wants us to do. He never demonstrates a thing, but we can still do it. I'm pretty quick with picking things up by just hearing them. You could just tell me what to do."

"Well, this ain't ballet now is it, little Miss Hoighty-Toighty Twinkle Toes?"

Emma turned her face up to him. He was smiling down at her. She sighed and acquiesced to his instruction with a slight nod of her head.

"Okay, so now we gonna practice movin' our arms and legs together," Anton continued. "Square up yo' shoulders and make sure yo' left hand is guiding yo' shot. Yo' right hand is there to help."

He raised the ball up and forward, guiding her with his hands over hers. He did this a few times before adding his legs, bending them up and down. She followed suit, concentrating so hard on getting everything right that she failed to notice when he backed away from her, leaving her in front of the basket alone.

"Okay, now shoot," he said.

She did, the ball hitting the backboard a little to the left of the basket and bouncing back to her.

"My aim sucks," she said disappointed.

"Nah, it's my fault. I forgot to tell you to follow through with yo' shot. Keep that left hand up until the ball goes through the basket," Anton said.

"How's that going to make a difference?" Emma asked.

"Just do it," he ordered.

Emma positioned herself again and this time held her left hand up after releasing the ball. The ball glided through the basket effortlessly, touching nothing but the net. She clapped and cheered for herself.

"There you go," Anton said pleased, walking up to stand beside her. "Didn't I tell you it all about form?"

"Uh huh," Emma answered. She thought this was as good a time as any.

"Anton?"

"Yeah?"

"My parents want you to come over for dinner," she said quickly then paused for his response.

"Where did that come from?" he asked looking all around him. "Girl, are you crazy?"

"I'm sorry. It's just that after they learned about this

assignment, they decided that they wanted to meet you."

"Has yo' parents ever had a black person in they house before?" he asked.

She looked at him perplexed.

"Okay, that means no," he said.

"I know it's a lot to ask," Emma continued, ignoring him. "But if you could just do it this one time, I think they'd stop getting all over me about you."

"What you mean by that? They got a problem with me?"

"No. It's not like that. They just don't know you. They know everyone I hang out with. They're my parents. It's their job. But they don't know you."

"They know you been to my house?" he asked.

Emma looked at the ground. "Not exactly," she admitted.

"Shit. What you been tellin' them about where we work?"

"I tell them we go to the library or to my friend Morgan's house," Emma said. She felt embarrassed.

"Hmm. Prolly better that way anyway. Once they see me they gonna prolly be wantin' to join us when we work so they can keep an eye on me."

"That's ridiculous," Emma said.

"I don't even know what I'm supposed to wear," Anton said. He was starting to feel worried.

"What you normally wear," Emma said. "Well, you could probably pull up your pants a little bit."

"Man, Emma. This is some bullshit," he said shaking his head.

"I know, I know," she replied.

"When they want me to come?" he asked.

Emma gave him an apologetic look.

"Tonight?! Shit, you didn't even give me no chance to prepare?!"

"I know. I feel awful. It's just that I've been meaning

to ask you."

"In the past week we been hangin', you been tryin' to ax me? You couldn't find any time in those seven days to ax me about dinner? Now you just spring it on me like this?"

He snatched the ball from her hands and drove it to the basket for an easy layup.

"They expectin' me?" he asked, turning to look at her.

"Yes."

"Man, Emma. What if I already had plans or somethin'?" he asked.

"I just assumed you didn't," she replied.

"Why you assume that? I got a social life," he said defensively.

"I know that, but you said we'd be working on our project all day."

"Yeah, day. Not night. I ain't workin' on no school work on a Friday night. Shit."

He dribbled the ball in and out of his legs, lost in thought.

"I'll take you to the movies afterwards," Emma offered.

Anton snorted. "That don't make it even. Movies for an entire evening with yo' parents. You gonna have to do better than that."

She bit her lip in concentration thinking of what she could give him.

"I know," she said, walking purposefully towards him. When she was within inches of him, she placed her hands on his shoulders pulling him towards her while lifting as high as she could on her toes. Her kiss barely reached his jawbone, and it shocked and delighted him. He never expected her to do anything like that.

He tried for casualness. "Well, I guess that's somethin'," he said. "But I think I might need another."

This time he bent lower to give her better access, and she kissed him softly on the cheek. He was tempted to turn his face quickly and trick her into kissing his lips, but he didn't want to chance spoiling the moment. She let her lips linger for a few moments, and when they left his face, he was certain all the warmth went out of the world.

"Now will you come to dinner?" she asked.

"What choice do I have after that?" he replied.

He straightened up, towering over her, fighting a strong urge to pick her up and squeeze her in a bear hug. He had no idea why he wanted to do that.

"Thank you," she said, smiling.

"Yeah," he replied resigned.

"I promise it won't be a big deal," Emma said.

"If you say so."

He dribbled to the outer edge of the three-point line. He positioned himself and released the ball into the air. It missed the basket, hitting the rim and bouncing out of sight.

CHAPTER 8
FRIDAY, APRIL 23

"Mama, I need the car," Anton said. He was standing in front of her in his church clothes looking terribly uncomfortable and visibly scared.

"Sure baby. Why you all dressed up like that?" she asked.

"I have a dinner I gotta go to," Anton replied.

He pulled at the collar of his shirt. It felt like it was choking him.

"What dinner?" she asked.

"Okay, so you know Emma and how we doin' this project for English class? Well, her parents want me to come over for dinner tonight."

Ms. Robinson burst out laughing. "Of course they do," she said between the laughter.

"I know, right? I don't know what they think I'm'll do to they daughter."

"Plenty, I would guess," she replied, still smiling.

"Mama," Anton chided.

"Honey, it's fine they ask you to go over there. They're her parents. They have all the right in the world to know who she's hanging out with whether it's social or school related. You just let them know that I'd like to have Emma over sometime for dinner." There was a twinkle in her eye.

"Okay, I'll tell 'em," Anton said, grinning. "Now how do I look?"

"Like you scared out of your mind. Come here," she ordered. "You don't need a tie on, baby," and she removed it from around his neck. She unbuttoned the top button of his shirt.

"Can you breathe now?" she asked.

"I don't know how I'm gonna do this," Anton said. "You know where they live? Avondale Drive, Mama."

Ms. Robinson whistled. "Maybe we should put that tie back on," she said grinning.

"Mama, be serious. I'm scared," Anton pleaded.

"Honey, they are people just like you and me."

"No they not! They rich!"

"So what? You need to stop thinking about how you're not good enough. That's what this is all about, and frankly, it's got nothin' to do with an English class assignment. Isn't that why they want to meet you? You're doing this assignment with their daughter?"

"Yes, but I know they gonna take one look at me and think to themselves that they don't want they daughter hangin' out with a guy like me," Anton said bitterly.

"Honey, you a good boy. And anyway, why do you care so much? She just a partner for a class assign—"

Anton wouldn't look at his mother. He knew the realization dawned on her. He kept his eyes glued to the kitchen floor.

"Oh dear Lord in heaven," she said, sighing.

"Are you upset with me?" Anton asked quietly.

"Upset with you?" Ms. Robinson asked. "Why would I be upset with you?"

It was almost too difficult to voice out loud, but he forced himself to. "'Cause she white, Mama."

Ms. Robinson stared at her son in disbelief. "White,

black, red, green, yellow, blue. Honey, I don't care."

She walked over to him and stuck her face underneath of his looking up at him. He smiled down at her.

"You really don't care or you just sayin' that?"

"Honey, if you like her and she's a good girl." Ms. Robinson paused. "She's a good girl, right?"

"Yes, Mama. She's a very good girl. Couldn't you tell when you met her?"

Ms. Robinson nodded.

"Are you two dating?" she asked.

"No. She don't even know I like her. At least I don't think she does," Anton said.

He noticed a great sense of relief on his mother's face.

"What's that look for, Mama? You hopin' she don't like me back? See I knew you had a problem with me likin' a white girl!"

"That's not it at all," she replied.

"Then what is it? Why that look of relief on yo' face?" he pressed.

"Because I know you're not having sex with her," Ms. Robinson said.

"Oh God, Mama!" Anton said, flushed with embarrassment. "How you gonna go there with me?"

"Because I'm your mother," she said. "And I have a right to go there with you."

"Mama, I'm eighteen! I'm an adult!"

"Boy, I don't care if you fifty. You still my baby and I have a right to know what you doin' with yourself," his mother replied. "And you still livin' under my roof."

He grunted.

"How old is she?"

"What?"

"How old is she?" Ms. Robinson repeated with emphasis.

"I think she seventeen," Anton said.

"And you better remember it," Ms. Robinson said.

He understood immediately, and not wanting to continue the awkward discussion, he lied and said that he needed to leave when, in fact, he didn't need to go for another half hour.

"You'll be just fine, baby," Ms. Robinson said, kissing his cheek. "Just be yourself. Minus all that cussin' you do."

"Mama, I don't cuss," Anton said.

"Oh who you foolin'?" his mother asked watching him disappear out the front door.

—

He sat in his mother's car in front of 560 Avondale Drive for twenty minutes studying the façade. The house boasted three stories with a large covered front porch. Though twilight was approaching, he could still make out every detail of the impeccably manicured lawn. Nothing looked real; it was too perfect, and he thought for a moment that perhaps heaven would look like this. He shook his head instantly, ridding his mind of that thought. He didn't want heaven to look like that. It wasn't inviting.

Taking a deep, shaky breath, he exited the Ford Escort and walked up the driveway. He noticed Emma's car and two other cars. One was an expensive SUV and the other a Porsche 911. He smiled sadly to himself thinking that he would die tonight of utter humiliation. He reached the door and rang the doorbell quickly. He knew if he did not, he would lose his nerve and run for the car. Emma answered.

"Are you okay?" she asked softly, moving aside to let him in.

"Yeah, why wouldn't I be?" he asked. His voice sounded strained.

"Because you look like you've seen a ghost," she replied.

"Aw, nah, that'd be your daddy's Porsche outside," Anton said.

"Porsche," Emma corrected.

"That's what I said. Porsche."

"No, no, it's pronounced Porsh-a," Emma explained.

"Do you want me to go?" he asked testily.

Emma smiled apologetically. She hadn't meant to be condescending. "No. I'm sorry. Come in."

She watched him walk into the house with trepidation.

"You're all dressed up," she observed. She wore a springtime dress, but then she always dressed nicely.

"I'm havin' dinner with yo' parents," he reminded her.

"You just need to relax. It's not like you're asking them for my hand in marriage," Emma said laughing.

Anton grunted. That was the best he could do for a reply as she led him through the entryway to the kitchen. He was too nervous to notice anything around him except for the high ceilings. They made the entire place look cavernous. Her mother was at the sink when they entered the kitchen.

"Mom, this is Anton," Emma said.

Emma's mother turned around and smiled.

"So nice to meet you, Anton," she said, but he wasn't sure he believed her.

She was a copycat of her daughter, or rather, her daughter was a copycat of her. Long auburn hair framing her face. The same light blue eyes and creamy complexion. She looked as young as Emma. He didn't think before he spoke.

"Wow, you two could be sisters," he said.

"Well, I'm flattered," Emma's mother said beaming. She didn't miss a beat.

"I'm not," Emma muttered.

"I'm sorry, Mrs. Chapman. Should I not of said that?" Anton asked anxiously.

"Are you kidding?" Mrs. Chapman replied. "What mother doesn't want to be told she looks as young as her daughter?"

Anton smiled and relaxed.

"And call me Kay," she added.

"Aw, no ma'am. I can't do that. Where I come from, that's disrespectful," Anton said.

"Fine, then call me *Ms.* Kay. Is that better?"

Before he could answer, Emma cut in. "Mom, you wanted us to set the table?"

"No, I wanted you to set the table. Anton is our guest."

"Oh, it's a'ight, er, alright. I can help," Anton said.

"That's very nice of you, Anton," Mrs. Chapman replied.

She handed Emma a stack of plates with utensils and cloth napkins—cloth napkins, he thought disbelievingly—and pointed to the glasses sitting on the kitchen island for Anton to take. Don't you drop those glasses, he thought, picking them up carefully with shaky hands and following Emma to the dining room.

He watched her set the table, holding the glasses all the while until she pointed to where they belonged. He placed them delicately on the table and breathed a sigh of relief.

"Call me Ms. Kay," Emma muttered under her breath.

"What's that?" Anton asked.

"Nothing," Emma said. "Just my mom being my mom."

Anton didn't know how to reply.

"Come on," Emma ordered, and he followed her out of the room.

They walked down a long corridor decorated with family photographs. The ceilings seemed higher in the hallway, Anton noticed, thinking that couldn't be right. How's a hallway gonna feel larger than a regular room, he thought, then remembered that they were rich. The guest bathroom was probably the size of his duplex.

They entered a large study where Emma's father sat behind a looming, dark cherry executive desk. He looked like he was in the middle of some important business, and Anton wondered why Emma didn't knock first. He felt immediately uncomfortable all over again just as he was beginning to relax after having successfully placed the glasses on the table.

"Baby girl," her father said looking up from his work. Anton noticed that it became completely inconsequential to him once he saw his daughter.

"Hey Dad," Emma replied. "This is Anton."

Mr. Chapman stood and walked around the desk to shake Anton's hand. He had a firm, authoritative grasp, and Anton tried hard to match it.

"Nice to meet you, son," Mr. Chapman said. "We're happy you came tonight. We've heard so much about this project of yours and Emma's. It's fascinating. I hope she's being a good partner to you." He looked at Emma who smirked at him.

"Oh, yes sir. She keeps me on track," Anton said, and then thought better. "Not that I don't do nothing, I mean, anything. It's just I have a hard time stayin' organized."

"Ha! So do I," Mr. Chapman said, pointing at his desk.

It was littered with stacks of papers, piled high and teetering on the verge of collapse. There were at least a dozen old coffee mugs sitting around. Anton could only imagine how long they'd been there. Folders and binders of all sorts were thrown about haphazardly. Anton wondered how this man could be so successful when he worked in such a mess. A lone picture frame sat at the corner, and he imagined the picture contained in it was of Mr. Chapman's wife or the family.

Mr. Chapman walked over to the desk and picked up the frame as if he read Anton's mind.

"This is my favorite picture," he said and showed it to Anton.

To Anton's surprise, it was not of his wife or the whole family. It was of Emma. And she was very young.

"Dad, why do you have to show everybody that picture?" Emma asked.

Her father offered Anton the frame, and he took it. He studied the little girl in the picture. She could not have been more than five years old. She wore a plaid dress with straps that went over her shoulders and buttoned in the front above her chest. Underneath of the dress she wore a white collar shirt trimmed in the same blue as her dress. She sat with her hands folded neatly in her lap, her long auburn hair flowing down past her shoulders and coming to rest at her lower back. Her eyes were large and bright. And innocent, he thought. She smiled sweetly looking every bit the epitome of a happy child. She was beautiful, and Anton thought that maybe this could be his favorite picture, too.

Emma snatched the picture from him and returned it to the desk.

"My father still doesn't know I've grown up," she said.

Mr. Chapman chuckled then asked about dinner.

"That's why we came in here to get you," Emma said.

Mr. Chapman placed his arm around his daughter's shoulders and kissed her forehead. She rolled her eyes and waved for them both to follow her to the dining room.

Emma's mother had laid the table, and it looked

delicious. Unfortunately for Anton, his nerves were too jumpy to really appreciate it. He noticed a bottle of wine and four extra glasses laid out that he didn't put there. That was peculiar, he thought.

Once everyone was seated—Anton across from Emma and her parents across from each other—the food was passed.

"I'll say the blessing before we eat," Anton offered, passing the mashed potatoes to Mrs. Chapman. They all froze then Mrs. Chapman regained her composure.

"That would be lovely," she said.

Anton noticed the awkwardness elicited by his offer. Did these people not say grace before dinner? And then he remembered Emma saying that she didn't "do church." Oh God, why did he open his mouth?

"Anton? We're ready," Mr. Chapman said.

"Oh, yes sir," he said quickly.

He looked around the table and folded his hands. They did the same. He bowed his head slowly still watching them, and they followed suit.

"Dear Heavenly Father," he began, closing his eyes. He took a deep breath. His mind went blank. What was he praying about again? Think, Anton, think. Why was he here? Oh, he was gonna kill Emma. Bye bye, sweet Emma. You goin' in the ground, girl. I can't even believe I'm sittin' here in this million dollar house about to eat with yo' parents who prolly think I'm some kinda thug or something. Why'd I offer to say the blessing? What kinda dumb shit do that at someone else's house they don't know?

Emma kicked him underneath of the table.

"Dear Heavenly Father," he said, remembering that he needed to bless the food. "Thank you for this lovely meal. Thank you for the hands that prepared it. Please make it a nourishment to our bodies, as I'm sure it will be because it looks real good. I can't even imagine how long it took to prepare such a lovely meal."

He paused for a moment not knowing what else to say. Should he thank God that he has the opportunity to work with Emma on their school project? Would her parents like that? He decided against it.

"It is such a lovely meal, Lord, and we are so grateful to you for the opportunity to eat it."

How should I end this, he thought?

"It is perhaps the loveliest meal I have ever seen, Lord. And we know that Mrs. Chapman worked real hard to prepare it. And that makes her a wonderful lady . . . uh, the most wonderful lady in the world, perhaps. Thank you for blessing us with this meal. In Jesus' name, Amen."

He looked up then and was greeted by two slightly perplexed faces staring at him. He knew he butchered that prayer, and he also knew who he'd be taking it out on later.

"That was so lovely, Anton," Mrs. Chapman said. "Thank you."

"Oh, you welcome," Anton replied.

He looked at Emma whose head was still bowed. She was grinning, he could tell. She tried to hide it, but he saw. Yeah, you go on and grin, girl. You don't even know what's comin', he thought sourly.

"So you go to church, son?" Mr. Chapman asked.

"Uh, yes sir," Anton replied. "Mount Zion Baptist."

He noticed an almost imperceptible look of relief on Mr. Chapman's face. He turned to Emma's mother and noticed that she, too, seemed more relaxed. He smiled to himself. So now they think I'm alright 'cause I go to church, he thought. They don't go to church. They nothin' but a bunch of freakin' heathens, but as long as I go. He wanted to be pissed, but the delicious aroma wafting from the chicken urged him to change his mind. He took a deep breath and forced himself to relax. He remembered how much he loved food and decided that he would make every effort to enjoy himself.

"Now Anton," Mr. Chapman began, reaching for the wine bottle. "We let baby girl here have a glass of wine at dinner sometimes. You certainly don't have to take any if you don't want to, but you are more than welcome."

Anton watched as Mr. Chapman got up from the table to pour his wife a glass and then pour one for Emma. Is this how rich white people do, he thought? Let they underage kids drink alcohol at dinner? It was prolly some fancy, expensive wine, he thought. This must be what cultured people do. And how they gonna think it'd be alright with his mama, them offering him wine? Well, maybe they didn't think he had a mama. Maybe they thought he was on his own, poor and black, and they'd try to give him a sampling of the finer things before he had to go back out on the streets.

"You don't have to have any," Emma said quietly.

"Nah, I'll have a glass," he said. "Thank you."

Mr. Chapman poured Anton a glass, and he took a sip. It wasn't like any wine he had ever tasted, certainly not the cheap stuff down on the corner at Ellie's Grocer, he thought. It tasted rich and dark. And pricey.

"So Anton, where do you live?" Mr. Chapman asked, seating himself once more.

"Uh, off Greenbriar Road," Anton replied. So much for enjoying his food and wine.

"Greenbriar Road, Greenbriar Road," Mr. Chapman said to himself. "I don't think I'm familiar with that road." He was clearly waiting for Anton to specify.

"West Highland Park," Anton said reluctantly.

Mrs. Chapman cleared her throat.

"Oh yes," Mr. Chapman said, seemingly unfazed.

There was an awkward silence.

"Dad, you should see Anton play basketball," Emma said. She smiled at Anton who stared back at her frowning, shoving a roll in his mouth.

"Oh yeah? You know, I was point guard in high school," Mr. Chapman replied. "What position do you play?"

"Oh, I play everything. I'm not on the school team. I just play for fun," Anton said.

"Well, maybe we should shoot some hoops outside after dinner," Mr. Chapman offered.

"That sounds like fun," Emma said.

Was she trying to be difficult, Anton wondered, or did she think she was actually being helpful?

"Okay," Anton said. He took another sip of his wine. He wanted to drown himself in it.

The conversation progressed more easily after that. Mr. Chapman talked mostly of his job. It was evident that it consumed him, and his wife looked bored throughout most of the dinner. She did perk up, however, when the subject changed to her volunteer work and then to Emma. Apparently Emma was the most gifted ballet dancer in the world, and they were sorely disappointed that this was her last year performing. Now Emma looked bored, Anton noticed.

Emma's parents asked questions about the class assignment. They seemed genuinely intrigued, and Anton did his best to clarify the purpose of the paper and what he thought Dr. Thompson wanted the students to get out of it. He also tried his best to keep the details of his world to a minimum. They knew where he lived now, and that was all he was willing to share. He didn't even want to share that, he thought bitterly. Thankfully they didn't ask him any more personal questions.

After dinner, Mr. Chapman excused himself to his office, shaking Anton's hand and saying regrettably that he had case work to do. Anton was relieved that he would not have to shoot hoops with him, Mr. Chapman apparently forgetting all about the offer. He helped Emma and her mother clear the table, and thanked Mrs.

Chapman once again for dinner. She told him she was glad he came and that he was welcome back any time.

Emma walked him out to his car.

"Well, that wasn't so bad, was it?" she asked.

"I guess not," Anton said. "Well, apart from my dumbass blessing and having to tell yo' parents where I live and them actin' like they wasn't completely embarrassed for me. Oh yeah, and bein' offered alcohol at eighteen and feelin' like I ain't sophisticated, like I don't understand that this what cultured people do—let they underage kids drink alcohol at the dinner table. Except for all that, it was great."

Emma shrugged.

"Look, I gotta get home. I wanna get outta these clothes and lay on my bed and listen to some music."

"Oh. Okay." She wondered if he would listen to "Hit 'Em Up."

He noted the look of disappointment on her face. "I ain't mad, Emma. I just feel like an idiot."

Anton opened the car door and climbed in.

"Please don't feel that way," she pleaded.

"Oh okay," he said irritably, and snapped his fingers. "I don't feel like an idiot no more!"

"Don't be mean," she said quietly.

"I'm sorry," he replied and looked her over. "Look, I gotta go."

"Well, when do you want to get together next?" she asked hopefully.

"I don't know. I'll call you," he said and pulled away before she had time to respond.

Emma watched as the Ford rounded the corner and disappeared. She tried to be reasonable, but the tightening in her chest was all too real. She didn't want him to go.

CHAPTER 9
SATURDAY, APRIL 24

Emma sat on the swing watching Anton.

"Are you still mad at me about dinner?" she asked.

"Girl, I was never mad at you," Anton replied. He was in the swing next to her. There were only two left out of the original six that weren't broken. He had taken her to the neighborhood playground because it was a lovely warm day, the breeze blowing occasionally, and he didn't want to be cooped up inside.

"You seemed like you were last night," Emma said. "I didn't think you'd call me today."

"Well, I did. Okay?"

Emma said nothing. Anton suddenly wished he hadn't called her. He was still annoyed by last night and wanted to punish her for it. He knew it was ridiculous, as though not calling her to hang out would punish her. The truth was that it would only punish him. He was angry that he liked her so much and she seemed oblivious. Or perhaps she did know and simply didn't share his feelings. He didn't know which was worse.

"Did you ever think you could swing so high that you would flip over?" Emma asked, breaking his contemplation. "You know, when you were little?"

"Yeah," he replied. "I would try real hard. Never got there though."

"Well, it's physics," she said.

"Yeah, I know," he said, although he didn't.

Emma scanned the dilapidated playground. There was an old metal merry-go-round. She had only seen them in movies. She didn't know they still existed and wondered how something like that could. She imagined a child getting caught underneath of it. The thought was horrifying. There was a metal slide as well. It was peppered with graffiti and looked like it had not been used in years. Where did the children play, she thought? In fact, where were the children? It was a perfect Saturday afternoon, and they were the only two people outside.

"Anton?" she asked.

"Hmm?"

"Where are all the children?"

Anton looked around. "I don't know. They prolly inside playing video games or down at the store. How should I know?"

"Look, if you want me to leave, just say the word. You've been pissy since I got here, and I don't need to hang around that," she snapped.

He looked at her and snickered. "Look at what you wearin'. Who wear that on a Saturday? You own any regular clothes? You know, T-shirts, jean shorts or whatever?"

Emma got out of the swing and started walking towards her car. Anton jumped up to follow.

"Emma, I'm sorry, okay? I don't know what my problem is," he said, catching up to her and grabbing her hand.

She wheeled around. "You can't talk to me like that! I haven't done anything to you!"

He wanted to say she had. She made him have dinner with her parents.

"You right. And I'm sorry."

He wanted to tell her how he felt about her right there, but he was too afraid. She would laugh at him, he was sure. Or she would slink away and never talk to him again, saying she'd be happy to do the entire project herself and put his name on it. The words were there; they were locked and loaded. But he couldn't.

"Will you just come inside?" he asked.

She thought for a moment then nodded grudgingly.

"I know what you think," Emma said. "You think I'm a priss pot."

Anton smirked as he let his eyes rove over her blouse and trousers. He was making a great effort to be in a better mood for her.

"Yeah, you a priss pot."

She had no reply but stood there in the center of his room taking in the wall posters. By now she knew most of the rappers. They were waving guns at her and giving her the middle finger. She thought she should feel offended, but she had gotten used to them.

Anton walked towards her and stood within inches of her body. He reached out to feel the soft fabric hugging her waist. She jumped at his touch, but he ignored it.

"Why you gotta be all put together all the time?" he asked, not looking at her but studying the fabric between his thumb and forefinger.

"I don't know."

Anton moved his hand to the pearl necklace around her throat. He tentatively touched the pearls one by one, this time watching her face. She was flushed and embarrassed, and he was glad for it. He thought that if he couldn't voice his feelings, he might touch her instead. Touching seemed easier.

"These real?" he asked, smoothing his forefinger over the pearls.

"Yes," she replied. She couldn't understand why there was a note of shame in her voice.

Anton laughed aloud again. "'Course they are."

"You're making fun of me," she said indignantly.

"Girl, I ain't tryin' to make fun. It's just so easy," Anton replied. "How you stay put together like this all the time?"

"They're just clothes. What's the big deal?"

"You all proper and uptight in that shit," Anton said.

He moved away from her towards his dresser. She watched as he opened the top drawer and removed a large sky blue hoodie emblazoned with the UNC Tar Heels logo across the front. She remembered that he wore it the day she introduced herself to him in English class. He threw the hoodie over his shoulder and turned back to her.

"Don't you ever get tired of always tryin' to be perfect and look perfect?"

"I'm not trying to look perfect."

"Oh, who you kiddin'? Look at you." And once more his eyes raked her body.

She said nothing but stood there determined. She lifted her face to him and willed the soft pink of her flushed cheeks to disappear. Anton approached her once more and looked down at her eyes. They were ice blue and angry and scared and excited. He made up his mind. If she punched him in the face, he would stop.

He started at the top of the blouse, undoing the ivory buttons one by one, never taking his eyes off of hers. His hands reached her waist and gently tugged at the shirt until he freed it from her trousers. He unbuttoned to the end of the shirt letting his eyes fall to the exposed lace bra. It was pure white. He slipped his hands under the fabric of the shirt on her shoulders and pushed it to the ground.

He watched her breathing rapidly.

"Now what you need is a makeover," he said lightly, and pulled the hoodie off of his shoulder. "Head first."

She helped him pull the hoodie over her head then pushed her arms through the sleeves. They were much too long. She felt silly and laughed as he pulled the hood up over her head. The material hung low over her brows, and she had to tilt her head back to see him. He was smiling at her, studying her.

"Almost there," he said and searched around the room until he found what he was looking for. He pulled a pair of black athletic shorts out of a pile of clean laundry and threw those over his shoulder. He approached her once more, a look of determination in his eyes, and her heart beat wildly at the realization of what he planned to do next.

Anton unbuttoned her trousers and slowly slid the material down her legs. They were soft and thin—skinny white girl legs. She placed her hand on his shoulder for balance as she stepped out of the pants. He knelt before her imagining her panties, but the hoodie covered them completely. He imagined they matched her bra—white and lacy, hugging her hips seductively.

He considered how easy it would be to lose control, let his hands slide roughly up the length of her legs, leave faint red marks as the sign of his claim on her. It was a primal need he'd never felt, and it grew in him the longer she stood there unresisting, letting him dress her. Why was she letting him do it?

He fought the animal urge and placed the athletic shorts on the floor for her to step into. She did, and she bent down to pull them up herself. He was relieved, not trusting himself with the shorts, only pulling on the drawstring as tightly as it would go once they were safely around her waist. He was glad, too, that he didn't get a glimpse of her panties. He felt his racing heart slow then, the animal instinct recede into the depths of his bones to mix with the marrow, and a calm return to the focus of his task. He stood back from her and studied her new image.

"That look better," he said thoughtfully, and then finding his humor added, "You look like a 'lil hood rat now. Well, except you ain't no ho." He paused considering. "So I guess you ain't look like a hood rat at all."

"What's a hood rat?" she asked.

Anton smiled at her. It was playful and incredulous. "You so funny."

He thought in that moment that he could own her. He had transformed her, given her the image of someone he understood, and now he wanted to possess her like a child possesses a baby doll, dress her up and keep her in his room to play with and love.

Emma looked down at her new outfit: the oversized hoodie and baggy athletic shorts that hung past her knees. She felt oddly comfortable standing in his room, in his clothes, taking in his scent.

"Okay, so how you think we should organize our paper?" Anton asked, grabbing a notebook off of his desk and sitting on his bed. "We got all these notes we gotta do somethin' with."

"What?" she asked.

"Our paper," he said.

"I . . . you just—"

"Yes?"

"Am I supposed to stay in these clothes?" Emma asked. She raised her hands up, the sleeves of the hoodie covering them completely and hanging limp.

"Why not? You uncomfortable?" Anton asked.

"No."

"Okay then. Are you ready to work?"

"I guess," Emma said.

"Then stop standin' there with that look on yo' face and get over here," he demanded. She walked to the bed and sat down.

He looked her over and chuckled. She looked like she had drunk an entire bottle of shrinking potion, dwindling down to the size of a dwarf while her clothes never altered.

"Why UNC?" she asked suddenly, staring at the logo.

"Oh, that'd be the school I'd get a scholarship at to play basketball," he replied. "You know, if I woulda done sports in high school."

"That good, huh? Why didn't you play for the school?" she asked.

"Girl, please," he said and handed her several sheets of paper. She pulled up the sleeves of the hoodie to take them.

"What is this?" she asked, finally taking her mind off of the fact that he disrobed her just moments before to concentrate on the pages of writing.

"It's my cultural summary thing," he said.

She flipped through the pages. There were ten total.

"Oh my God," she said.

"What?"

"You did all of this? When did you do this?" she asked.

"Here and there. When a thought popped into my mind, I wrote it down."

"You've had a lot of thoughts lately," Emma said.

"Well, this project's important, you know? I wanna do a good job. And I don't wanna let you down neither," he said.

She smiled at him.

"I thought you could look it over and tell me what you think. I'm sure I got all kinda grammar and spelling mistakes in it. I figured you could help me out with that."

"Yeah, sure," Emma said, distracted.

She had already begun reading. He watched her face nervously. He couldn't tell if she liked what she was reading or thought it was horrible. He couldn't stand the silence as she absorbed his words, not knowing what went on in her mind.

He jumped up and offered her a drink. She nodded preoccupied. He left her immersed in the pages he had written, walking to the kitchen to grab some sodas. He thought that she might hate it, and then it would have been a lot of wasted work. And he had worked hard; he couldn't remember the last time he cared so much about a school assignment. It was her. It was everything about what was happening inside of him every time he looked at her, talked to her.

He stood at the kitchen counter in contemplation. He couldn't believe she let him disrobe her like that. He couldn't believe his brazenness. He didn't see anything, or at least not everything he wanted. And while it excited him—taking off her clothes—he knew it wasn't the right time to make a move. The strong urge was there—it almost overtook him—but he fought it down remembering the goal. It wasn't to kiss her, to touch her body intimately, to be romantic with her in any way. He needed to understand her, to transform her into something that fit nicely into his world.

He wanted to remain casual about it when it was over. He knew she was confused afterwards as he moved on to the subject of their paper. She wanted to talk about it, too, but what would they say? It was one of those movie moments, he decided. Something that would never happen in real life. He wanted to keep the memory of it, not ruin the magic of it by talking.

He left her alone for awhile, putting clean dishes away and washing the few dirty ones in the sink. When he entered his bedroom, she was sitting staring at the opposite wall. She still had the papers in hand, but she was finished reading.

"I just really had no idea," she said quietly.

"What are you talkin' about?" he asked.

He sat down beside her on the bed and offered her a drink. She took it automatically, not looking at him, still staring at the wall.

"I really never understood this life," she said.

He noticed a tear spill over. Oh God, he thought, he didn't mean to make her cry!

"Well, it ain't all bad," he said.

"I'm so spoiled. I really am," she replied, the tears flowing freely.

"What?"

He felt uncomfortable. He was not prepared for her reaction. He thought he'd come back into his room and she would be marking up his paper with a red pen. He now wished she were, and thought about looking for a red pen.

"How you gonna feel bad for havin' things?" Anton continued. "There ain't nothin' wrong with that. Everybody in the whole world want things. Nobody work hard to live in the ghetto."

Emma placed the unopened soda can on his bed and buried her face in her hands. She was sobbing.

"Oh my God. Emma? It ain't no big deal," Anton said.

"Your mother works hard," she bawled.

"Well yeah. And she ain't gonna be here much longer," Anton replied. He tentatively put a large hand on her back and rubbed it gently.

"I'm a spoiled brat!" she wailed.

Anton fought the urge within him to laugh. She was being unreasonable, crying uncontrollably into her hands. He thought long and hard before answering her. He wanted to make sure he said the right thing.

"You ain't a spoiled brat just 'cause yo' family is

wealthy," he said grinning. He was glad her face was still buried in her hands. "Yo' parents work hard for that money. They wanna give you a good life. That's what good parents do. It's all about how you handle that money. And you fine about it. You ain't snotty or stuck up. You a nice girl, Emma. And anyway, I like that you gotta car. It mean I gotta ride home most afternoons."

She laughed at that, wiping carelessly at her eyes. She looked at him finally, and he made an uncertain face.

"What?" she asked.

"You just be lookin' like a raccoon, that's all," he observed.

"Oh God," she said embarrassed, and made a move for the bathroom. He caught her arm and kept her seated.

"Relax. Like I ain't never seen make-up run on a girl's face."

The truth was that he didn't think he'd ever seen make-up run on a girl's face. It looked comical, and he wondered why they bothered to wear it at all. She didn't need it, he thought. He searched his cluttered desk until he found a box of tissues. He took one and handed it to her.

"Blow," he ordered.

"I don't want to blow my nose in front of you," she said.

"Good grief, Emma. Who cares? You want snot runnin' down yo' face instead?"

She hesitated then blew her nose. He took another tissue out and gently began wiping away the mascara from underneath her eyes.

"You too sensitive, Emma. That's yo' problem," he decided.

"You think?" she asked, feeling not at all uneasy that he was wiping her face. She felt strangely like a little girl whose daddy was comforting her after a fall off of her bicycle. She felt warm and safe with him.

"Yeah. But maybe I shouldn't say that's a problem," he said thoughtfully. "Maybe the world need more sensitive people in it. Maybe then we wouldn't have all this killin' and rapin' and shit."

"Maybe," she agreed.

"Then again, my pastor always be talkin' about how people sinful by nature. We born into it, so maybe it don't matter. Maybe the world just a bad place, and we gotta do the best we can," he said.

"Well, I think people are basically good at heart," Emma said, and Anton burst out laughing.

"Girl, you so crazy," he said, finishing his task and studying her face. "Okay, you don't look like a raccoon no more."

"Thank you," she said.

He took the tissues and disposed of them in the bathroom. When he returned, she was searching the floor for her clothes.

"I don't think I can handle anymore of this assignment today," she said, locating her pants.

"My mind too intense for you?" Anton asked lightly.

"Something like that," she replied, pulling off his shorts and replacing them with her pants.

Anton turned his face away to give her privacy. It was absurd, he thought, when he had just disrobed her earlier. She switched out the hoodie for her blouse and walked over to hand him his clothes. He took them reluctantly. She was no longer his baby doll to dress up and keep in his room. He had to let her go, and wondered suddenly what he would do for the rest of the day. It didn't occur to him until she was gone that he had friends.

He stood in the doorway observing the empty parking spot where she had just been. His clothes were still in his hands, and he instinctively lifted them to his face breathing in. Her scent lingered on them, light and fruity, like a tropical island, he thought. He stood inhaling her, feeling as though he had been transported to somewhere warm and sandy and sunny. He had never been to a place like that, but he could see it vividly. There were palm trees like he'd seen on T.V. and hammocks swaying in the breeze. And she was there lying beside him like a golden goddess, her body cradled in the warm sand. It stuck to her naked skin. It was seductive. Her hair shimmered in the sunshine, and he ran his fingers through it. And then he kissed her, and she let him.

The sudden appearance of his friend in the doorway shattered the enchanting vision, jolting him back to his reality, and tossing the clothes on the couch, he went out to smoke some weed.

CHAPTER 10
SUNDAY, APRIL 25

Anton was at her house at three o'clock as promised. He had not changed out of his church clothes, and he thought that her parents might start believing that he always dressed up. But her parents weren't there. Her father was golfing and her mother was visiting with friends. Did they know he was there? But she assured him that she had told them. He wanted to believe her, but he was skeptical. He thought that perhaps he should go, but she insisted that it was alright.

She led him up a massive staircase to her bedroom. She wanted to show him her world, she said. His heart beat wildly. For so long he had imagined it. He never thought he'd actually get to see it. And even though she told him things, described aspects of her room for him, it wasn't the same as actually seeing them. He felt like he was about to enter into a sanctuary, become privy to the secrets of her world, and it filled him with intense joy.

Emma opened the door and invited him in.

"This is it," she said indifferently.

Just as he had expected, her room was very large. She slept in a queen-sized bed, he thought incredibly. His was a twin, one of those extra long twin-sized beds because he was so tall. The quilt on her bed was speckled with tiny pink embroidered roses. There were creamy white nightstands on either side of the bed that matched the large bureau opposite them. A chest of drawers lined another wall. It, too, matched the nightstands and bureau. There was a small sitting room that housed a desk on which sat perfectly organized binders and books. Everything matched, he noticed. Everything was pristine. He was afraid to touch anything. He didn't want to leave a fingerprint on her highly polished furniture.

It was only after she excused herself to the bathroom that he noticed she had one in her room. A master suite, he thought amazingly, and followed her. The door stood ajar and she was washing her hands. He walked in and laughed when he noticed the garden tub. It was enormous. She couldn't possibly soak in that thing, he thought. She'd drown.

"What's so funny?" she asked, drying her hands on a hand towel and then folding it back the way it originally hung on the towel rack.

"That," he said pointing to the towel.

She looked confused.

"Hold up. Lemme try somethin'," he said, and snatching the towel from the rack, he threw it up in the air letting it fall wherever it may. It landed on the edge of the tub.

"What are you doing?" she asked.

"I'm gonna see how long you'll let that towel sit there," he said.

She grinned. "I like to be organized."

"No girl, this ain't no organization," Anton replied. "This called bein' majorly Obsessive Compulsive."

"No it's not," she said, laughing.

He saw her glance at the towel.

"You wanna get it, don't you? You wanna hang it up all pretty and perfect, don't you? It's killin' you."

"Shut up," she said lightly.

"Well, I ain't gonna let you. At least not while I'm here," he replied and led her out of the bathroom with his large hand on the small of her back.

He noticed her ballet shoes sitting near a nightstand. He walked over and picked one up to examine it.

"You stand on yo' toes in this?" he asked.

"Yes," she replied.

He felt inside of it. "There ain't no cushions or nothin'?!"

"Some dancers go without pads or lambs' wool. I don't," she answered. She grabbed the bag sitting next to the nightstand and pulled out a pair of toe pads to show him.

"It still gotta hurt," he said looking at the toe pads doubtfully. "What's in this thing? Wood?" He rapped his knuckles on the shoe.

"Layers and layers of fabric glued together," she said, smiling.

"You crazy. Really?"

"I'm not kidding," she said, gently taking the shoe out of his hand.

"What do you call them things?"

"Pointe shoes," she said.

"Pointe shoes," he repeated, as if trying on the words. He had never said them before. "So when's yo' show?"

"My show?" she asked, confused. "Oh, my dance recital?"

"Mmhmm."

"Yeah, I don't think so," she said.

"You don't want me to see you dance?" he asked.

"Absolutely not."

He smiled.

Emma invited him to take a seat in a chair next to her bureau. He plopped himself on her bed instead. He was mindful of taking off his shoes before sprawling out on her quilt.

"Now see, this what I need. A nice big bed like this," he said, snuggling her pillows. "You like four feet tall. What you need a big ass bed like this for?"

"I don't know. It came with the set," Emma replied shrugging. She moved over to the chair she had offered him.

"You don't gotta sit there," Anton said. "I don't bite."

She was uncertain about sitting on her bed with a boy, but she didn't want to come across as prudish. He already thought she had Obsessive Compulsive Disorder. Why did she clean her bedroom so thoroughly before he came over?

"You comin'?" he asked.

She attempted humor. "Why? So you can get me into bed with you?"

Anton laughed. "Yeah, I have plans on gettin' freaky with you in yo' parents' house. Girl, I know you didn't tell them I was comin' over."

"I did too!" Emma said, walking over to the bed and sitting on the edge.

"How they gonna be okay with me bein' here alone with you?" Anton asked.

"They think we're outside," Emma said sheepishly.

"Oh I see."

"And they know you go to church," Emma said.

"You people crazy. You tellin' me they fine with me comin' over here when they not home because I go to church?" Anton asked.

"They figured it makes you a decent guy, I guess," Emma responded.

"Well, I am a decent guy," Anton said.

"I know."

"And I'm respectful," he continued.

"I know."

"And gentlemanly," he added.

"Uh huh."

"Now lemme see yo' panties," he said.

He meant it to be silly and lighthearted, but it had the opposite effect. The tension it created was palpable. Emma didn't know what to say. She leaned forward to fix the lamp on her nightstand that was slightly off center.

"I can't even believe I said that," Anton said after a time. "I'm sorry. I was just tryin' to be silly. You know, after I said I was a decent guy. It was supposed to be a joke."

He felt mortified, and hoped that she would ask him to leave. He had an overwhelming need to be very far away from her at that moment, and if he never saw her again, he would think of her fondly.

Emma seemed to have decided something. She got up from the bed and walked to her bureau. She opened the top drawer and pulled something out. He couldn't see. He was still painfully replaying the last few moments of his life wishing he weren't such an idiot.

Something floated into his lap, and it took him a moment to realize what it was. He held it up, looking at it, looking at her, looking at it again. He was in disbelief. Her panties. Black and silky, trimmed in pink ribbon and lace. He stared at them as if he held an object of great worth— a signed Babe Ruth baseball card or the Hope Diamond. They were everything he wasn't—feminine and soft, sensual and delicate.

He looked at Emma. She stood in the doorway transfixed. She had been watching him, watching the way he responded to her panties. Her lips curled into a grin as if to say, "Game on." And then she disappeared from the room, beckoning him to follow.

He wanted so much to put them in his pocket. Maybe she wanted him to, he thought. He knew he was wrong, though. Perhaps she only showed him her panties to make him feel better for saying something so inappropriate. But then wasn't what she did totally inappropriate as well? He didn't understand. Was she giving him a signal? He didn't dare to hope. But how he wanted to—he wanted to hope.

He placed the panties on the bed. And before he left the room, he made sure to go around rearranging her things, shifting stacked books and moving the objects on her bureau to other places like her nightstands and desk. He wanted everything to be slightly askew. He was about to leave before remembering her dance recital. He walked swiftly to her desk looking around for a planner or calendar. He found neither, but he did discover a mockup of the dance program. He grinned devilishly noting the time, date, and place. He returned to the doorway and studied his work. Her room was in perfect disorder. She would freak out, and he chuckled. Game on you little cutie, he thought, and went in search of her.

He didn't mention anything about the panties when he found her sitting at a table outside in the back yard. He wondered if this was like the clothing incident when he disrobed her and put his hoodie and athletic shorts on her. It wasn't meant to be discussed. A movie moment, he thought.

She affected complete ignorance to what had just occurred, and he was grateful for it. He sat beside her and dumped his book bag in a vacant chair. He had no motivation to work on a paper today. He wanted to go back upstairs and see what other things she would pull out of her dresser drawers. He wondered how long they would refrain from doing anything more than flirting. They had so many more weeks together, and he could think of nothing but getting her naked and exploring her body.

"Are you listening to me?" she asked.

"Uh, yeah. You was sayin' how we gotta tighten up that third paragraph 'cause, you know, the syntax be all wrong and, um, those commas all over the place make it sound bad."

He grinned at her.

"Pay attention!" she ordered, and slapped a piece of paper down in front of him.

"How 'bout we go do somethin' fun today? Like go to the park and shoot hoops?"

"No."

"Well what about seein' a movie or somethin'?"

"No."

"Game of cards?"

"No."

"Damn, Emma. Why you gotta be all studious all the time? We got plenty of time for this paper. We already done half of it. Can't you just relax?" Anton griped.

Emma looked at him evenly.

"And anyway, it Sunday. Day of rest? We can't be doin' all this work on the Lord's day. That's just disrespectful."

Emma slammed her binder closed. "Fine. What do you want to do?"

"I don't know. Why don't you show me some of them ballet moves you so good at," he offered.

"I don't think so," she said.

"You could teach me. Like I taught you how to shoot a ball," he said.

"You're insane," she replied laughing.

"Well, it's a pretty day and we ain't gonna waste it by doin' no school work," he said.

"I thought you liked this project," she said.

"I do. I just can't get focused today."

Emma knew why. She knew it was because of her panties. Even now as she sat across from him, she knew he was thinking about them, the way they felt in his hands. He probably put them in his pocket to take home. She disregarded the thought, and then making up her mind, she got up from her seat.

"Alright. Stay here," she ordered.

She disappeared for a few moments and then returned with a chess board and pieces.

"You fuckin' kiddin' me, right?" he said.

"Um, language. It's the Lord's day, remember?" she said.

He gave her a level look.

"Do you know how to play?" she asked setting up the board.

"No."

"Then I'll teach you."

"I don't wanna learn," he said.

"Too bad. You don't want to work, we don't have to work. We'll sit here and play a game."

"This ain't no game," he argued.

"How is this not a game?"

"Because it ain't fun."

"How do you know? You've never played before," she said, and he rolled his eyes.

She walked him through the pieces and how they moved on the board. He thought he would never master it, but she was patient with him, explaining and correcting throughout their practice game. To his surprise, he actually began enjoying it. He thought it was fitting that the queen had so much power on the board—how she was able to move anywhere—while the king could only move one or two spaces at a time. Not much different from human relationships, he thought. The woman always has the power, and he looked at Emma. She was so pretty sitting there with her brows furrowed in concentration, pretending that he was a worthy opponent, and he smiled at her kindness.

She beat him. That was to be expected, and she was surprised when he wanted to play again. And when she beat him a second time, he asked for another game. They played chess all afternoon, stopping only for bathroom breaks and to rummage through the refrigerator. They played until the sun set and her parents came home. She won every time, but he never got frustrated. He never gave up. With each game he was studying the way she moved. He began realizing that she had her go-to moves, her same set-ups. He had simply been too amateur to recognize them before. But now he knew them; he knew what she would do. And next time, he would be ready for her. He would anticipate her moves, and he would beat her.

—

That night Anton had an unsettling dream. She was there, a tall elegant queen on a chess board and he a miniature pawn standing opposite her. He moved to the only space he could, knowing his fate. He watched her, eyes pleading, but she drew her sword nevertheless. She came towards him slowly, controlled. He was ready for the blow, probably to his throat, he thought, and would feel her slice his head cleanly from his neck. But he never felt the pain in his throat. Instead, his eyes went wide with agony and disbelief as she cut through his chest. He thought he should fall down, but he was fixed to his spot. He watched as she plunged her hands into his chest, pulling out his rapidly beating heart and holding it up in triumph.

"I didn't want to kill you," she said. "I only wanted this."

He watched as she strode away gracefully, like gliding upon water, carefully cradling his heart in her hands. She could have it, he thought, and then his knees went out. He collapsed on the floor still watching her though his vision blurred. His eyes never left her until she walked off of the chess board and disappeared into the night. Then he closed his eyes and died in her hands.

CHAPTER 11
MONDAY, APRIL 26

"You are not coming to my recital," Emma said firmly.

"Why not?" Anton asked. "Why can't I see you dance?"

"Because you just want to come to make fun of me," Emma said.

"That's not true," Anton argued. "I know ballet important to you. It's part of who you are. Yo' culture and all that."

"I'm so sick of this assignment," she muttered.

"Whoa. Where'd that come from?" Anton asked.

They sat on his bedroom floor after school that evening amidst strewn papers.

"I don't know," she said. "I guess I'm just frustrated with it. You're so good at articulating where you come from and what it means to you. I don't even know what my culture is. I come from a wealthy white family. That's all I've got."

"Well, that ain't all there is to you," Anton pointed out.

Emma grunted.

"You tell me all about yo' family and how they

successful in they jobs and stuff. Wouldn't education be part of yo' culture? Something that's shaped you?"

"Whatever," she said flippantly.

"Okay," Anton replied. He was trying to help, but she seemed distracted, irritable. He wondered if it was something he'd done.

"Why don't I know your friends?" she asked suddenly.

"Why don't I know yo' friends?"

Silence.

"You've never introduced me to them," Emma said. "Do they know we're working on this assignment together?"

"You know they do."

"And what do they think?" Emma prodded.

"They don't think anything. No, correction. They think Dr. Thompson a lunatic," Anton said, chuckling.

"They never say anything to you about me? They laughed at me when I confronted you that time," Emma said.

"Why you gotta bring that up? Can't we just let that go?" Anton asked. "And anyway, why you care what my friends think?"

"I don't know," Emma said. "It's just weird to me that we've been hanging out a lot . . . I mean, I know it's because of this project, but still. We've been hanging out a lot and neither one of us has ever introduced our friends."

"And how you think yo' friends would react to meetin' me?" Anton asked. "Be for real, Emma. They'd be like, who the hell is this guy?"

Emma said nothing. She stared at the papers on the floor.

"What's really botherin' you?" Anton asked. "'Cause I don't think it's about meetin' each other's friends."

"I don't know," she mumbled. She flipped carelessly through the novel, careful not to look at him. "Are we friends?" she asked quietly.

"What?"

"You heard me. Are we friends?"

"'Course we're friends," Anton said.

"So after this project is done and after we graduate, we'll still be friends?" she asked.

Anton thought for a moment. "Well, sure, if you want."

"Please," Emma said coldly. She felt an unjustifiable anger rising within her. "We'll never talk to each other after this. What the hell is the point of all this?"

"Do you wanna be friends with me after this project?" Anton asked. He was confused by her sour mood. "It ain't no big deal. If you wanna stay friends, we can stay friends. What is yo' problem?"

She could not voice her frustration. She was not sure exactly what that frustration was. She panicked at the thought of the project ending, school ending, and the very real possibility that she would never see him again. She had not even known him for that long—a week and a half at most—but they had spent so much time together. Nearly every day, she realized. And she liked being with him. He made her laugh constantly. She wasn't sure how they ever got any work done. They seemed to always be laughing. She liked coming over to his house. She liked wearing his hoodie. She wore it even now because his bedroom was cold. He had it ready for her—told her she could wear it anytime—and helped her put it on. Then it hit her like a hurricane force wind. She was in love with him. Oh God, she was in love with him! It had taken less than two weeks!

"You on yo' period or somethin'?" she heard Anton ask.

"What?!"

"You just all pissy today. I can't figure it out. Look, I didn't mean no disrespect when I axed you that."

Emma shot him a nasty look.

"Okay, I guess you on yo' period," he mumbled to himself.

She got up to leave.

"Wait, I was just playin'. Come on, Emma, don't be like that," Anton pleaded.

"I'm not being like anything," she said, taking off the hoodie and throwing it as hard as she could at his face.

"What the hell?" he asked behind the fabric.

The hoodie fell from his face revealing a large grin. He tried to suppress an urge to laugh. She wanted to smack him, knowing all the while that she was being ridiculous. He had come to realize that this was the way of women. Never know what you're gonna get, he thought. She'll be all sunshine and smiles tomorrow.

"I have to go," Emma said, gathering her papers and books. "It's late anyway."

"A'ight then," he said.

He moved to open the door for her, but she stormed out before he could. She didn't bother to say goodbye.

—

She didn't know why she returned. She had just left. It was getting late and she knew her parents would be angry. She called them on her cell phone and explained that she needed to stay a little longer. They believed she was still at Morgan's, and the guilt of lying to them made her chest feel tight.

She knocked on the door softly. At first there was no answer. Maybe he had gone somewhere, she thought panicking. She prayed silently that he was still home, knowing she would never have the courage to try again. She knocked for a second time more determined. He opened the door then, his brows furrowed in a question.

"You forget somethin'?" he asked.

She pushed past him into the small living room.

"I don't know. I . . . I think I might have," she lied.

He said nothing but led her to his room. He stood in the doorway and watched as she pretended to look around.

"What you think you forgot?" he asked.

"I'm not sure," she said unable to look him in the face. Did he know her true intentions?

"I didn't notice anything," he continued.

He seemed oblivious which only made it harder for her. She would never be able to voice out loud what she wanted. She was too afraid that he would reject her.

"I had on a bracelet," she lied. "I'm sure I had on a bracelet and now it's gone."

"No you didn't," he said.

"Yes I did!" she screamed unexpectedly. She looked at him then, her eyes beseeching him, and his lips curled into a smile.

He knew.

"Come 'ere," he said softly.

"I don't know what I'm doing," she said desperately.

"Come 'ere."

She obeyed and walked towards him. She was inches from him and felt like she would die if she could not touch him. She reached her hand to his face—she needed to feel the silk of him—but he drew back.

"You really wanna go there?" he asked. "You wanna get with a nigga?"

He watched as her chest rose and fell rapidly.

"Don't talk like that," she whispered. She was fighting down the urge to jump on him. But she didn't know if she wanted to hold him or claw at him. She thought that perhaps she needed to do both.

"Talk like what? 'Nigga?' I'm a nigga if you hadn't noticed," he teased. He flashed his teeth in a brilliant smile then licked his lips. "I don't normally kick it with white chicks," he continued watching the contortions of her face. He knew she was thinking fast and hard. She was in emotional turmoil, and it was amusing to watch. "Not that I got anything against white chicks. They can hang, I guess."

"Forget it," she said bitterly. She tried to push past him for the front door, but he grabbed her upper arm.

"Who you think you fuckin' with?" he asked, the ghost of a laugh in his voice. He bent low to whisper in her ear. "There ain't nothin' wrong with wantin' it. I ain't even gonna lie." His lips brushed her ear, and she shivered. "I want it, too. I want you. I've wanted you from day one."

She didn't know if he meant from the first day they began the project or from the first day he ever saw her. Frankly she didn't care; it was all she needed to hear, and she pressed her body against him feeling his arms envelop her. They were strong and dark, contrasting starkly with her white skin. She lifted her face to him and only then felt the tear slide down her cheek. He bent to kiss it, but it evaded his lips and fell to the floor. He looked at her face and smiled. She was crazed inside. He couldn't help but imagine for a moment what she would do to him in bed.

"Please kiss me," she said hoarsely.

"I will," he said and released her from his embrace.

She stood there confused. The warmth of his body still lingered on her, but she felt it fading fast and was reluctant to let it go.

"What do you want? You want me to beg?" she asked angrily, wheeling around to look at him. He was sitting on the edge of his bed watching her.

"Nah. I want you to come here and sit on my lap," he said patting the tops of his thighs.

She was at a loss for words.

"You comin'?"

"I have to be home soon," she said.

"That's your answer?" he asked.

She paused for just a moment before going to him and settling herself on his left leg. She tugged on her skirt, trying to pull it down over her knees, but it covered her just to mid-thigh.

"You so tiny," he said playfully. "You prolly weigh, what? Eighty, ninety pounds?"

She shook her head as he bounced her lightly with his knee.

"I don't wanna just jump into bed with you," he said. He brushed her hair over her shoulder and turned her face to look at him.

"You must think I'm a ho or something," she said. Her face was red with embarrassment.

"Please, girl. You the furthest thing from a ho." He placed his hand on the back of her head pulling her gently towards his face.

"Wait. You've got to say something else."

"Huh?"

"The last thing you say to me before we kiss for the first time can't be 'you're the furthest thing from a ho'," she pleaded.

He laughed. "A'ight." He pursed his lips and looked up at the ceiling in consideration. "Okay. How 'bout this? I think you kinda cute."

"Kind of cute?" she asked.

"Okay really cute," he said. "Actually, you fine."

She couldn't wait for him to make the first move. She grinned and pressed her lips hard against his. They were soft and plump, silky and foreign. She relaxed and softened then, letting him gently explore her lips with his own. She opened her mouth to him feeling his tongue search her tentatively at first, then more forcefully. Her tongue mingled with his, tasting honey, and she felt the tingling moving down her throat, through her chest, twisting through her belly to rest in between her legs. She couldn't understand her inability to restrain her desire. It was animal. She didn't want to sleep with him. She wanted to fuck him.

He knew he should keep it strictly at a kiss. Going any further would be too fast, and he wasn't sure exactly what she wanted. He imagined she wanted more, and he tried to justify his own desire by convincing himself that they had actually spent more time together—an inordinate amount of time—in the last week and a half than most couples do in their first month of dating. Yes, he thought, that sounds right. It wouldn't be imprudent to assume she'd want his hands all over her.

He moved his hand down the side of her neck to rest lightly on her breast. It was a question, and she answered by pushing herself against his hand, inviting him. He wasted no time going up her shirt, fumbling with the clasp of her bra until it came undone in sweet success. He fought to control himself as his hand pushed under her bra to rove over her soft breasts, feeling her shake slightly, kissing her harder even as he willed himself to slow down.

He wanted to take his time with her, but he couldn't. He felt the mixture of power and shame at his unchecked sexual excitement. He should stop. It's only been a week and a half, he thought. We've only just kissed. He knew he should send her home even as his hand left her breasts to touch her in between her legs.

She gasped but did not resist. His fingers moved her panties aside and stroked her softly. They slipped in and out of her tenderly, and she heard herself moaning into his mouth, fighting the rising climax. It hovered dangerously close to the edge.

"You have to stop," she said into his mouth.

"Are you crazy?"

He continued his exploration with more urgency knowing what it was doing to her, knowing she wouldn't last long. She was charged from the moment she walked through the door, and he knew his decision was the right one. A kiss wasn't enough. She needed release.

"Please," she whispered.

She tried to get up, but he held her firmly on his lap with his left arm around her waist. She could do nothing but wrap her arms around his neck and bury her face in his shoulder. She felt her hips moving against his hand, his fingers stroking her in a hip hop rhythm.

Her climax came violently, and she was powerless against it. All of the heavenly bodies burst, exploding in her stomach and rushing like white waters through her legs. She held onto him, saying his name over and over as the rapids coursed through her, slamming against her bones, obliterating them. He turned her to liquid. She cried out tasting the tears at the corners of her mouth. She could not control them. They flowed freely and abundantly, and she pushed her face harder against his shoulder trying to hide. She shook hard, sobbing, and he wrapped his arms around her firmly, pressing her to him, stroking her back.

"How do you do this to me?" she cried softly into his shoulder.

He did not answer but continued to stroke her back.

Her shaking eventually subsided, but she was too afraid to look at him. She wanted to die like this: her face buried in the muscles of his shoulder. But he gently pulled her away forcing her to look at his face. She was flushed and beautiful, her eyes glassy and transparent, her hair cascading around her face in lovely, untamed curls. He smiled at her sweetly, and she returned her own.

"I'm so embarrassed," she said.

"Why?" he asked.

"Because I'm crying and I don't know why. Why am I crying?" She wiped at her face and looked at him waiting for an answer.

"I don't know why girls do what they do," he said.

He didn't even try, and it made her laugh.

"Me neither," she said.

She was still breathing heavily, and he watched the slow rise and fall of the tops of her breasts. He wanted to touch them again. He wanted her naked in his bed. But it was late. He knew it couldn't be tonight.

"You betta go home," he said reluctantly. "I don't want you gettin' in trouble."

She opened her mouth to protest.

"We got time," he said. "We got all kinds of time. Why rush it?" He thought the question absurd. He had just gone from kissing her for the first time to touching her intimately within the span of fifteen minutes.

"But I'm the only one—"

"What? Who got off?" he asked.

"You put that so eloquently," she replied.

"You think I didn't get anything outta this?" he asked. "I got to touch all over yo' pretty body. You don't even know how long I been waitin' to do that. Never thought I'd get the chance."

She placed her hands over her face in embarrassment, but he peeled them away. He raised his eyebrows at her in a question, and she giggled.

"Don't worry. I'll get mine," he said. The statement sent a shiver down her spine. He felt it and tightened his arm around her waist even as he knew he should let her go. He just couldn't. He wanted to keep saying things to her that made her nervous. He liked the way her body responded to it, and he wanted to keep affecting her.

"I don't want to go," she said softly.

"You wanna get in trouble with yo' parents?"

"No," she said.

She stood up too fast and stumbled to the side. He caught her and helped her regain her balance.

"Man, I ain't never did that to a girl before," he said. "Cryin', shakin', fallin' all over the place. I really got you."

She rolled her eyes wishing he'd stop staring at her as she situated her clothing.

"I really got you," he repeated more thoughtfully, placing his hands on her hips and pulling her close to him. He pressed his face against her stomach and kissed it. He looked up at her then, his large amber eyes searching her face, and she was sure that if she didn't pull away at that moment she would melt into him.

"I have to go," she said, gently releasing him.

"Then you betta go."

She let herself out.

CHAPTER 12
WEDNESDAY, APRIL 28

Emma checked the bag once more, but she knew everything was there. She had made a list—a sex list, she thought, grinning like the Cheshire cat. She checked it a dozen times for something to do while she waited for his call. They chose this night because he wasn't working and his mother was at the hospital. The call came, and she tried to sound casual when she answered. She sensed that he was doing the same thing. His mother had left for work, he said, and she could come over whenever she liked. She took it to mean that he wanted her to come over that instant, and she wasted no time. She hung up, grabbed her bag and threw it over her shoulder, and checked herself in the mirror before leaving. Her cheeks were flushed, her eyes bright. She wondered if she would still look the same tomorrow.

—

He led her to his room without a word. She could tell that he was nervous, and she didn't know how to calm him. She was nervous herself. When he opened the door, she saw the candlelight. She looked at him, and he shrugged.

"You think I'm corny," he said.

"Not at all," she replied. "I think you're sweet."

She placed her bag on the desk chair and sat down on his bed. There were three lit candles on his desk emitting a low, soft glow. She wondered where he got them.

He sat down beside her placing his large hands on his knees. Suddenly, he was too afraid to touch her. How had it been so easy the other day?

"I'm just going to say it," she said. "I'm a virgin."

He didn't reply at first. He let the information sink in. He wasn't sure why he wasn't prepared for it. She looked like one. She dressed like one. But from the other day, he thought, she didn't act like one.

"I understand if you don't want to," she said quietly.

"So am I," he said softly.

"What?"

"I said so am I," he repeated, still not looking at her.

"You're lying," she said. He could hear the smile in her voice and relaxed some.

"I ain't lyin', okay? You gonna give me shit for bein' a virgin?" he asked.

"No, not at all. I love that you're a virgin," she said. "I'm surprised that you're a virgin. You don't act like you're a virgin."

"Can you stop sayin' 'virgin'?" he asked. "Man, this hard enough as it is. I don't even know what my problem is. Why don't you come back through that door like you did the other day? You come in here lookin' all sweet and saintly. Where's that girl come in here the other day wanna jump my bones?"

She took his hand in hers.

"So like I said, I'm a virgin."

"We established that," he said.

She took a deep breath. "This is so embarrassing."

"What's embarrassin'?"

She made herself look at his face when she said it.

"I might bleed. I mean, I'll probably bleed."

He said nothing. She started to feel anxious.

"So I brought a towel. I didn't want to mess up your sheets."

He thought for a moment before responding. "I know all that," he said. "You don't gotta worry about that."

"Does it make you uncomfortable?" she asked quietly.

He shrugged his shoulders. He wasn't sure. He suddenly felt a great weight of responsibility for what he was about to do and wondered for a moment if he was ready for it. He looked at her, searching her face for any sign that she felt the same weight—the weight of taking something from someone that can never be given back.

"We don't have to do this," she whispered. She needed reassurance.

"I want to," he replied determined. "If you let me, I want to. You crazy if you think I don't want to."

They sat in silence for a time, holding hands, waiting for the other person to make a move.

"I know I clown around and all," he said. "But this is important to me. If we do this, it ain't just 'cause we two horny teenagers. And I'm sorry if that's too heavy for you, but it's how I feel. If we do this, you a part of me. You mine."

He watched her closely but could not read her. He thought that perhaps he scared her. He didn't mean to.

"I want to be yours," she said, and she kissed him softly on the lips.

It took great effort to control himself. She was so sweet and yielding. He wanted to tear her apart. But he didn't. He removed her clothing slowly then laid her gently on his bed. He removed his own clothing quickly, and moved on top of her.

She let him look at her though it made her feel uneasy, exposed. He made a sound from deep within his throat, and she knew he was fighting hard to restrain himself. He kissed her again.

"Wait, the towel," she said into his mouth.

"Fuck the towel," he replied, and kissed her lips harder.

There were other things in the bag, she thought absurdly. What did she bring? Why did she bring those things? Was she doing it right? She felt stiff and anxious.

"Okay, you gotta relax," he said. "You stiff as a board. It ain't like you not fool around before. Why you actin' like you never been kissed even?"

"I'm sorry," she said, looking in the direction of her bag. "I don't know what my problem is. I put all of these things in my bag specifically for this, and I can't remember. I can't remember what's in my bag." Her chest was rising and falling rapidly, and she was sure she was having an anxiety attack.

He placed a hand on either side of her face, gently forcing her to look at him.

"Emma, we don't need nothin' from yo' bag. Okay? I gotta condom, a'ight?"

"You're going to use a condom?" she asked.

His eyes went wide with shock. "Emma, do you know where babies come from?"

"Oh stop it!" she said, pushing him off of her and sitting up in the bed. She pulled her knees to her chest hugging her legs.

He sat up, too, leaning against the wall. Her back was to him, and he wondered what she was thinking. He was beginning to think that this was a mistake. Nothing about it seemed easy, though he was unsure why he thought it would be.

"I meant that I'm on birth control," she said.

"Oh," he replied. He was so confused. "Why you on birth control if you don't have sex?"

"Birth control is used for many things," she said patiently.

"So why you use it?" he asked.

She turned around to face him, sitting Indian style, completely exposed to him. He liked what he saw.

"Well, since you want to know. I take it to regulate my period. And no, I'm not going to explain that to you," she said when she saw his mouth open to ask a question. He closed it and smiled.

"I can't help I ax a lotta questions. I just wanna know everything about you," he said.

"You want to know about my menstrual cycle?" she asked sarcastically.

"Okay, maybe not that," he said laughing. "I just can't figure you out. Did you come over here thinkin' we wasn't gonna use protection?"

"No," she said. "I brought condoms. But once you said you were a virgin, I figured what's the point?"

He was bewildered. "Look, I ain't even tryin' to get a girl pregnant at eighteen."

"And I'm not trying to sound irresponsible. But facts are facts. If I've never done it, and you've never done it, then we obviously don't have any STDs. And if I'm on birth control, then I won't get pregnant."

"That shit ain't a hundred percent, though," he pointed out.

"And condoms are?" she asked.

He thought for a moment. "Well, no, but maybe the birth control and condoms together are."

She smiled at that.

"Why you not want me to wear a condom?" he asked.

"Oh my God, nevermind. Wear the fucking condom. It's not about the condom," she said.

He looked at her. She was biting her nails.

"I know it don't feel the same," he said. "I mean, I ain't ever had sex, but I know it don't feel the same."

"I just want you to get as much pleasure out of it as I will," she said quietly. She stopped biting her nails and traced circles on the bed sheets with her forefinger.

"You the strangest girl I ever met," he said. "Come 'ere."

She was no longer tense and anxious. She relaxed during their conversation, allowing his eyes to rove over her nakedness while they talked.

She moved on top of him, straddling his hips, and let her body sink down onto him slowly.

"Oh my God," he whispered, and she laughed.

"You're not even inside of me yet," she pointed out.

"Hush. Don't say a word. Just lemme take all this in." He drew in his breath slowly, moving his hands down the sides of her face to her shoulders and finally her breasts. She sighed softly as he played with them.

"You have the most perfect breasts," he said. "But you prolly knew that, huh?"

She kissed him quite hard suddenly, and he wasted no time laying her down on the bed once more. He began his tender assault, kissing her everywhere. He kissed her lips and cheeks, her neck and breasts. He let his mouth and tongue taste her all over. She stiffened when he licked her hip, moving his tongue down her thigh. He wanted to, he was dying to, but he wasn't sure. Instead, he let his fingers do what he wanted his mouth to. He stroked her while he kissed her mouth, feeling her relax and submit to his touch.

His fingers were clumsy putting on the condom, and he cursed his awkwardness. Before she knew it, he was between her legs, poised and ready. He just needed her to signal that it was alright. She tentatively touched him, guiding him into her, and he thought he would come right then at the feel of her hand. He was determined to be slow and controlled. He didn't want to hurt her; he thought vaguely of remembering someone telling him that it hurt girls the first time. Did she know that? She must know that, he thought.

He pushed slowly, hearing the sharp intake of her breath.

"You okay?" he asked hoarsely.

"Yes," she replied.

He pushed farther in, feeling her body blocking him, fighting him. She was so tight, and it took every ounce of his strength not to take her hard and fast. He was starting to feel trapped within his own physical needs, wanting to please himself, wanting to hear her scream, he thought shamefully. He couldn't make sense of his desire to at once forcefully possess her and yet be gentle to her.

"It's okay," she whispered. "Just do it."

She barely got the words out. He drove into her completely, hearing her cry quietly, ignoring it as he found a gentle rhythm. She wrapped her legs around him, her thighs tight against his hips, and he was certain that she was wishing for it all to be over soon. Why did it have to hurt her? Why couldn't she feel what he was feeling? It was ecstasy. He was consumed with it, no longer caring to be gentle. He tried, but he couldn't. I'm just eighteen, he thought. I can't be perfect. And he thrust into her harder.

He felt her fingernails on his back. He wished desperately that she would remove them. They only made him want to take her harder. But she didn't remove them. She raked his back with them, fueling within him a desire so intense he was sure he would wound her beyond repair.

It did not take long. He came into her hard, his body drenched with the sweat of physical exertion and mental havoc. He wanted to collapse on her, but he knew he would crush her. And it was selfish, he thought. He had already taken so much. He felt ashamed at his own inability to be gentler with her. He rolled off of her and took her in his arms, cradling her head against his chest.

"I'm sorry," he said. "I'm so sorry."

"For what?" she asked. She sounded genuinely confused.

"For bein' so rough." He stroked her hair and kissed the top of her head.

"It's okay," she said. "It started feeling good towards the end."

He was surprised.

"It did?" he asked.

"Mmhmm," she said lazily.

"Why you not say anything?" he asked incredulously.

"Didn't you feel my fingernails in your back?" she asked.

He wasn't sure what to say.

"That's supposed to let me know you enjoyin' it? God, I thought I was rippin' you apart!"

She had no reply. She simply nuzzled closer to him, feeling his heartbeat slow until she thought it was back to normal.

"You okay with everything?" he asked tentatively.

"Yes. Are you?"

"Yes."

There was a moment of contented silence. He moved his hand up and down her back feeling the softness of her skin. It tickled her slightly, and she squirmed.

"Do you want to do it again?" she asked quietly.

"Right now?!"

"No," she laughed. "Later. In the future. Is it something you'd want to do with me again?"

"What kinda question is that?"

"An honest one," she replied.

He rolled her onto her back and looked down at her. "Girl, I wanna do that with you all day, every day, 'til the end of time."

—

It was almost nine, and Emma knew that she needed to be home soon. She walked out of the bathroom dressed only in his hoodie. He was sitting up in bed wearing a pair of boxer shorts. The strong desire to do it again glowed in her. The hard part was over, she thought. She wanted to see what it felt like now.

Anton looked at her standing in the doorway. "You know you can't wear that home. Yo' mama and daddy go to pieces if they see you like that."

She walked over to him with purpose, climbing on top of him and straddling his hips.

"Emma, you know you gotta go home," he said as she kissed his neck.

"Oh shut up," she said, and kissed his mouth hard.

She fumbled with his boxers until she found him, gripping him tightly in her hand. He was hard, but then he had been that way all evening.

"Emma—"

She ignored him, guiding him into her, sinking down on him slowly. He made no move to stop her, only groaning with delight. He forgot all about a condom.

She moved her hips tentatively at first, unsure of what she was supposed to be doing. She thought she was moving right; she could feel the soft shocks of electricity traveling up and down her legs and throughout her belly. He watched her face as she moved on him, taking for herself with no thought of what he wanted. He could see the pleasure of it in her eyes. He wanted to lose himself in them, thought that perhaps he already had, long ago, the first time he really looked at her.

He was vaguely aware of her hand down there, and realized suddenly that she was touching herself. He wanted to lift up the hoodie and watch, but she wouldn't let him. So he contented himself with watching her eyes. They were getting darker, a stormy blue, and then she exploded quite suddenly without warning. She wanted to hide her face from him, but he held her so that she was forced to look at him. The storm waves danced in her eyes, crashing blues around her pupils, and he felt her body shudder over and over. There was no end to it until she cried out for release, and then he let go allowing her to bury her face in his shoulder, feeling her body tremble from the aftermath.

"Is that what you needed?" he asked gently after a time, stroking her back underneath of the hoodie. It was slick with sweat.

She nodded into his shoulder, and he laughed. He wanted to roll her over and take from her then, but he knew it wouldn't be right. He had already taken so much. He had to keep reminding himself.

"I've got to go home," Emma groaned into his shoulder. She sat up then and looked at him.

"That's what I kept tryin' to tell you," Anton replied.

"Yeah, like you didn't want me to climb on you just then and do that," Emma said. She smirked.

"I could take it or leave it," Anton replied, and she punched his arm. "Ow! You know I'm playin' with you."

She climbed off of his lap and dressed. He watched her the whole time aware of the unsettling feeling spreading throughout his chest making his heart rate increase to an uncomfortable, rapid rhythm. He realized that he had perhaps just complicated his life beyond what he could handle. His future with her was as uncertain as the present. No one knew about them. He couldn't imagine what his friends would say. He failed to even think about where she was going to college. Why had he never bothered to ask? She could be going across the country for all he knew. And did he honestly think that her parents would be accepting of him? Sure, they were polite at dinner. They seemed to be okay with him, he thought, but only as a partner for a school project. He was sure they'd go ballistic if they learned he and she were together romantically. Suddenly, everything began changing, becoming more serious, dangerous even. He should have kept it at a mild flirtation, he thought panicking.

"Are you okay?" Emma asked.

"Yeah," he lied. "I'm great." And he forced a smile.

"Because you look like you're thinking about something," Emma went on. "Are you thinking this was all a huge mistake?"

"God no!" He jumped out of the bed and went to her.

What *was* he thinking, entertaining the idea that he had made a mistake being with her? Never, he thought. It would never be a mistake. And he voiced that to her as he held her possessively.

Later that night he actually prayed, kneeling beside the bed in reverence, his large hands folded in supplication. He prayed earnestly, prayed that he could be with her forever because he knew he could never love another woman.

CHAPTER 13
THURSDAY, APRIL 29

Dr. Thompson reminded his students for the fifth time that the class time he so generously provided them should be used for the sole purpose of working on their term papers. It appeared that most students actually were working, and that only a few were indifferent or distracted by the more important details of being a teenager.

Emma and Anton sat in a corner of the room by the windows talking in whispers.

"This is weird," he said.

"I know."

"I don't know how we supposed to be actin', you know?"

"I know."

"I mean, are we supposed to be holdin' hands or something?"

"I don't know."

"Okay, Emma? You ain't helpin' at all," Anton said impatiently.

"I know," Emma replied, putting her face in her hands. "I just don't know, I don't know!"

"Okay, take it easy," Anton said softly. He looked around, but no one was paying any attention to them.

She took a deep breath and regained her composure.

"Let's just not worry about it, okay?" Anton said.

He didn't know what they were going to do, and suddenly the pressure of telling his friends about her seemed much scarier than the first time they had sex.

"Okay," she said quietly. She knew it was no solution, but she had none. What would her friends think? What would they say to her?

They tried to resume work on their paper, but it was pointless. It was so frustrating, in fact, that Anton gave up and went back to his seat before class was over. Emma was grateful that he left her alone. She felt an explosive mixture of emotions inside of her threatening to detonate. She wanted to laugh and cry and scream all at the same time. It was miserable being trapped inside those emotions, but she could do nothing. She had to cope until she could find a way to deactivate the bomb.

She did not acknowledge him when she passed him out the door after the bell rang. She headed straight for her locker and began changing out her books. She thought he would follow her and want to talk some more, but he didn't. She turned around to see him joking with his friends. It irritated her. She was a mess inside and he was laughing. How could he be so calm when she felt out of control? She thought that perhaps he was putting on a show, but he seemed genuinely at ease. How do guys do that, she wondered? Do they have limited emotions, or are they simply able to handle them better? Either way she felt the cards were dealt unfairly, and she sunk into sullenness behind her locker door.

She did not see much of Anton for the rest of the day. It was almost as if he weren't at school. She usually saw him at the lockers between classes, but he showed only a few times and was always flanked by his friends. She watched him chat and laugh and rough house with them. They seemed very close, and her heart stiffened with envy. What was wrong with her, she thought? She felt herself transforming into that girl—the jealous girl who wants her boyfriend all to herself all of the time. And then she laughed derisively, hiding her head in her locker, thinking that she was a fool for even contemplating the idea that he was her boyfriend. They never said anything about that last night.

She knew her anger was unjustified. She wanted to be frustrated with him for his casual manner, but he was only doing what he normally did at school. She was the one who pushed him away with her behavior earlier in English class. Did she expect him to go running after her all day? And she couldn't shake the feeling that she didn't want anyone to know. Certainly not Morgan, she thought. At least not yet. If whatever it was they were doing blossomed into something more, she knew she would have to tell her. But it seemed easier to keep things as they were however confused it made her feel.

He came to her at the end of the day. She was walking to her car when he caught up with her.

"I gotta work today," he said. "So I guess I won't be seein' you later."

"Okay."

"And I gotta work tomorrow night, too," he added.

"Alright."

"You okay?" he asked.

"Mmhmm."

"Well, I don't believe you, but I ain't got time to go into it," he said. "You still want me to come over on Saturday?"

"If you want." She tried for indifference.

He chuckled. "A'ight then. I'll call you." And he hoofed it to the bus.

She couldn't understand why he didn't ask for a ride home. She would have gladly given it, and then she spotted one of his friends. He was hanging around the bus watching them, waiting for Anton. He slapped Anton on the arm when he approached and said something that made them both laugh. They disappeared onto the bus, and she stood watching as it pulled away.

Saturday, May 1

"I didn't leave nothin' in Dr. Thompson's room that time," Anton said watching her squeeze juice from a lemon into her water.

"What are you talking about?" she asked.

They were sitting at the table in her back yard working on their project. She had gotten over her moodiness from the past few days the moment her doorbell rang. It was instantaneous; her emotions lifted and she was a different person as soon as he stood at her front door.

"Remember when this whole thing started and how you had to go complain to Dr. Thompson about me not bein' serious enough for you?"

"Oh that," she said. "What about it?"

"Well, I was walkin' by the room and saw you in there. I knew what you was up to. I knew you was mad and tattlin' on me," Anton said.

He grabbed her water and took a long gulp.

"Hey! I did the work there! Next time you're slicing and squeezing the lemons," she said, watching him drain most of her glass. "And anyway, I wasn't tattling."

"Oh who you kiddin'? You was all up in that room whinin' 'cause you couldn't get yo' way," Anton replied handing her the nearly-empty glass.

"Whatever."

"So that's why I went in and acted like I forgot somethin'. I didn't want you to get yo' way. I wanted to make sure we was still gonna be partners."

Emma looked at him as he made the realization

known.

"You liked me then?" she asked quietly.

"Yes."

They were silent for a moment.

"And you don't even know what that was like for me. All that waitin' and hopin' you was gonna like me or make a move or somethin'. I thought I was gonna die when you came back to my house Monday. It was so hard to play it cool, and I don't know how I was able to do that after waitin' so long."

"What do you mean?"

"I wanted to grab you and kiss you as soon as you walked through my door. I knew what you was up to. Missin' bracelet. Please, girl. I ain't never seen you wear no bracelet."

Emma grinned. "You made me pretend to look around for a bracelet and then when I finally found the courage to ask you to kiss me, you made me wait for it?!"

"Yep. That was so hard," Anton replied.

"Hard? Hard for whom?!" she asked.

"Hard for me."

"Oh, you're impossible!" she cried throwing a lemon at his head. It bounced off his left temple and landed on the stone patio.

"Ow! That hurt!" he said, jumping from his chair and reaching across the table for her.

She evaded his grip and sprinted across the patio to the center of the lawn feeling him behind her. She dashed to the left and hid behind a bench swing. He was on the other side.

"Where you think you gonna go?" he asked.

She was breathing fast and thinking fast. Which way would she go? To the right and back towards the house to hide in her room? Or to the left deeper into the back yard to hide behind the rose bushes? Which way? She chose the left, and ran with all her might. She was almost there when she felt his arm come around her waist and pull her to the ground. She screamed and squirmed to get away, but she was no match for his strength. He had at least eighty pounds on her.

Anton pinned her arms overhead, deciding what to do with her.

"Okay, so you hit me with a lemon," he said. "What's a good payback?"

She squirmed and fought to release her hands. He had them clasped with his one.

"I could tickle you," he said placing his free hand on her ribcage.

Her eyes went wide with fear.

"I could kiss you," he said.

She nodded at that.

"But that ain't no punishment," he argued.

She fought a bit more before giving up completely.

"I do love kissing you, though," he decided. "It's no punishment really, but it'd still be somethin' for me."

He released her hands and cupped her face softly making sure to put most of his weight on his elbows.

"You so pretty," he said tenderly staring into her eyes. He pressed his lips to hers feeling her body respond beneath him. He let his lips linger on hers before drawing away from her face to look down at her again.

"God, you so pretty," he said as he felt her pull him towards her lips once more.

—

She was glowing and her friends saw it. They were sitting around Morgan's room deciding what to do that night. Emma knew what she would rather be doing, but Anton had to work. It was probably a good thing, she thought. Space from him would remind her that she was still living in the real world. And she had friends who she deeply cared about. She did not want to turn into one of those girls who abandons her girlfriends for a guy, no matter how cute, she thought with a grin.

"Okay, spill it," Sarah said, sitting on the floor painting her nails.

"Spill what?" Emma asked.

"What is up with you? You've been grinning all night," Sarah replied.

"Have I? I didn't notice," Emma said, and went back to flipping through the pages of her magazine.

"Are you high?" Morgan asked. "And where can we get some?"

"Oh my God, Morgan! No, I'm not high! Can't I smile and be happy?"

"Are you in love?" Aubrey asked.

Yes, she wanted to say. My God, yes! But she didn't.

"Have you seen me with anyone?" Emma asked.

Aubrey and Sarah shrugged, but Morgan was not convinced. She decided to trap her into confessing.

"How's your project going with Mr. Thug?" she asked, brushing her hair in the mirror.

"You're seriously calling him that?" Emma asked.

"Whatever. Tell us about your project," Morgan replied. "You've been spending a lot of time with him."

"It's going fine. We're almost finished with it," she said. She hoped that her face wasn't blushing.

"Does he actually work, or does he expect you to do everything?" Sarah asked.

"He works. I work. We both work."

"Emma, I'm gonna be honest with you about something. And I don't want to hear any shit from you, Morgan," Aubrey began.

Aubrey, too, was on the bed with Emma flipping through fashion and gossip magazines. Morgan made a face at her.

"I think he's cute," Aubrey confessed.

Emma laughed.

"What? Yes, I know he's black. But there's just something about him. He's like a nice bad boy, or at least that's what I imagine. When he came into Calculus class that one day and apologized to you, I thought I was gonna die. So sweet!"

"I'm gonna throw up," Morgan muttered.

"You know, Morgan, you haven't got one romantic bone in your body," Aubrey said.

"What happened in Calculus class?" Sarah asked.

"Oh, I never told you?" Aubrey said excitedly. She loved the opportunity to tell stories.

Emma forced herself to remain detached as she listened. She sensed that Morgan was on to her and wanted to squash her suspicions. She was not ready to tell her friends.

"So, he comes in after the bell already rang," Aubrey began. "And Mrs. Hartsford was like, what are you doing in my class? And he was like, hold up, I just need to talk to her. And he pointed at Emma. Emma, what's his name?"

"Anton."

"Okay, so Anton points at Emma and she looks petrified. And the whole class is listening as he tells her he's sorry for calling her a bitch," Aubrey said.

"He called you a bitch?!" Sarah cried. She fanned her hands trying to dry her freshly-painted nails faster. "Where have I been?"

"It was a misunderstanding," Emma said lamely.

"What does that mean?" Morgan asked. She had stopped brushing her hair and was looking Emma square in the face.

Emma didn't want to explain, but she felt she had no choice.

"He was angry," she began.

"Okay. So that gives him the right to call you a

bitch?" Morgan asked.

"Will you let me finish?"

Morgan grunted which Emma took as an invitation to continue.

"I had gone to Dr. Thompson to complain about him before I even gave him a chance. He caught me doing it," Emma said sheepishly.

Sarah grinned. "Not a good way to get things started."

"Tell me about it," Emma replied.

"Um, hello? Can I finish my story now?" Aubrey asked.

"Yes, Aubrey. Sorry," Emma said smiling.

"Okay, so anyways, the class is listening to him saying that he's sorry he called her a bitch. Then he wouldn't leave until she promised to meet him after school so that they could talk some more. And then Mrs. Hartsford ruined everything by calling someone from the office down to her room to get . . . what was his name?"

"Anton."

"That's right, Anton. And so Mr. McCullum came to get him. And he walked out of the room all happy because Emma had accepted his apology," Aubrey said. "It was really cute."

"Are we finished with this subject?" Morgan asked, but Aubrey ignored her.

"You brought it up," Sarah reminded Morgan who had moved on to scrutinizing her face in the mirror.

"Like I said, Emma. I think he's cute, but I would never date him," Aubrey said.

"And why's that?" Emma asked.

"Um, hello? He's black. Maybe I would sleep with one just to see what it's like, but I would never ever in a million years date one. Could you imagine?"

Emma remained silent.

CHAPTER 14
MONDAY, MAY 3

She felt an uncontrollable rage deep inside. She could kill someone; she was sure of it. She could kill him. She watched as he spoke to the girl playfully. He was at ease, looking more at home with that girl than he ever did with her. What did she expect, though? She was white. That girl was black. Sooner or later the black girl would win. She could never compete with the people he understood the most.

It was almost the end of the day, and she had a strong urge to check herself out and go home. Nothing had gone right at school since they had sex. They didn't know how to act around one another. None of their friends were aware of their relationship. They didn't know how to make it public or even if they should make it public. Perhaps it wasn't a relationship at all but merely sex. She panicked at the thought of a one-night stand. But how could that be after the things he confessed to her on Saturday? It sounded like he wanted more. A relationship.

But he was a different Anton at school, rarely venturing to talk to her but instead stealing glances in her direction from time to time that she would ignore if her friends were around. She tried to smile at him when her friends weren't around, but that never worked because he was always with his friends. He looked through her like he had no idea who she was. On the rare occasions that they did find themselves alone with one another, they both pretended that they hadn't ignored each other throughout the day and that they weren't embarrassed by the way they treated each other. It was hurtful and immature, and she was just as guilty as he.

And now she stood and watched him flirt with another girl. How could he do that? She felt ashamed that she had given him her virginity. How could she be so naïve? How could she let him trap her like that? Showing her a side of him no one else saw, a sweet side—a side that lured her into his bed. Was it merely an act to see what she'd be like? Maybe he just wanted to be rid of his virginity and she happened to be available. As much as it hurt her, she had to confront the possibility that it was nothing more than sex.

She was a fool, partially hiding behind her locker door as she watched them. The girl wrapped her arms around Anton's waist and squeezed him. He looked happy, saying something that was evidently funny because his friends laughed. The girl laughed, letting her forehead rest on his chest while she giggled with delight. Fucking bitch, Emma thought, aware of the tear gliding down her cheek. She didn't wipe at it. She continued to stare until they moved down the hall and out of sight, the girl's arm wrapped around Anton's waist and his arm falling comfortably over her shoulder.

—

She stood in his room as far away from him as she could get. They were already deep in the fight. She couldn't believe the things she had said. They poured out of her without control. She knew she was crazy, but she couldn't stop. She had to keep saying things—awful, hurtful things to rid her heart of the anger.

"Can you try for one second to understand where I'm comin' from?" he asked, trying desperately to control his temper.

"Where you're coming from?" she screamed. Her voice sounded strange and shrill. "Are you fucking kidding me?"

"You don't come from the ghetto. You don't know what it's like to be black. You don't know what kind of pressure that is, the way you gotta act around yo' friends and have street cred and still try to work to get outta that life without lookin' like you some kinda sell-out."

"What the hell does that have to do with earlier? That girl?" Emma snapped.

Anton ignored her as he continued. "Not to mention datin' people different from you and how yo' boys gonna react to that. Cause they matter, whether you like it or not."

She was furious, her face tightening with a mixture of anger and humiliation. *She* was to blame for his flirting earlier in front of his friends?

"And then on top of all that shit, you gotta deal with not havin' the same opportunities as other people," he finished.

"Give me a break. This isn't 1963. No one's keeping the black man down," she spat. "Get over yourself."

He wanted to hit her. He couldn't believe the rush of rage—that in that short second he could have brought his hand up to her soft cheek and struck her violently like a poor angry black man who justifies abuse because he's put upon. He was glad that she was on the opposite end of the bedroom.

"You might wanna check yo'self," he said calmly.

"Go to hell," she said. "I don't see how not having the same opportunities as other people has anything to do with you flirting with that girl!"

He was exasperated. "She's a friend," he said slowly, emphasizing every word. "I've known her since first grade. She used to live like two doors down from me. And anyway, what the fuck you care who I talk to? When you around yo' little posse, you act like I don't exist."

"That's not true," she argued.

He laughed derisively. "Oh really? You wanna tell me what happened today at lunch? I tried to approach you since I realize we need to start bein' a little bit more mature, and you shrink down in yo' fuckin' chair like I'm some sorta bad muthafucka gonna git you."

At those words, he took a sudden step towards her just to watch her body jump. It did.

"I did not shrink," she argued. "I was caught off guard."

"Girl, what the fuck does that mean?" he asked. "Face it. You was ashamed."

She opened her mouth to reply, but he cut her off.

"And yo' little punkass bitches was lookin' at me like, 'How the fuck you gonna come over to our table and talk to our girl?'" he spat. "You need to check the people you hang around. They nothin' but some bitchass muthafuckin' hos."

"Don't talk about my friends like that!" she screamed. "Like yours are so much better. They are so disrespectful to me!"

"Get over yo'self," he said, laughing. The laughter was hard and cold. "They don't care 'bout you. They not takin' any time to worry 'bout disrespectin' you."

"This was a huge mistake," she said suddenly.

"What? Gettin' together?" he asked.

"Yes," she said. "Maybe you should just go date your little Latasha or Shaquita or whatever the fuck her name is. We obviously can't do this."

It was shamefully passive aggressive, a way of

manipulating with words. She hoped it would elicit the response she wanted, the assurance she needed from him that he did, in fact, like her and want to be with her.

They stood for a few moments staring at one another from across the room. He finally broke the silence.

"Whateva," he said shrugging. "It make no difference to me. I got what I wanted from you anyway." He was looking for a reaction from her, and she knew it.

"Oh really?" she asked. "Because I didn't. In fact, I was left very unsatisfied."

The words were a challenge, and while he knew she didn't mean them, couldn't possibly mean them, his pride was hurt. He had opened up to her completely that night. Confessed himself to be just as new and inexperienced as she was, and glad for it. Glad that he would share himself for the first time with her, knowing afterwards that he would only ever want to share himself with her. Her words wounded him in his core, and his anger intensified.

"Is that right?" he asked harshly, moving towards her with purpose.

She tried to sidestep him for the door, but he was too fast, trapping her against the wall with an arm on either side of her head, hands pressed firmly against a poster of Warren G.

"Well, I don't remember it quite like that."

She squirmed to get away, trying to retreat underneath one of his arms, but he simply moved it lower blocking her escape.

"See, I remember you moanin' into my mouth," he said quietly, his face inches from hers. "And sayin' my name over and over again while you fuckin' came to my hand. That's what I remember. I hadn't even put my dick in you and you already comin' for me."

She was desperate for something to say, something else that would sting him. She hated the control he wielded over her, trapped against the wall, listening to a recount of how she yielded to him so easily, exposing the most vulnerable side of herself.

"Yeah, well it was all a show," she replied, her voice quavering.

He laughed genuinely then. She watched for the flashes of his white teeth as he snorted with laughter, all the while keeping his arms on either side of her. She wanted to hit him.

"Girl, you outta yo' mind," he said. "If that was a show, then you need to get yo' ass to Hollywood 'cause you be a real big star."

He was unprepared for what came next. She pushed against his chest with all her might, making him stumble backwards slightly, and before he regained his balance, she slapped him hard across the face. It was a white-hot burn, a blast of hate, and he could feel his heart pumping in his cheek.

She stood there with a look of triumph on her face—snide and smug—watching him rub his jaw slowly. He was thinking about how he would retaliate, she could tell, and she knew it was time to leave. She made for the door but he jumped in front of her. She moved to the other side, but he was already there. She backed away from him, but he moved towards her as if there was an invisible chain connecting them. He never took his eyes off of her face. She felt for a moment like she was prey being toyed with before the kill.

He came at her then, pushing her violently against the wall and kissing her angrily. His lips and teeth were everywhere: her mouth, cheeks, chin, ears, neck. Every place his lips touched burned and stung. He was hurting her, and she tried desperately to throw him off of her once more. But this time he was wise to it. He leaned into her, making it easy to pin her against the wall with his weight.

He bit her neck hard and listened to her cry out,

ignoring her protests as he lifted her skirt, hands roving over her thighs and bottom. Damn, he loved when she wore skirts. He ripped her panties cleanly, and she vaguely felt them float down her legs to the floor. He lifted her up forcing her to wrap her legs around his hips for support, fooling with the zipper of his pants until he was exposed and ready to take her. She protested as she felt him enter her.

She was wet and ready for him. Little tease, he thought chuckling, and he held her hips still, watching her face as he slid in and out of her. She was trapped between lust and anger—it was evident by the look in her eyes—and it made her that much more desirable. He neither went slowly nor fast with her. He knew that he must find a perfect balance in between or he would lose it before making her yield to him. And he wanted her to yield to him. He wanted to prove a point, prove her a liar, humiliate her sweetly. He was focused on reading her, pushing away the thought of his own sensations, watching her intently. Her face went tight with rage and then relaxed to submission. She was the pendulum swinging between two emotions, and he wondered which would win out.

He kissed her mouth softly then, and to his surprise and delight she kissed him back. So submission would win out, he thought, drawing away from her lips to smile at her victoriously. She wouldn't smile back; she had to hold on to some vestige of pride still even as he had her pinned, opened to him, with no chance of escape.

His eyes never left hers as she came. She was terribly beautiful, caught in between the humiliation of defeat and the rapture of physical satisfaction. Even when her climax was through, he continued stroking her. It was payback, she knew, and while she begged him to stop, crying that she couldn't bear to feel it anymore, he continued unmoved, watching her eyes, falling into them as he came for her. It was intense, hard and quick. He felt in that moment like a star that imploded, collapsing within, debris and wreckage everywhere inside while the outside remained intact.

He leaned his forehead against the wall, feeling the beads of sweat dropping off of his face to hit her shoulder. He felt drained of everything: his anger at her earlier, his will to fight, even the constant nagging fear of their blossoming relationship and what that meant for him as a black man and her as a white woman. He found the tiny bit of remaining strength within him and carried her to the bed, laying her down gently.

He crawled in beside her and felt he could sleep for a hundred years, thinking absurdly of Rip Van Winkle and his fate. What would be Anton's fate, he thought? Would he wake up in a hundred years to see her still lying beside him, face flushed and shining, hair tumbling about, still the young beautiful seventeen-year-old whose love he stole away? Or would she be old and gone, perhaps someone else's lover, and he would be in a desperate search for the rest of his life to find her and win back her love? He turned to face her. She was staring at him. Had she been staring the whole time?

"I love you," she said softly. "I love you and I don't know how to handle that."

"I love you, too," he said.

It was so easy to say. He loved hearing it. He had never said it to a girl, could not, for he never understood it until he laid eyes on her for the first time, touched her arm, felt her breath on his shoulder.

"What are we going to do?" she asked.

"We're gonna stop bein' scared," he said. "We just scared of everybody and what they think. We have to stop carin' what they think."

She nodded.

"But I don't wanna think about that right now," he

continued. He sighed deeply and contentedly. "I just need to lay here with you."

She saw him truly vulnerable then, watching the slow rise and fall of his chest as he breathed, the flutter of his eyelashes as his eyes moved behind closed lids. She put her hand on his chest and he instinctively closed his over hers. It was strong and warm, no longer demanding from her. Simply thanking her for giving to him. She did not know until then how much he needed her.

She could feel the slow and steady beating of his heart. Hers was beating wildly still, but now from the realization of his intense need for her. She would give him everything, she resolved. Turn herself inside out for him if he wanted. It was a dangerous feeling, but she was not afraid of it. It was her assurance of his love for her. She had gotten her assurance.

CHAPTER 15
WEDNESDAY, MAY 5

Emma froze in the doorway staring at the group of boys gathered in Anton's bedroom. They were laughing about something, but it petered out once they realized she was there. They stared back at her, studying her as if she were an alien specimen, something they'd never seen before. She was uncomfortable and quickly grew angry. Why did he invite her over if his friends were there?

"Okay, so I brought you all together for a reason," Anton said.

No one said a word, so he continued.

"You my crew," he said looking at his friends. "So I wanna be straight with you about what's goin' on. I didn't want you caught off guard or anything at school. And how you feel is important to me, know what I'm sayin'?"

His friends nodded, uncertain.

He took a deep breath and looked at Emma. "So I like this girl. And I know she white. She the whitest girl I ever met. But I'm workin' on some things. At least now she know how to shoot a ball right."

He was nervous, playing with his fingers while looking back and forth between Emma and his friends.

"But she a good girl. She good to me. She good for

me. Can you understand that?" he continued.

There was a moment of silence before one of them finally spoke.

"Man, I don't care who you date."

And then another: "She that same girl who yelled at you at the lockers?"

"Yeah," Anton replied.

"I thought you said she was a bitch?"

"I was wrong. I assumed it, and I was wrong," Anton said.

Another moment of silence. And then the largest of the four friends got out of his seat and walked over to Emma.

"I'm Kareem," he said, extending his hand. She took it tentatively. It was large, soft and warm. It matched the way he looked, like a giant teddy bear.

"Oh shit, I ain't even made no introductions," Anton said. He looked at his friends. "So this is Emma."

He took her purse from her shoulder and placed it on his bed.

"Emma, this is Kareem the Dream, Johnny D in the white T-shirt, Nate Dog on the bed—you met him already—and Lazy L at the desk. His name Lamar, but we call him Lazy L 'cause he never do anything."

"Man, not true. I do things. I do important things," Lamar argued. He spoke with a drawl so that even his words sounded lazy.

"Bullshit, man. You so fuckin' lazy. You ain't even get up today 'til three," Kareem pointed out.

They laughed.

"How you gonna graduate, man? Can't even get yo' ass outta bed," he continued.

"Man, don't you worry 'bout me. I got plans," Lamar replied, completely unaffected by Kareem's teasing. "Don't you never stay in bed late, Emma?" he asked.

Emma began feeling a bit more relaxed listening to

the conversation around her with detached curiosity until she was addressed directly. Her nerves jumped.

"I . . . sure, I guess," she replied.

"See, now you gonna say she lazy and give her all kinda shit about not graduatin'?" Lamar asked.

"She actually go to school," Johnny D said. "That's the difference, you dumb fuck."

"Fuck you, man. I ain't even tryin' to be upset by any of y'all. And I ain't sharin' my weed later, neither," Lamar said.

The friends groaned and argued, cajoled and entreated until Lamar agreed to share his weed for a small price. Each had to buy him lunch sometime the following week. Emma noticed one friend who remained quiet during the conversation: Nate. He looked her over, sizing her up, scowling from time to time as the others gently teased her and peppered her with questions. His silence was unnerving.

"Girl, you ain't never did weed?" Johnny D asked bewildered.

"No," Emma replied. Oh God, were they going to make her smoke weed, she thought with panic?

"And she ain't gonna," Anton said. "Don't even be axin' her 'bout doin' drugs or nothin' like that."

"Relax, papa, I wasn't offerin'. I just ain't never met no one who hadn't tried it," Johnny D said. "I am genuinely amazed."

Emma smiled at that.

"What you see in this dumbass nigga anyway?" Lamar asked, pointing at Anton.

"Um, I don't know," Emma replied. "I see a lot."

"I see a lotta bullshit," Kareem said, playfully punching Anton in the stomach.

"Whateva nigga. You mad 'cause you ain't eva had my skills on the court," Anton replied, forcing Kareem into a headlock.

"Who the fuck cares? I got mad skills on the mic," Kareem argued.

His head was still locked in Anton's arm as he addressed Emma. "See Emma, that why my name Kareem the Dream. I flow on the mic like Biggie. I got the dreamlike flow, see?"

"I think so," Emma replied.

Finally Nate spoke up.

"What you mean you see?" he asked aggressively.

Emma did not reply.

"Do you even know what the fuck he just said?"

"Hey man, take it easy," Kareem said as Anton released him from the headlock.

All eyes were on Nate.

"I am takin' it easy. I'm just axin' our little friend here a question." He looked at Emma. "You know what he meant by what he said? You eva heard of Biggie Smalls? You know who he is? Has you eva listened to rap music before? You undastand what it mean to flow on a mic?"

"Chill out, Nate," Anton said.

"Nah, man. This is bullshit," Nate said. "How you gonna bring this bitch up in here talkin' 'bout you datin' her? Then she gonna stand around actin' like she know what the hell we talkin' about."

"I said chill out," Anton said evenly.

"Man, whateva," Nate said and stormed out of the room. Anton followed being careful to close the bedroom door behind him.

Emma, Kareem, Johnny, and Lamar could hear the argument clearly. Kareem tried to start up a fresh conversation to distract Emma, knowing that she would undoubtedly hear words that would upset her, but she put her hand on his arm to signal silence.

"Don't call my girl a bitch," Anton said.

"Man, you called her a bitch! Remember that?" Nate spat.

"I told you, that was a mistake. What's yo' problem, anyway? She ain't eva done nothin' to you," Anton replied.

"She not our kind, man. What you doin' datin' some white chick?"

"I like her," Anton said pointedly.

"Nigga you lost yo' mind," Nate said.

"She a nice girl. A good girl. Give her a chance, Nate."

"Fuck that. I don't care if she nice and good. It ain't about that. It's about you rejectin' where you come from," Nate explained.

"That's crazy, man. I'm rejecting my blackness 'cause I gotta white girlfriend? You hear how retarded that sound?" Anton said laughing.

"I ain't laughin', nigga," Nate replied. "You a black man. You date black girls. That's how it is."

"Maybe for you," Anton said. "Why it always gotta be about color anyway?"

"Because it is! That's the world we live in! And we from the projects, man. We ghetto. Thug. Weed and K's."

"What the hell, Nate? Nobody gotta damn AK-47," Anton said, trying not to laugh. "Crazy nigga."

"Fuck you, man. You know what I mean. How you gonna make yo' world and her world happen together? It can't. Unless you plannin' on bein' a sell-out."

"What the hell does datin' a white girl have to do with bein' a sell-out?" Anton asked.

"It's the first step," Nate said coolly. "Then you be dissin' yo' friends for her, wantin' to sound like a preppy white muthafucka for her, gettin' a big time job in her daddy's company."

"Nigga, you lost yo' mind. I don't even know what the hell you talkin' about," Anton said. "I'm just a senior in high school datin' a white girl. I ain't lookin' for no corporate job."

"Stop downplayin' this shit, man. I ain't comfortable with it. I don't like it."

"So what are you sayin'?" Anton asked.

"I don't want you datin' her," Nate said.

"Now you really lost yo' damn mind."

"You said our opinions important to you," Nate reminded him.

"They are, Nate, but come on. You really tellin' me who I can date?" Anton asked.

"No, I'm tellin' you who you can't date."

Anton bristled. "Well, I think I'm'll make that decision for myself. I'm eighteen years old, Nate."

"She come into yo' life, I go out. It's that simple, dog," Nate said.

There was silence.

"You really gonna do this over a girl?" Anton asked. "That stupid, man. Come on. You know that stupid."

"She come in, I go out," Nate repeated.

Anton said nothing and Nate understood. He walked out of the apartment, and Anton stared after him, bewildered and angry. He expected Nate to be the least accepting of the four, but he didn't expect that reaction. He walked back into the bedroom. Everyone tried to act casual, like they were hanging and talking while the argument ensued, but he knew they all heard every word. Finally, Kareem spoke.

"He come around," Kareem said. "You know how he is. Hot head."

"Yeah," Anton said quietly.

"He just wanna look like a badass in front of Emma," Lamar offered, and then after a thought added, "Maybe he jealous. She cute."

"Shut the hell up, man," Kareem said. "You ain't helpin'."

Emma wanted nothing more than to leave. She felt like a foreigner, unwelcomed, though his friends made an effort to get to know her. Well, most of them. She didn't belong there; she felt it deep within. And she wouldn't break up a friendship. She didn't want to be held accountable for that.

"I'm gonna go," she said.

"Why?" Anton asked.

"I've got things to do," she lied. It was pathetic. She didn't even try to make it sound genuine.

Anton nodded but said nothing.

"You sure you don't wanna stay and get high with us?" Johnny D offered. He grinned at Anton.

"Man, you ain't smokin' that shit in my house. And no, she ain't gettin' high with you," Anton said.

"Thank you, but no." Emma grabbed her purse from the bed. "It was nice meeting all of you."

The boys grunted replies.

"I'll walk you out," Anton said.

"No. You stay here with your friends. It's fine."

"You sure?"

"Yes. Please just let me go," she said quietly and left the room before he could respond.

Nate was a few doors down sitting on the stoop of his apartment building. She noticed him immediately when she walked out, and tried to pretend that he wasn't there. She felt his eyes boring into her and fumbled with her car keys. She couldn't get away fast enough. She felt panicked, her hand shaking as she searched for the unlock button on her key ring.

"Nice ride," Nate called. "Yo' daddy buy you that?"

She didn't respond.

"He prolly buy you whateva you want, don't he?"

"Emma, put your finger on the button," she said quietly, her voice weak and unsteady.

"Daddy's little girl," Nate continued. "So good and sweet. He know you fuckin' a nigga?"

The doors unlocked. Sweet relief. Emma climbed into her car and shut the door. She was shaking fiercely. She fumbled again trying to start the ignition. She hadn't noticed that Nate had walked over to her car. He rapped his knuckles on her window. She jumped violently.

"Yo' daddy know you fuckin' a nigga?" he called to her through the window.

She sped out of the parking lot not bothering to look for traffic before pulling onto the road. She felt the tears coursing, wiping at them clumsily as she tried to focus on driving. She felt like a fool. How could she think this would work? Why did she go back that night? If she had never gone back that night, how would things be different? They would still be just partners on a school assignment who entertained a mild flirtation. Then school would be over and he would be gone and she would think nothing of it.

But now she was in something terribly deep, connected to him in the most intimate way. She had given herself to him completely, and there was no way to undo that. She cried out of fear. She was afraid of Nate, afraid of what her friends would say when they found out. She pulled into the nearly-empty parking lot of a gas station and wept hard. She wept until exhaustion overtook her, resting her head against the steering wheel and closing her eyes to the world.

CHAPTER 16
THURSDAY, MAY 6

Emma was careful to avoid Anton all day. She ducked in and out of rooms, going frequently to the bathroom to hide in between classes, carrying all of her books for the entire day to avoid seeing him at the lockers, even going off campus for lunch—a senior privilege. She acquired a nurse's pass to be excused from English class and sat far away from him in history, never giving him the opportunity to talk with her because she stayed close to Morgan. She knew it was childish, but she could not yet face him. She did not know what she wanted or needed to say to him. She just knew that she felt she had messed everything up for him and perhaps for herself.

When the final bell rang, she found herself back in the girls' bathroom to wait out the clearing crowd. She did not notice Morgan follow her in.

"What is going on?" Morgan demanded peremptorily.

Emma whirled around to see her best friend standing, hands on hips, eyebrows raised in question.

"What do you mean?"

"Please. Don't play stupid. You've been acting weird

all day. Like you're hiding from someone," Morgan pressed.

"I'm not hiding from anyone."

"Is it that guy you're working with? That partner for English class?" Morgan's tone became more urgent. "Did he say something to you? Do something to you?"

"No," Emma said. "It's nothing."

Morgan cocked her head to the side. "You wanna try again?"

Emma let her bags fall to the floor and walked over to the window. She pretended to look out though the panes were frosted.

"Emma?"

"I had sex with him." She expected an immediate reaction but got none. "Did you hear me? I had sex—"

"I heard you," Morgan said.

Emma turned around to face her friend. Morgan looked concerned.

"Did he force you?" she asked.

"Jesus, Morgan! No! Why would you say that?"

"Because he looks like the type," Morgan replied.

"He looks like the type? What the hell does that even mean? What, because he's black? You assumed he forced me to have sex with him because he's black?" Emma felt the anger bubbling over.

"Oh my God. You like him?!" Morgan asked.

"We're dating," Emma said quietly.

"So, you've had sex with him more than once?"

Emma gave her friend an exasperated look.

"I'm sorry, Emma, this is just a lot to take in. My best friend has been dating a black guy for how long, and she hasn't told me anything until now?"

"It hasn't been that long. But you're right, and I'm sorry. I should have told you the moment we got together," Emma said.

"Is this just, like, an experiment or phase or

something? Are you trying on black guys to see if you like them?" Morgan asked.

"No, Morgan. I'm not trying him on. I genuinely like him." And she added softly, "I love him."

"Oh my God."

"Why can't I love him?" Emma asked defensively.

"Because he's from the projects, that's why," Morgan said. "What do you honestly think will come of this?"

"What are you talking about?"

"You think you two will stay together? You think you'll be able to make this whole black and white thing work?" Morgan asked.

"I don't know. I'm not thinking ten years down the road."

"Well, maybe you should. Do you want to be living in the projects with some nobody who doesn't have a job because he has zero motivation and he's stupid and—"

"He's not stupid! Don't say that about him," Emma snapped.

"Okay, who are you and where's my best friend?" Morgan asked.

"I can't help I fell in love with him," Emma said.

"What do you even see in him, Emma? He called you an uptight white bitch? Remember? Now you're telling me you've had sex with him? Excuse me if I'm a little confused," Morgan said.

"I told you we cleared up the bitch thing," Emma said lamely.

"Oh, that's right. You cleared up the bitch thing. How could I forget?"

"Don't be like that, Morgan," Emma pleaded. "I love him. I fell in love with him. I've been spending nearly every day with him, and I've gotten to know him. He's funny and smart and insightful. He hides a lot of that at school, but I've seen it. I can't help it. I love him and I don't know what to do."

Morgan watched a tear glide down her friend's cheek. She wanted to hug her, but she was too angry with her, an anger she knew was completely unfair, but it was there all the same.

"How do you think you guys will be able to make it work? You're from completely different worlds," Morgan pointed out.

"We just will," Emma said, though she was doubtful.

"You're living in a fairytale, Emma."

"No I'm not!"

"Yes you are. You think you can make it work—your world, his world. It can't. Sooner or later one of you is going to have to choose the other person's world, and frankly, I'd like to not see my best friend go ghetto on me."

Emma wiped at her face and said nothing.

"Do either of you have any of the same dreams?"

"I don't know," Emma confessed. What does that have to—?"

"Exactly. You want to go to college and you are. You want to be successful and you will. Is he even going to college? Does he even want a job, or is he more worried about buying his next stash of weed?" Morgan asked.

"Why are you being so nasty?" Emma said.

"I'm being realistic because I love you."

"He doesn't smoke weed," Emma said.

Morgan let out a disdainful laugh. "You really are living in a fairytale."

"Stop saying that," Emma demanded.

"What do you want me to say, huh? You want me to give you my blessing? I'm not your parents, Emma."

"I want you to be okay with it," Emma pleaded.

"Well, I'm not, okay? And you're putting me in a really awkward position here. I mean, come on Emma, have you looked around our school lately? It's not exactly that melting pot we keep learning about in history. Blacks stay with blacks. Whites stay with whites. Mexicans stay with Mexicans. Are you seeing the pattern?"

"I don't care about the factions in our school, Morgan. I care about your opinion. And anyway, we're done in, like, four weeks. Who cares?"

Morgan was silent for a moment. She wanted to continue chiding Emma, making her feel uncomfortable for the choice she made, asking her the difficult questions she knew Emma could not answer, but curiosity over her friend's new, potentially risky relationship won out.

"Is he big?" she asked, her tone completely changed.

"What?"

"You know. Does he have a big dick?" Morgan asked.

"Oh my God. I'm so not answering that question," Emma replied mortified.

"Well, I keep hearing about how black guys have big dicks," Morgan said.

Emma cracked a smile.

"So he *is* big," Morgan said. She could not help it as the grin broke out on her own face.

"I didn't say a word," Emma replied, and both girls giggled.

"This is just so weird, Emma," Morgan said trying for seriousness. "I'm sorry for being mean about it, I really am. But you've got to see where I'm coming from. My best friend is getting it on with a black guy."

"It's not just about sex," Emma said.

"I know, I know, but that's all I can think about," Morgan confessed.

The girls were silent for a moment.

"Do you really think I'm living in a fairytale?" Emma asked.

"Yes. Look Emma, I'm just gonna be straight with you. I think you're gonna get hurt. And I'm not saying that he'll necessarily be the one to hurt you. I just think that the situation is not going to work out the way you want it to."

"I'm not going to get hurt," Emma argued.

Morgan grunted and walked into a bathroom stall.

"I won't, Morgan," Emma insisted, but the image of Nate standing at her car door flashed into her mind making her doubt her resolve. *"Yo' daddy know you fuckin' a nigga?"* he had said, and she shivered involuntarily.

"Do Aubrey or Sarah know?" Morgan asked from inside the stall.

"No."

"Good, because I'd have been pissed if you told them before telling me," Morgan said. "What about your parents?"

"Are you insane?" Emma stood in front of the bathroom mirror and studied her reflection. "They think we work on our project at your house," she said finally. "When we're not at mine."

The bathroom stall door flew open. "Excuse me?"

"I'm sorry," Emma replied. "I really am. But I can't tell them I've been going to his house."

Morgan was shocked. "You've been going to his house?!"

"Well, yeah. Where did you think we did our work?"

"I don't know. At the library. At a damn park!" Morgan said, scrubbing her hands ferociously. "His house? Emma, isn't that, like, dangerous or something? Where does he live exactly?"

Emma didn't respond.

"Hello? I'm talking to you. Where does he live?" Morgan insisted.

"West Highland Park," Emma said quietly.

Morgan rolled her eyes. "God help us," she muttered wiping her hands with a paper towel and tossing it in the trash can.

"It's not that bad. I mean, it's not like there's drive-by shootings or blatant drug deals going on."

Morgan shrugged. "Well, at least it's not those projects on Davidson Parkway," she observed. "Still ghetto, though." She studied her friend for a moment. "Is that where you're having sex?"

"Well, yeah," Emma said, feeling her face blush. "Where did you think we were doing it? My house?"

"No. I guess I figured you were doing it in a car somewhere like every other teenager in America," Morgan replied.

Emma said nothing.

"You have a lot to tell me, you know," Morgan decided.

"I know."

"But right now I'm late for some yearbook crap," Morgan continued. "Call me tonight so we can chat. Okay?"

"Alright."

"You better call," Morgan yelled to her friend as she exited through the door.

Emma watched her leave and then gathered her bags. When she reached the parking lot of the school, Anton was leaning against her car waiting. Her heart fell. She was not prepared to face him, but now she had no choice. She walked towards him, a hollow aching in her stomach that wouldn't go away.

—

She drove them to the park. They were silent on the drive. She didn't know what to say, and he was visibly angry. It wasn't until she parked the car and turned off the ignition that he spoke.

"Are we really back there again?" he asked. "Ignorin' each other at school? I introduced you to my friends, Emma. I thought we was past all that now."

Emma couldn't look at him. She would not tell Anton what Nate said to her when she left his house. However cruel it was, she almost felt Nate was justified in being upset. After all, she was the outsider. She was the wedge that had come between two best friends. The guilt she felt was unbearable.

"Are you not even gonna talk to me?" Anton said.

"Anton, I like you, but—"

"Oh my God. What the fuck is this? You dumpin' me? After everything?" He was panicked.

"No. I'm not dumping you," she said looking at him.

"Then why the hell did you say that? And when did you start likin' me? The other night you said you loved me," he said. He was charged and defensive.

"I do love you, but I can't be responsible for breaking up a friendship!"

"What are you talkin' about?" he asked.

"You and Nate."

"Oh." Anton thought for a moment. "Look, it ain't ideal, okay? But if Nate wanna be mad at me over who I date, then that's somethin' he just gonna have to live with. It ain't my problem."

"But he's your best friend," Emma said.

"I know that," Anton replied. He shifted in his seat. "It's hot as hell in here."

He got out of the car and she followed. They walked to the lake and sat down near the edge watching the ducks paddle languidly in the water. They looked content, Emma thought.

"Man, I need to be a damn duck," Anton observed. "You know how much easier it be to be a duck?"

Emma smiled. "I imagine it'd be kind of boring though."

"But I wouldn't have to be dealin' with all this bullshit," he said and then quickly added, "Not you. I didn't mean you. I meant Nate and all that."

"I know you didn't mean me," Emma said.

"I love Nate, you know? He my homey. My best friend. We go back a long way. Kindergarten." Anton was silent then, brooding.

Emma watched as the ducks plunged their heads under the water, searching for food, cooling off, she didn't know. She wondered what her life would be like if she were an animal. The simplicity of instinct. The absence of emotion. It was a tempting thought, being an animal, but then she was no magician.

"He wasn't always so angry," Anton said after a time. "Truth is I been tired of his bullshit lately. Mad about everything. I mean, I know he got a right in some ways. You seen where we live. But everything? He can't just chill and be happy. That's always been what's different about him and me. I know my situation ain't ideal. I wish I be livin' in yo' house. But I ain't gonna be some angry nigga about it all the time."

Emma listened. She was conscientious of Anton's need to express his feelings about Nate, to get it all out, and made sure she didn't interrupt.

"I mean, how he gonna get that mad about me datin' you? He talkin' like I'm betrayin' my kind, like nobody in the whole damn world ever got with someone who wasn't they same color. I mean, I get how it be a big deal in high school because high school just stupid, but in the real world? It ain't a big deal with adults, is it? I see those kinda relationships all the time. It ain't no big deal."

Emma nodded.

"You got any opinion on this?" Anton asked looking at her.

"Oh, well, I was just letting you talk," Emma replied.

"Well, I want you to talk back."

"Okay."

"Okay."

"Alright then," she said.

"Jesus, Emma! Tell me what you think."

"Oh, okay. Well I think you're right. I think interracial relationships aren't a big deal. In the real world, that is. But I think they are a very big deal in high school," she replied.

"Why you think that is? High school kids just stupid or somethin'? It can't be all high school kids 'cause we ain't stupid."

"I don't know. I think high schoolers are just trying to fit in somewhere. Find a group and feel safe, you know? And it's easy to split up into groups according to color."

"That's stupid."

"Gee, thanks. I was just putting something out there."

"No, not yo' comment. The truth behind it. I can't believe I used to think that way. It's just so fuckin' stupid," Anton said. "I can't wait 'til I'm grown and done with all this, you know?"

"Yeah," Emma replied.

"It'll be different for us then," Anton said.

Emma's heart gave a small leap. Was he including her in his future? The thought was exhilarating, and she suddenly leaned over and kissed him on the cheek. He smiled at her, not understanding the motivation behind her kiss but liking it.

"I told Morgan about us," Emma said. Anton's smile faded.

"Yeah? I'm sure she had some things to say," he replied coolly.

"She was shocked, that's for sure," Emma said. "But I think she's okay with it."

"And if she wasn't? Would you not be with me?"

"Don't be ridiculous! I don't do things according to what my friends think," Emma said.

Anton grunted.

"I know you don't like her," Emma went on.

"She always givin' me these dirty looks. I ain't never done nothin' to her," Anton said defensively.

"She's just looking out for me," Emma replied. "She's a fierce friend."

"Fierce friend," he muttered. "She need to take that shit somewhere else."

Emma scooted closer to him, linking her arm with his.

"She just wants to be sure that you're going to treat me right," she said sweetly.

"Yeah, well she just need to worry about her own damn self," Anton replied.

"Don't be mad at her," Emma said, and kissed his neck.

"Don't even be doin' that. I'm still mad at you for earlier. Avoidin' me all day. Now you think you can just talk all sweet and kiss my neck and that's that? I forget about how you treated me?"

"I'm sorry I avoided you," Emma said into his neck.

She kissed him again and heard the familiar low rumble in his throat. He was fighting the urge to respond to her, but she was relentless, and she pushed him down on the soft grass, climbed on top of him and straddled his hips.

"There people out here!" he said.

"I'm just going to kiss you," Emma said innocently. The sun was to her back framing her face with light, and he was sure that she transformed into an angel.

She bent down and kissed him, long and slow. He responded to her then; he had no choice. He'd swim with hungry sharks or sky dive without a back-up parachute if she wanted him to, he thought absurdly. He'd do anything for this girl. He thought he would even renounce his faith in God, would go with her to hell just to be with her. He'd burn for eternity to feel the softness of her lips.

He kissed her hard realizing he wanted more and could not get it. His mother was home. They had no place to go. He would have to content himself with simply kissing her here out in the open for all of the park visitors to see. Fuck 'em, he thought. *They* could go to hell.

He inched his hands up her thighs to rest under her skirt on her bottom, squeezing her playfully and breaking the magic of their kiss as she sat up abruptly slapping his hands away.

"We're in public! Hello?" she said, looking wildly around.

"Girl, you kiss my neck then climb on top of me and then you gonna give me shit about squeezing yo' ass?" Anton asked.

Emma grinned and crawled off of him.

"You just a little tease," he said, sitting up. "Someone need to teach you a lesson 'bout bein' a tease."

"Yeah? And if that someone were you, what would you do?" she asked.

"I'd bend you over my knee and lift up that ruffley skirt of yours and—"

"Stop! That's enough," Emma said. Her face was beet red.

"Yeah, that's what I thought."

They fell into a comfortable silence with one another, watching the lake, running their hands over the spring grass, listening to the conversations of birds overhead.

"You know, I don't know who got who in this relationship," Anton said at last.

"What do you mean?" Emma asked.

"Well, it's like this. I can make you come by just lookin' at you—"

"Anton!" Emma squealed.

"Now wait, just lemme finish. I can do that to you, and it make me feel like I got all the power in the world over you. And then you say somethin' or you touch my arm or kiss my cheek or somethin' simple like that, and I feel like gettin' on my hands and knees and worshippin' you. And then you got all the power. I can't figure it out. I really can't."

Emma smiled at him. She watched his face, his brows furrowed in concentration.

"I don't understand it either," she said finally.

"I like it though. I mean, it weird and frustratin' sometimes, but I like it."

"Me too."

"So this what bein' in love is like? I ain't never felt this before," Anton said.

"I guess it is," Emma replied softly.

"Well, okay then," Anton said, taking hold of her hand and staring back out on the water.

CHAPTER 17
FRIDAY, MAY 7

"Hi girls!" Emma said cheerfully, plopping her purse and lunch bag on the table. Morgan, Aubrey, and Sarah stared back and forth between her and her company. "I brought along some friends today. Mind if they sit with us?"

Kareem wasted no time wiggling his large body in between Aubrey and Sarah. Settling in, he took note of their facial expressions and couldn't decide which one looked more terrified. Johnny D and Lamar—who actually made it to school that day—acted as bookends, nestling the three as tightly together as possible.

"So, I'm sure Morgan informed you two that I'm dating Anton," Emma said, addressing the two frightened girls on the other side of the table. She had taken a seat beside Morgan.

"Well, I wanted to avoid any awkwardness," Morgan noted with sarcasm.

Anton couldn't help but laugh. "Kareem, don't be lookin' at her like that. It's obvious she don't want you near her."

"Baby, that not true, is it? Tell me that not true," Kareem begged Aubrey. He grinned at her.

"Oh my God. Can you scoot over please?" Aubrey said.

"Um, no he can't," Sarah said from the other side of Kareem.

"Say, is that a real Louis Vuitton?" Lamar asked Sarah. He fingered the purse.

"Yes, and please don't touch," Sarah replied, snatching the bag away from him.

"Man, Emma, why yo' friends gotta be so uptight? They need to relax," Lamar said. And then looking at Sarah, he added, "Baby girl, I didn't mean no harm by touchin' yo' purse. It's just so pretty. Like you." He let his fingers lightly brush the top of her hand as he winked at her.

"Emma, I'm changing tables," Sarah said, standing up suddenly.

"What? Like in third grade? Come on, Sarah, he's just playing with you. Chill out," Emma said laughing.

Sarah narrowed her eyes at Emma and slowly sank back into her seat.

"Okay, introductions," Emma said. "Aubrey, Sarah, Morgan, this is Johnny D, Kareem (he placed his arms around the girls flanking him when he was introduced), and Lamar. And obviously you know this is Anton."

"Hey," Anton said.

Neither Aubrey nor Sarah responded as they were busy trying to shrug off Kareem's heavy arms. Morgan turned to face Anton.

"It's nice to meet you, Anton," she said, and he realized that it was the first time she actually smiled at him. It was strained, but still a smile. He'd take what he could get. "It's nice to meet the rest of you, too," she added, looking at the other boys.

They all smiled, and Emma began feeling hopeful. Perhaps this could actually work, she thought.

"Aubrey, is that yo' real hair?" Johnny D asked.

"What does that mean?" Aubrey asked affronted.

"I mean it so thick and shiny. It all yo' hair?"

"Yes, it's all my hair."

"Well, I know you girls be gettin' those extensions or weaves or whatever. I don't know what you be doin' to yo' hair half the time. It just look so perfect, I had to ask. Was I out of line?" Johnny D asked.

"Yes," she snapped, and he chuckled.

"No, see man, the black girls, they get the weaves," Kareem explained. "The white girls, they get the extensions."

"Nah man. It the other way around," Lamar pointed out.

"Man, is you stupid? You ever seen a white girl with a damn weave?" Kareem asked.

Lamar considered the question.

"I think it true what people say. You hang out with people who look like you," Johnny D said. "All you girls got perfect, shiny hair. You all look alike. It's like some twins up in here."

Morgan rolled her eyes. "Except that there's four of us," she muttered.

"You all pretty," Lamar chimed in. "But you all prolly know you pretty."

Aubrey couldn't help but grin. She'd never been talked to this way—so frank and honest—and she wasn't sure she didn't like it. It was silly and fun.

"So how long y'all been friends?" Johnny D asked.

"A long time. We went to private school together," Sarah answered.

"Private school?" Anton asked, looking at Emma. She shrugged. "You ain't never tell me about private school."

"Well, you only just met her, remember?" Morgan said. She instantly regretted her words.

Anton chose to ignore her. Emma flashed her an

angry look. Kareem was too busy making eyes at Aubrey. And Lamar kept trying to touch Sarah's hand.

"We went to a private school together until sixth grade," Emma pointed out.

"So why you not go there now?" Kareem asked, addressing the question to Aubrey.

"It closed down," she answered, feeling more comfortable by the minute.

"And they ain't no other private schools around?" Johnny D asked.

"I'm sorry, do you want us to be going to a private school?" Morgan asked. As much as she tried, she could not keep her mouth shut. "I'm just confused. Why all the questions?"

"They just wanna know about you," Anton replied. His voice was controlled though he felt his temper rising.

Morgan said nothing.

"My parents couldn't decide on one they liked," Sarah said, noting the tension between Morgan and Anton. "And once they found out that the others were coming here, they figured it was okay to send me too."

"I see," Johnny D said. "So you four travel 'round in like a pack or somethin'."

"We kill as a pack, too," Aubrey replied.

The boys laughed out loud.

"Okay. You funny," Kareem decided. "Now how 'bout you be my girl?"

This time Aubrey burst out laughing.

"What?" Kareem asked, feigning confusion.

"So which one of you fine ladies is going to prom with me?" Lamar asked.

The girls looked at one another grinning.

"Prom was four weeks ago," Sarah pointed out.

"Man, I can't even deal with keepin' up with this schedule. All this school shit goin' on all the time. I can't keep nothin' straight," Lamar said.

"No man, it's called, you ain't been at school since March. Why you even here today? You know you gonna have to go to summer school," Anton said.

"Man, you trippin'. I planned to go to summer school all along, man," Lamar replied.

The entire table erupted with laughter. Nate watched from a distance, alone with his thoughts of jealousy and rage. There were his friends sitting with strangers, laughing and talking like they shared so much in common, like they could ever hope to understand one another. His anger intensified when he saw Kareem hug Aubrey, no doubt teasing her about something. He watched her try to push him off, and noticed, too, that she did it with a smile on her face. Fucking bitch, he thought. What the hell was going on at this school? Damn campfire kumbayah bullshit, he thought. He was sure the whole world was going crazy.

—

"Just for a little bit," he pleaded tugging at her waist.

"I can't, Anton," she said. "I have rehearsal this afternoon." She swatted at his hands, but he ignored her and drew her closer to him.

There were people everywhere, packing their bags and moving briskly down the hallway for the exit, and he was so happy not to care. The relief of finally coming out in the open was the elixir he had been waiting for, and now all he wanted to do was hold her to him and kiss her, let everyone see, and damn them to hell if they had a problem with it.

"I promise it won't take long," he cooed into her ear.

"For you or for me?" she asked.

"Well, I ain't no expert lover yet, so prolly me," he said truthfully, laughing lightly. "I ain't even gonna lie. It's hard sometimes holdin' out with you."

"I think you're a fantastic lover," she replied, pulling on his shoulder until he bent down. She kissed him on the cheek.

"A'ight then. Let's go," he said, tugging on her arm.

"I cannot be late for my rehearsal, Anton," she said.

"Emma, I promise you won't be late for yo' rehearsal," he said.

He looked at her in desperation. He had to have her or he would die. He could think of nothing else, the image of her naked body consuming him ever since their first time. And he knew she wanted him too. He could sense it in the way her body moved, how it responded to him when he stood close to her. It cried out to him silently, and he was determined to heed the call.

"Okay, but you promise," she said.

He pulled her along with force pushing people aside who got in his way. He heard them curse at him, and he didn't care. He had to get out of the building, get home to where he could do with her as he wanted. The urge intensified the closer they got to her car. He grabbed the keys from her hand and opened the door for her nearly shoving her in. He was on a mission with no time to delay. He drove them to his house perhaps faster than he should. And once there, he grabbed her arm, pulled her out of the vehicle, and forced her up the stairs to his apartment. She stumbled on the steps, but he held her up, gripping her tightly as though afraid she might run away.

There was no prelude. There were just his hands all over her, stripping her down to nothing, pushing her onto his bed. He told her to be quiet when she tried to speak. He didn't want to talk. He wanted to fuck her quickly. And he wasted no time taking her hard, letting her squirm in discomfort as he took for himself. It was self-seeking and uncontrolled and terse. And he didn't care.

He rolled off of her and breathed deeply. He noticed he did not even sweat. It had taken so little time. He felt like a typical teenage boy, inexpert and selfish. She had gotten nothing out of it, he knew. She was just the instrument he used to get off. He exploited her so blatantly and was bothered that he didn't care.

He heard her giggle.

"What?" he asked, looking at her.

"Nothing."

"No, you can't do that. Just tell me," he said.

"Did you get what you needed?" she asked. "I just want to make sure you got everything you needed."

He grinned. "I'm sorry, okay? I told you it wouldn't take long."

"Could you be any more selfish?" she asked smiling.

"Again, I'm sorry. But I'm eighteen. What you expect?" he asked.

She shrugged getting out of the bed and dressing. He watched her.

"I know I was selfish right then. I know. I won't be selfish the next time," he promised.

"Next time?" she asked, buttoning her shorts.

"Oh, you funny. You know you can't get enough of me," he said stretching his arms overhead and then flexing his muscles. He grinned and wiggled his eyebrows at her. She rolled her eyes and grabbed her bag.

"You goin' that quick?" he asked. "You don't wanna cuddle or nothin'?"

She laughed brightly. "Cuddle?"

"Yeah, cuddle. What's wrong with that?"

"Nothing. You're just weird. You drag me here all the way from school, rip my clothes off, tell me to be quiet, fuck me for two minutes, and now you want to cuddle?"

"Yeah," Anton replied. He reached his arms out to her.

"Well, you'll just have to cuddle with yourself because I've got to go," Emma replied.

She leaned over and kissed his lips, fighting his attempt to wrap her up in his arms.

"Emma?" he said as she stood in the bedroom doorway.

"Yes?"

"I love you."

"I know you do," she said smiling, and walked out the door.

—

She danced with complete abandon. She never felt so light and free. She could stretch her arms forever, touch the heavens and pull down the stars. She would give him the stars to keep in his pocket, she thought. They would bring him good luck. She jumped and laughed and drew giggles from some of the other girls. She felt high, though she never before experienced a drug high. But then what was she thinking? He was her drug, and she felt high on the dark, rich honey. Honey that matched the color of his eyes. She could drink him to overflowing and never be satisfied. She was filled with the honey even now; it coursed through her limbs—a powerful, exotic, demanding potion that ordered her to dance. And so she did. She danced.

CHAPTER 18
SATURDAY, MAY 8

His mama wanted to come too. At first he was hesitant, certain that she had some ulterior motive. She wanted to meet Emma's parents, he thought, and that simply couldn't happen. They had no idea Emma was dating him. And he was just fine with that. In fact, he was fine with Emma never telling them, at least not until they got married and had their first child. He figured that with a child, they couldn't get rid of him then. But his mama promised that she only wanted to go to see the dancing. It was as simple as that.

"Since when you like ballet, Mama?" Anton asked, standing in front of her as she straightened his tie.

"I've always liked dance, Anton," his mother replied. "Just 'cause I never shared that with you doesn't mean it ain't true."

Anton grunted.

"And I want to know her better," his mother added quietly.

"I told you everything already," Anton said.

"I'm sure you didn't," his mother replied, and he chuckled.

"I can tell she important to you," Ms. Robinson said.

"So is it alright that I get to know her a little more? Is that alright with you?"

"Yes, Mama," he said. She pinched his cheek and he drew back rubbing his face.

"Why you always gotta do that?"

"'Cause I love you," she replied.

Anton grinned and grabbed the car keys off the kitchen counter.

"Does she know you goin' to see her dance?" Ms. Robinson asked suddenly.

"Um, not exactly," Anton replied.

"Baby, how you know she even want you there?"

"Well, I don't know. But Mama I'm curious. I can't help it. Her parents be talkin' 'bout how she so amazin'."

"So lemme get this straight. You blowin' off your friends on a Saturday night to see Emma dance when you don't even know if she wants you there?" Ms. Robinson asked.

"Pretty much," Anton replied.

"Well, you really do like her then, don't you?" she asked smiling.

Anton paused for a moment before responding.

"I think I love her, Mama," he said quietly.

"Baby, I already knew that."

They left the tiny apartment for the community cultural center on the other side of town.

—

"You look beautiful!" Emma's mother said. "How do you feel?"

"Nervous," Emma responded. She scanned the dressing room.

Everyone was scurrying around, putting last-minute touches on their costumes, securing their hair with pins, darkening their eyes with kohl eye liner. A haze of hairspray permeated the room, and Emma's mother coughed as a fresh wave assaulted her face.

"You better go now," Emma said. Curtain call was in fifteen minutes. She was in the first and last numbers, as was tradition for the senior class.

Her mother leaned in to give her a kiss on the cheek.

"Good luck, honey," she said, and disappeared out the door.

Emma never felt nervous before a recital. But this one was different. Anton had discovered the show time information in her bedroom; he confessed when she asked him how a large smiley face appeared on the front of the pamphlet. And now she was panicked that he might actually show up. She tried to reason with herself. It was Saturday night after all. Surely he had plans with his friends. But he did say he wanted to see her dance. He was insistent until she made him promise he wouldn't come. Surely he wouldn't break his promise to her.

She could stand it no longer. She made her way to the side stage entrance and peered out into the audience. The lights had not yet dimmed. She scanned the auditorium, her heartbeat beginning to slow until she spotted him. With his mother! She felt the rapid increase of her pulse, certain that her heart would burst, and then she wouldn't have to worry about performing for anyone. How could he do this?

"Psst! Emma!" called a fellow dancer. "Back here. It's time."

Emma moved into place, vowing to get a grip on her emotions. She would not let him distract her. She would not make a mistake. She took a long breath, listened for the music cue, and then burst onto the stage with the rest of her class. It was a lively dance—a jig—and as she moved, gracefully bouncing about the stage, she forgot all about Anton. She was performing this dance for herself.

Anton found her immediately. He leaned over to his

mother and pointed her out amidst the sea of dancers. They were moving so fast, up down, up down on their toes. He remembered she called them pointe shoes. Her arms were so graceful, he thought. Her body sinewy and light. He observed her costume. She looked like a little Irish maid, he thought, then wondered how he even knew what an Irish maid looked like.

He could have watched her forever, and was sorry to see her exit the stage as fast as she entered it. The audience exploded in applause. Apparently everyone had been swept up in the dance. There was energy emitting from all around him, and he wondered how a dance could be so powerful.

He looked down at the program and realized he would not see her again until the end of the show. He felt he'd been teased, been given a small taste, and now he would have to wait an eternity to taste it again, taste her again. He hadn't realized ballet was so sexy, or perhaps it was just her.

Anton's mother whispered comments to him throughout the program. She seemed enraptured. These girls danced like professionals, she said. He was bored. The only ballet he wanted to watch was Emma's, and he still had a dozen dances to sit through until she came out again. He closed his eyes and listened to the music, mostly classical. It was perfect to sleep to, he thought, the strings lulling him into a contented slumber.

He was nudged hard sometime later. He woke with a start. How long had he slept? Did he miss her?

"Anton, Emma's number is coming up," his mother whispered.

He straightened up immediately, rubbing his face roughly to wake up completely.

A low, mournful sound of a violin pierced the auditorium. The curtain rose gradually, and he saw dozens of girls lying on the floor. Their bodies rose slowly, arms lifting high overhead, reaching. Reaching for God, he thought. They were wearing all black, and as they stood slowly, Anton could see that their skirts hung to the floor, barely brushing it. They were barefoot.

He found Emma easily. She was in the front, long and lean as she stretched her arms high, her body so taut that he was sure he could count every rib. When he thought that she would die from stretching herself so thin, she let her arms fall to her sides, always graceful, always controlled. The girls moved in circles, following one another one by one like a funeral procession. They were the saddest people he had ever seen, he thought. These girls, rich enough to afford ballet lessons at the most expensive studio. How could they look so sad, he wondered?

He watched Emma intently. He could feel her pull him into her dance as if he were the only one in the audience and she were the only one on stage. She was dancing for him, and he didn't know what to make of it. She was asking him something he didn't understand, and he felt trapped between feelings of sadness and lust. She needed him to do something, she was crying out to him for it, but he couldn't help her. Her arms stretched out to him, and he sat immobile. He wanted to go to her, in spite of the people around him. He wanted to go to her and rescue her from the stage, cradle her in his arms and keep her safe. He wanted to.

The music stopped as the girls froze on stage. It felt incomplete, and he thought that maybe that was the point. The curtain fell and the audience burst into applause once more. They stood, and he and his mother followed suit, clapping and cheering for an encore. The curtain rose suddenly, and the girls walked forward, curtsying before exiting the stage.

Anton fidgeted with his tie while he waited in the

lobby of the auditorium. He wasn't sure if he should stay, but his mother said it was rude to leave without seeing Emma to congratulate her.

"You were the one who wanted to come," she reminded him.

Just then he saw her walk out flanked by her parents. She cradled a large bouquet of yellow roses in her arms. His heart dropped, and he turned to his mother.

"Maybe we should just go," he said. Why had he not thought about her parents being there? Why did he not think to bring her flowers?

"Absolutely not," his mother replied, and upon seeing Emma, she hurried towards her. Anton had no choice but to follow.

"Hi Ms. Robinson," Emma said. She sounded tired and happy.

"Emma, you were beautiful!" Ms. Robinson said. "Anton, wasn't she beautiful?"

"Yeah," Anton said.

Emma beamed. "Thank you," she said shyly. "Ms. Robinson, these are my parents."

Her parents introduced themselves in turn and commented on how nice it was that Ms. Robinson and Anton came tonight. They chatted politely for a few moments as Emma pulled Anton aside.

"So you came anyway," she said. She didn't sound mad.

"Yeah, and I feel dumb. I didn't even bring you no flowers," he said.

"Who cares? I'd rather you give me something else anyway," she said, and he looked shocked.

"Yo' parents are right there," he reminded her.

She grinned at him and winked.

"You sure do wear a lotta make-up for these things," he observed.

Her eyes were heavy and dark with the black liner

and mascara. Her cheeks were caked with blush, and her lips looked blood red.

"I know," she said. "I look like a clown up close. But it's so that you can see my face on stage."

He nodded with understanding.

"You were really good tonight. Really pretty," he said. "How come you never told me you could dance like that?"

"Well, I didn't want to brag," she said affecting nonchalance.

"It's like you was dancing for me," he said. "In that last number." It was more of a question.

"I was," she said, all playfulness in her tone gone.

Anton looked over to their parents and then back at her.

"I want you to do that for me again," he said quietly. "Will you?"

"Yes," she said, and then they heard their names called.

They parted ways, each charged with the anticipation of their next meeting.

Anton called her late that night. It was almost midnight, and he was sure she was sleeping. She answered the phone groggily, and he felt mildly guilty for waking her. He invited her to church, figuring she would say no, and was surprised when she agreed. He apologized for such a late invitation, and told her to be at his house by ten thirty. Church started at eleven. She asked how long it would last, but he evaded the question. It was obvious she knew nothing about black churches. They'd be lucky to get out by two. He told her that his mother wanted her to stay for lunch, and she agreed. It was a pleasant, quick conversation. He hung up the phone thinking that now he could sleep well.

CHAPTER 19
SUNDAY, MAY 9

Emma's parents were sitting in the breakfast room drinking their morning coffee and eating toast. She walked towards the table with purpose.

"I'm going to church with Anton and his mother," she said.

They looked at her dubiously.

"Where is his church?" her mother asked.

"Near his house," Emma replied. There was no point in lying about it.

"Near West Highland Park?" her father asked. He was picking through the Sunday paper for the business section.

"Yes Dad. Right down the road."

"Hmm," her father replied.

"Well honey, I don't know how comfortable I feel with you going over to that side of town," her mother confessed. She took another sip of her coffee.

"I've already been there," Emma said boldly.

They looked at her, eyebrows raised in question.

"I mean, I've taken Anton home from school a couple of times," she clarified.

"Does he not have his own car?" her mother asked.

Her tone was laced with conceit, and Emma hated it.

"I don't know, Mom. He lives in West Highland Park. Do you think he has his own car?"

"Emma?" her father said testily.

"I'm sorry," Emma replied quickly.

There was a brief moment of silence before her father spoke.

"And his mother will be going with you?" he asked.

"Yes."

"Is this for your class project?" he asked.

Emma smiled. "No. He invited me to go and I said yes."

"Hmm," her father replied.

Emma checked her watch. She really needed to be leaving at that moment.

"When will you be home?" her mother asked.

"I don't know. I'm eating lunch with them afterwards," Emma said.

"Where?" her mother asked.

Jesus, she thought. They've never before asked her so many questions. Most of the time they didn't have a clue what she was doing.

"At his house," she replied. "Mom, Dad, I really have to go now. I don't want to be late."

"Very well," her father said. "Be careful and call us after church and before you come home."

Be careful, she thought amused. Did they not hear her say she was going to church?

"I will," she said and turned to leave.

The urge to say it boiled over. She really just wanted to see their reactions, but she had to make sure she could escape before they made her stay home. She was standing in the entryway and could still see into the breakfast room. They had gone back to eating their toast and reading the Sunday paper. It was now or never.

"Oh yeah, I almost forgot," she called to them, and

she watched as they looked up from their reading. "I'm dating him."

She was out the front door in no more than three strides. She couldn't believe how nimble she was wearing heels. She didn't turn around when she heard her parents at the door. She never moved so fast in her life, and was in the car pulling out of the driveway before she realized she had started it. She looked up then and saw them standing in the doorway. They didn't look angry. They looked clearly puzzled, like they had no idea who this child was that they had raised for seventeen years.

—

Emma hesitated before entering Mount Zion Baptist Church. Anton noticed it and told his mother that they would be right in. Ms. Robinson went ahead to find seats.

"You a'ight?" he asked her. She was wearing a summer dress with a short-sleeve cardigan. She had on her pearls as usual and looked the perfect picture of a churchgoer.

"I'm too embarrassed to say it," she said blushing.

"What?"

"I've never been inside a church. Well, I mean not to worship or whatever. I went to a few weddings." She fidgeted nervously. "I don't know what to expect. Will God see me and know I don't go to church? Will he strike me down with a bolt of lightning as punishment?"

It took everything within him not to fall to the floor laughing. She looked genuinely frightened. He maintained his composure and squeezed her hand.

"God don't do that. He know you don't go to church. He God after all. But he not gonna strike you down with no lightning," Anton assured her.

She seemed mildly relieved and let him lead her into the sanctuary.

It was hot as hell. She thought that couldn't be right. How was a church going to feel like hell? Shouldn't it feel heavenly inside? Where was the air conditioning? She noticed ladies in large hats fanning themselves. There were large hats everywhere. They were fabulous, she thought. Feathers, wide brims, bright colors, even rhinestones. It was as though the ladies were in a competition to see who could impress God the most with her hat. Suddenly Emma wanted her own hat. She thought that maybe that would put her in better standing with the Almighty.

They found Anton's mother near the back of the church and had a seat. Only then did Emma realize she was one of the few white people in the congregation. She knew to expect it, but it still made her uneasy. Would they wonder why she was there? Were they wishing she'd leave, knowing she didn't belong there, that she wasn't one of them, that she could never understand their faith or the way they worshipped?

"Here Emma," Ms. Robinson said handing her a fan. "It can get real hot in here. The air conditioning ain't workin' right now."

Emma accepted the fan with gratitude. She was sure she would not be able to make it through the service without it. She began fanning herself immediately, feeling the rush of coolness hit her face and neck. It felt delicious.

"You can fan me too if you want," Anton said, his face glistening. He was all buttoned up, wrapped in a tie, looking hot and miserable.

"Maybe later," she replied. He laughed quietly.

The service began shortly after they had taken their seats. There was music—music like nothing Emma had ever heard. It was loud and powerful, urging the congregation to clap with joy, lift their hands to the ceiling and sway, even holler. She heard a lot of "Praise Jesus's" and "Glory, Hallelujah's." It was hard to not be affected by the emotion pouring forth from the pews and pews of people even if she did not understand it. They believed in something powerful—that she understood. And she thought that she wanted to feel it, to believe in something like that, to raise her hands to the ceiling and let the certainty of it fill her up. The emotion never waned, even when the pastor took his place behind the pulpit to preach. In fact, Emma noticed that it seemed heightened.

"I had a sermon prepared," he began.

"Mmhmm," came a chorus of voices.

"But God spoke to me this morning and gave me a new one."

"Praise God!" the congregation shouted.

"You see, some of you here today are hurtin'. And you need a message of hope. I know the pain of livin' in this world. Just 'cause I'm a pastor don't mean I don't feel it."

"Yes," came the agreement.

"I know the pain of adversity. When you feel the whole world is against you. You work hard. You try hard. But the world push you down. The world make you feel like you nothin'," the pastor continued.

"That's right," his congregation said.

"You know what God say?" he asked.

"Tell us!"

"He say, 'Rise up! You my warriors! Pick yo'selves up because I give you the strength!'"

There were shouts all around.

"Lean on me! And then you can do anything. You can rise up on them wings, just like the eagles. You can run and not be weary. You can walk and not faint," the pastor said.

"Praise Jesus!"

"Glory, Hallelujah!"

"Amen!"

"Thank you, Lord," Ms. Robinson said quietly,

fanning herself rapidly.

Emma could not ignore the lump in her throat. It had crept up during the singing and now sat waiting at the back of her mouth. She did not know what it meant, but it felt like the lump in one's throat before the tears come. She could not understand why she felt like crying. She had nothing to cry about. She experienced no adversity. They all did, she thought, as she looked around her. They were poor and struggling. They were from rough neighborhoods. But she wasn't. The pastor couldn't possibly be addressing her, she thought. But then why did she feel like he was?

"You see, when you try to do it on yo' own, you gonna fail," the pastor said. "Every time, you gonna fail. And then you stay trapped in that adversity. You stay victim to this world. But when you give it all to God, and I mean all. You can't be holdin' nothin' back. You got to give it all. When you do that, he bless you beyond measure. And then you see yo' strength return. You see yo' smile return. You see yo' life return!"

There was an eruption of clapping so hard throughout the building that Emma feared the walls would give way and crumble to the ground. She fanned herself harder, pushing down the lump in her throat until she felt her emotions were under control. The power of the message, though she understood so little of it, infused her heart. She had the urge to shout out as they did, but she wasn't sure she was allowed. She was a guest, after all, and white. It might not be her place to cry "Glory, Hallelujah!" And so she contented herself with shouting it quietly in her heart where no one but God might hear.

She was quiet on the car ride back to their house, deep in reflection about what she just witnessed. She was not aware that they had been there for three hours until Anton told her. She felt she could have sat there all day listening to the pastor shout hopefulness into her. It was the hope that made her believe she could do this, that she could be with Anton, that she could fight her parents later on when they objected. As long as the pastor kept giving her hope, she could do it.

Anton's mother got to work straight away once they arrived home. Emma offered to help, but Ms. Robinson said she had it under control. She said the best help would be for them to find something to do for the next half hour since Anton was getting in her way while she was in the kitchen.

"Get out from under my feet!" she yelled at him as he picked at a plate of fried chicken she had prepared in advance. "And stop picking at that plate!" she said slapping his hand away.

"I can't help it, Mama," Anton replied. "I'm hungry. We was at church for like a million years. I'm starvin'. Emma, didn't you hear my stomach growlin'?"

Emma shook her head. She took no notice that he was even beside her during the service.

"Well it was," he said, and his hand went back to the chicken.

"If you touch that chicken I will whoop you so hard," Ms. Robinson said.

Anton looked at his mother and grinned.

"Mama, you ain't gonna whoop a grown man," he said, his hand poised over the succulent meat. Emma wished she could pick at it too. She didn't realize until she saw it that she was hungry.

"Try me," Ms. Robinson said flatly.

He withdrew his hand reluctantly and walked out of the kitchen.

"Go down to Ellie's and get some soda. Why don't you do that?" she asked, and turning to the stove added, "And get outta my hair."

"A'ight," Anton replied. He grabbed Emma's hand

and pulled her along out the door and down the stairs.

Emma instinctively walked to the car and Anton stopped her.

"We ain't drivin'. It's just down the road," he said.

"Oh," she replied, uncertain. She looked down at her Prada heels and bit her lip.

"What?" he asked, watching her look at her shoes.

"Nothing."

Anton grinned. "You want me to carry you to the store? So you don't mess up your little shoes there? What you think? We gonna be takin' a hike? The store literally right down the road."

She ignored him, lifting her chin indignantly, and started walking.

"You goin' the wrong way," he pointed out.

Without missing a beat, she turned on her heel and started in the opposite direction. Anton caught up with her and fell into step beside her.

"You on a mission or somethin'? Slow down," he said, grabbing her hand.

She slowed her pace and let him entwine his fingers with hers.

"How much them snazzy shoes cost anyway?" he asked looking at her feet.

"Six hundred dollars," she said, head still raised in the air. She felt her body jerk as Anton stopped short still holding her hand.

She turned to face him.

"What?" she said. "You asked."

"Maybe I *should* be carryin' you then," Anton replied.

Emma looked at him evenly.

"Is this going to be a problem?" she asked. "Because you know my family has money. And you told me I shouldn't feel bad about that. You wanted to know what my shoes cost and I told you. Not all of my shoes cost six hundred dollars. These are a special pair, and I wore them today because I wanted to look good for you for church." She looked at the ground while she awaited his response.

Anton smiled, releasing her hand. "Nobody worried about how wealthy you are. I know you are. And I appreciate you wearin' yo' fancy shoes for me, but I prolly should of told you not to. We in the ghetto, you know. Someone might come steal 'em right off yo' feet."

"Well, that's why you're here, right?" she asked.

Anton smiled. "Baby, I'm a lover, not a fighter."

He watched the expression on Emma's face change. It brightened ever so slightly.

"You've never called me that before," she said.

"What? 'Baby?' Sure I have."

"No. Never. You always call me 'girl.' Sometimes you say my name."

"Girl, you crazy. I've called you 'baby' lots of times."

He started walking again, taking her hand and leading her along. Emma felt herself glowing. She was his baby, and she liked it.

Ellie's was literally right down the road, no more than two blocks. It was a small locally-owned corner store. The outside was littered with brightly colored advertisement signs and old cigarette butts. There were metal bars on the door and in the windows. A few men hung around the outside of the building smoking and drinking from long brown paper bags. Emma noticed the neck of a bottle poking out of the top of one bag, the contents within a clear liquid.

Anton opened the door for her. She walked in hesitantly and looked around. There was the strong smell of grease coming from the back and she noticed a deli counter up front with every deep fried food she could imagine. Some foods she didn't recognize. A large man stood behind the counter counting change to a customer. He looked up when the door opened and nodded to Anton. Apparently they knew each other.

"'Course I know him," Anton said when Emma asked. "I come here almost every day."

He took her hand and led her to the refrigerators that housed the sodas. Kareem, Johnny D, and Lamar were there, faces stuck to the glass of the refrigerator doors trying to decide on a drink.

"What trouble you get yo'selves into today?" Anton asked approaching them.

"Man, it's the Lord's day. You don't get in no trouble on the Lord's day," Lamar replied bumping Anton's fist. The strong smell of weed wafted from him.

"You got yo' girl here?" Johnny D asked. He did some sort of handshake with Anton that involved snapping fingers and bumping fists. Emma made a note to herself to ask him to show her how to do that.

"Yeah. We just got back from church," Anton replied.

"You take her to yo' church?" Kareem asked then burst out laughing.

"What's wrong with my church, nigga?" Anton asked.

"Man, it ain't yo' church. It's any black church," Kareem replied, and then addressing Emma he said, "Girl, I can't even believe you still alive."

Emma smiled shyly. She did not understand what he meant.

"Man, Emma, was you scared in there?" Lamar asked.

"No," she replied. "Why would I be?"

"That's just a lotta black folks to be around at one time," Johnny D said. "And for such a long time, too."

"Yeah, man. That's why I can't be doin' no church. It just take too long," Lamar said. "I just gotta worship the Lord in my own way, know what I'm sayin'?"

"How's that? By smokin' a blunt?" Anton asked. The boys laughed.

"Man, whateva," Lamar mumbled.

"Girl, wasn't you afraid when everybody be shoutin' and yellin' things and singin'? Didn't that singin' make you nervous? They can get rowdy when that singin' starts," Kareem said.

Emma shrugged. "I liked it. I liked everything, actually." And then after a moment she added, "I really liked the hats."

They all stared at her.

"You know. The ladies' hats. They were beautiful. I'd like to have a hat like one of theirs."

The boys looked at each other and grinned.

Anton put his arm around her shoulder. "No baby. You can't have a hat like theirs."

They burst into laughter after that. Emma was confused. She didn't get the joke. Why couldn't she have a hat like theirs?

"You seen Nate lately?" Anton asked.

"Nah man. He doin' his own thing. I think he hangin' with that nigga from those Holly Springs projects. You remember that kid? He go to our school," Johnny D replied.

"That 'lil punk?" Anton asked. There was a note of irritation in his voice. "Nate used to always be tellin' me what a 'lil shit he was."

"I know, man. I remember. But apparently he got a good weed connection. I even heard Nate started doin' some other stuff," Kareem said.

"Other drugs? Like what?" Anton asked. He was in disbelief. He never thought Nate would go that far. They smoked weed occasionally, not nearly in the amount that Johnny D and Lamar did, but they never went past that. Anton never needed to. He thought it was the same for Nate.

"I don't know. Crack maybe," Kareem said shrugging. "That nigga need an intervention or somethin'.

Other day I tried to talk to him at school, and he brushed me off. I don't know what he so mad about. I can't believe it could still be over you and Emma."

Emma stiffened slightly.

"I don't know, man," Anton replied. He thought for a moment then added," Maybe I just gotta go talk to him."

"Well, you better catch him on a day he ain't jacked up," Johnny D said.

"Yeah," Anton replied, thinking.

He pulled a two liter of soda from the refrigerator and said goodbye to his friends. Emma waved goodbye as they made their way to the counter to pay—Anton chatting with the owner for a few minutes—and then out the door for home. They walked hand in hand at a slow pace though Anton was anxious to get back to the house. The smell that permeated the small grocery store reminded him of his intense hunger. He couldn't wait to sink his teeth into his mama's fried chicken. He thought that Emma would never taste such good food. Suddenly all thoughts of Nate vanished.

"Why couldn't I have a hat like the ones those ladies wore?" Emma asked, interrupting his thoughts.

Anton looked at her patiently. "Emma, lemme explain somethin' to you about hats. There hats for white people and hats for black people. And they don't look the same. Now I can't explain to you how to tell 'em apart. But you just know when you look at 'em which ones belong on a white woman's head and which ones belong on a black woman's head. And all those hats you saw today belong on a black woman's head. So no, you can't have one. You'd look ridiculous."

Emma had no response. In fact, she remained quiet until they got to his apartment door.

"How do you know so much about hats?" she asked as they made their way into his house.

"I just do," he replied, but she was not listening.

CHAPTER 20
SUNDAY, MAY 9

She was instantly transported somewhere else. She did not know the place. She had never before been there. It was a place with the most delectable smells, so tempting that they made her stomach grumble and ache the moment she walked over the threshold of the front door. She saw the food laid out on the table. There was the fried chicken that Anton had assaulted earlier, a large casserole dish of homemade macaroni and cheese, a bowl of fried somethings she could not identify, another bowl of leafy greens she was sure she had never tasted, and corn bread. She couldn't believe her instant starvation and was longing to sit down and pile her plate.

"Okay you two," Ms. Robinson said. "Come eat." She was glistening with sweat, and for good reason Emma thought. She had created a feast in thirty minutes!

Anton held out the chair for Emma, and she thanked him as she sat down. Ms. Robinson smiled at her son's manners. She asked him to say grace when they were all seated with glasses of iced tea and soda. Emma chose the iced tea. She remembered its delicious sweetness from awhile back.

After Anton said the blessing, he addressed Emma:

"Okay, so what on this table have you never tasted?"

Emma looked around. "Well, what's that?" she asked pointing to the bowl with the leafy greens.

"Those are collard greens," Ms. Robinson replied. "You never had collard greens, honey?"

Emma shook her head.

"I know right?" Anton said. "Shouldn't that be child neglect or somethin'?"

Ms. Robinson ignored him as she scooped a small portion onto Emma's plate.

"Well go on and try it," Anton said.

"Anton, where's yo' manners? You ain't gonna sit here and watch her eat. Lord child, you are so rude sometimes," Ms. Robinson said.

"I just wanna see how she react," Anton said. "'Cause it so good."

"Emma, would you like some fried okra?" Ms. Robinson said ignoring her son.

"Sure. I've never had that either," Emma replied.

"Now *that* might be considered child neglect," Ms. Robinson said winking at Emma, and she laughed.

When their plates were filled, Emma dug in. She tasted the collard greens first and decided that there was no better side dish in the world. She wished Ms. Robinson had given her more. The fried chicken was so tender and juicy she wished she could have several pieces though the one on her plate was enormous. But when she moved on to the fried okra, her love affair with Ms. Robinson's food really began. She could not describe it. She felt like she could eat an entire tub of it, like popcorn. When she finished the first helping, she asked for a second. And even though she knew it would be unmannerly to ask for a third, she did anyway. She couldn't help it. The switch in her brain that signaled she was full had malfunctioned. She was certain she could sit at the table all day and eat. And eat.

It was not just the taste of the food. There was something in it that she couldn't get enough of. She thought it had something to do with Ms. Robinson. She tried hard to understand it. It was as if all of the food was laced with love, hard work, and sacrifice. And she could taste each thing specifically. She had never tasted love in food before. Not her mother's food. Not the food she prepared for herself. And she wondered how to put it in. What was Ms. Robinson's secret? Was it the way her hands moved as she prepared the dishes? Did she speak it into the food and that's why she asked them to go to the store? To give her privacy, so that she could work her magic? How did she do it, making Emma feel she could eat forever and never be satisfied?

They chatted pleasantly as Emma ate. She enjoyed listening to the banter between Anton and his mother. It was so easy and natural, and she wished she could talk to her mother like that. Theirs was a special kind of relationship, she thought, one that develops into intense loyalty and absolute love in spite of an absent father. Emma realized she never asked Anton about his father, and he never offered her any information about him. Perhaps he knew nothing about his father, and that made her sad.

"Girl, you done ate yo' weight in fried okra," Anton said, yanking her out of her contemplation.

"I'm so embarrassed," she said quietly. And then turning to Ms. Robinson she added, "I have manners. I really do. I cannot believe I just ate like that."

Ms. Robinson laughed. "Emma, you so thin you can eat as much of this food as you want. How 'bout I send you home with the rest of this fried okra?"

"Now hold up a minute," Anton said.

"Oh hush, Anton," Ms. Robinson said.

Emma felt selfish. She nodded watching Anton scowl at her playfully.

"Okay then. Now we gonna clean all this up and then I got to get myself ready for work," Ms. Robinson said.

Emma was glad she was expected to help clear the table and wash the dishes. It made her feel like she was part of their family and not just a Sunday guest. She enjoyed their company and liked watching the way Anton teased his mother and how she playfully swatted him on the back of his head. Her heart leapt into her throat when she saw him pull his mother close and kiss the top of her head. So much love, she thought, and she wanted to stay at their tiny apartment in a rough neighborhood forever.

Anton kissed her cheek unexpectedly, and she jumped.

"Anton," she chastised quietly, feeling embarrassed.

"What? My mama know we're datin'," he said and leaned down to kiss her again.

She drew back.

"Anton, stop makin' her feel uncomfortable. You doin' it on purpose," his mother scolded. She had just finished wiping down the kitchen table.

"I ain't tryin' to make her feel uncomfortable," Anton said grinning.

Ms. Robinson looked like she wanted to say something, like it had been on the tip of her tongue the entire time they cleaned the dishes. She had just scolded Anton for making Emma feel uncomfortable, and now she realized she had to do the same.

"Come on over here to the living room, you two," she said finally. Her heartbeat quickened, but she was his mother, she decided. It had to be discussed.

Anton and Emma sat together on the couch, and Ms. Robinson took a seat opposite them. Emma thought how not so very long ago it was Anton who sat across from her. Then she had barely known him, and she remembered that she looked him over that day deciding if he was as cute as he thought. She smiled to herself remembering that time, when love had not yet been spoken but was hovering above them, ready to descend when they were finished playing their game of flirtation.

Ms. Robinson cleared her throat. "You know I gotta go to work," she began.

"Mama, you ain't gonna make me do a bunch of chores for you today, are you? I had plans with Emma," Anton whined.

"We have plans?" Emma asked suddenly.

"Girl, be quiet," Anton replied.

"I'm not gonna make you do chores. Just hush and listen, okay?" his mother said.

Anton looked relieved, but Emma started feeling mildly uneasy.

"I don't even know how to say this, so I'm just gonna say it," Ms. Robinson said.

"Mama, what is it?" Anton asked impatiently.

Now Emma wanted to tell him to be quiet. She knew, and she didn't want to hear it out loud.

"It's my business and it's not my business," Ms. Robinson said. She paused for a brief moment. "I need to know if you're having sex and if you're bein' safe."

"Oh my God, Mama!" Anton yelled, covering his face with his large hands.

"I know it's embarrassing to talk about, but we have to," she replied.

"No we don't! No we don't!" Anton said.

"Yes we do," Ms. Robinson insisted. "I'm gone a lot workin' and doin' school things. And it bothers me I'm gone so much. It's always bothered me. But now that you two are together, I gotta whole other set of things to be worried about."

Emma wanted to crawl under the couch and die.

"Mama, everything fine. You don't gotta be worried about a thing, okay?" Anton said hurriedly. "You can go on now to work."

"Anton, stop," his mother said. "And be serious."

"Yes, we're having sex." It was Emma who spoke up. She was mortified, but she wanted to get it over with.

Ms. Robinson looked at her and then Anton. Her face fell a little, and she was visibly worried.

"And we're being very safe," Emma continued noting Ms. Robinson's unease. "We're using protection. I'm on birth control."

Ms. Robinson nodded. She looked slightly more relieved.

"Can I go die now?" Anton asked.

Ms. Robinson ignored him. "Emma, baby, how old are you?"

"Seventeen. I'll be eighteen in July."

Ms. Robinson sat silent for a moment. Anton shifted uncomfortably in his seat.

"I just really need you two to be safe. Anton here is legally an adult, and you're not," she said.

Emma had never thought about it. She had been treated like an adult all her life. She was the more mature one out of the two of them. But facts were facts. She was still considered a child in the eyes of the law. He was not.

"Emma? Do your parents know you datin' my son?" Ms. Robinson said.

"Yes," Emma replied, and Anton looked at her. This was news to him.

"And they're okay with it?" she asked.

"I'm not sure yet," Emma confessed.

"What'd you mean?" Anton asked.

Emma bit her lip. "Well, I kind of told them as I was leaving this morning."

"What?! You dropped the bomb on them then went runnin' out yo' house?" Anton asked nonplussed.

"Sort of," Emma replied. Her face felt hot with shame.

"Dear Lord," Ms. Robinson said softly.

"I'm going to sit down and talk to them tonight," Emma said.

"'Course you are. You don't gotta choice. You gotta go home," Anton said, and then he looked at his mother. "Unless she can stay here tonight."

Ms. Robinson drew in a deep breath. "Do you wanna get beaten? 'Cause you this close," she said holding up her thumb and forefinger slightly apart.

"It'll be fine. My parents will be fine," Emma said, though she did not believe it.

Ms. Robinson looked at the clock hanging above them.

"I've got to go," she said. "And I don't want to. I don't want to leave you two here alone. I'm still havin' a hard time wrappin' my head around this." She rubbed her forehead and sighed deeply.

"Mama, I'm eighteen," Anton said softly.

"I know, baby," she replied.

"You know I love this girl, Mama," Anton continued. "I ain't messin' around. You know I'm serious."

Ms. Robinson smiled wearily remembering when she was eighteen and the certainty of her convictions could not be shaken. She remembered when she turned twenty and those convictions foundered, vanishing along with the man who vowed to love her for a lifetime. He left her alone holding a tiny baby in her arms.

She stood up suddenly and addressed the humiliated couple on the couch. "Go do something today. Go see a movie or something. I don't want you hanging around in this house. You understand?"

"Okay Mama. We'll go somewhere," Anton said.

He watched his mother walk reluctantly to her room to change into her scrubs. He and Emma sat in silence until she returned reminding them to "go do something" before leaving.

When his mother had closed the front door behind

her, Anton spoke.

"I can't even believe she just did that. I am so embarrassed. I cannot believe my mama just sat there and axed if we was havin' sex. Can you believe that?" he asked, turning to Emma.

She was bent over holding her stomach.

"I don't feel so good," she said.

"I know, right? My mama thinkin' she can just ax us about our personal business."

"No, I really don't feel good," Emma said, and jumped up from the couch.

She ran to the bathroom, slammed the door behind her, and bent over the toilet. She vomited violently, her body shaking and the tears pouring involuntarily. It kept coming, and she had to kneel down for the weakness she felt in her knees. She thought regrettably that she was vomiting all of the love she had just eaten, as though her body were rejecting his mother, his home and family.

There was a break in her sickness, and she wiped at her mouth with some toilet paper. She heard Anton knocking on the door and forbade him to enter. She felt a fresh wave coming, and no sooner had she gotten the words out to him then her head was back in the toilet, her stomach contracting and ridding itself of everything she had put into it. All of the love, she thought. All of the warmth of family.

She wiped at her mouth again, flushed the toilet, and sat back against the wall. She took deep ragged breaths and let the tears slide down her cheeks. She never understood why vomiting induced tears. She heard a tentative knock once more, and reluctantly invited him in.

Anton entered the bathroom and left the door open. He didn't mention the smell, but she knew he was thinking it. And she wanted to be embarrassed, but she was too weak to care.

"You okay?" he asked softly.

"I threw up," she said.

Anton tried not to laugh. "I know you threw up, baby."

"I threw up my entire lunch," she said, the tears still spilling over.

Anton went over to her and sat down beside her. He wiped at her tears.

"Baby, that's gonna happen when you eat fifty pounds of food," he said tenderly.

She laughed softly, tasting the vomit in her mouth.

"You didn't throw up," she pointed out. "You ate as much as me."

Anton couldn't help but laugh. "Girl, do we look like we anywhere near the same size? Plus, I'm a black man. I'm used to eatin' that food. You prolly never had so much fried food in yo' life."

Emma nodded. "It was so good."

"I know," he said, pulling her close to him. She resisted.

"My breath is disgusting," she said.

"Well, go brush yo' teeth," Anton suggested.

"How? I don't have a toothbrush here."

"Use mine," he offered.

"Hmm, I don't know. That sounds pretty gross," she said.

"It is. But what else we gonna do? Have you walkin' around all day with dragon breath? I can get another toothbrush," he said.

"No, I meant gross for me."

Anton burst out laughing. "Girl, you kiss me all the time. You put yo' tongue down my throat, and you gonna be grossed out by my toothbrush? Baby, you crazy," he said hugging her close.

She let him hold her feeling the love seep back into her. Her heart felt better and the panic subsided. It was there—the love. It was there in many different forms. So maybe she couldn't eat so much of it. But she could let him hold her, let it flow into her from his strong dark arms.

He helped her up and handed her his toothbrush and toothpaste. She brushed her teeth while he sat on the toilet and watched. He gave her a paper cup filled with mouth rinse, and she was tempted to swallow it. He laughed listening to her gargle. She thought she should be embarrassed doing that in front of him, but she was too busy relishing the feel of a clean mouth.

"I feel like a new woman," she said after spitting into the sink and rinsing it out.

She looked at Anton who appeared to be thinking about something.

"What?" she asked nervously. "You didn't have to watch me do that. I know it's not attractive, brushing your teeth in front of someone."

"No, I ain't thinkin' about that," he said. "I'm thinkin' that this is the only time I haven't felt like havin' sex with you."

Emma felt slightly irritated.

"Look, I know I threw up and you had to smell it when you walked in here and then you sat there watching me brush my teeth and—"

"Girl, no. It ain't about all that. It's my mama. She just made me feel all weird about it," he said quietly.

"Oh," Emma said with a sigh. "I know."

She stood in front of him waiting for the invitation. He moved his arms to let her sit on his lap. She settled in and felt his arms go around her waist.

"It's because I'm seventeen," she said.

Anton sighed. "You more mature than I am," he said frustrated.

"I know."

He made a face at her, and she giggled.

"It's also because she's your mother," Emma pointed

out.

"I'm eighteen! What she expect?"

"It doesn't matter. She's still your mother. She's looking out for you the way a mother is supposed to."

Anton shrugged. "I really wanted to have sex with you today."

Emma laughed at his disappointed tone.

"Look, I don't want to have sex either," she said. "I just threw up all my insides."

Anton squeezed her lightly and she winced.

"It's just weird now, you know? My mama know what we doin'. I mean, I think I always knew she knew. But now it's out in the open."

Emma made a noise and shrugged.

"You in for it tonight," he said after a time.

Emma's heart dropped. "I know."

"I can't believe you did that, Emma," he said chuckling. "What was you thinkin'?"

"They were just giving me a hard time about going to church with you. You know, because it's on this side of town. I just got pissy. It was the complete wrong way to go about it, I know. But they just made me so mad."

Anton grinned. "Well, that's 'cause you scrappy."

"Hmm."

"What if they make you stay away from me?" Anton asked after a moment. His tone was suddenly serious.

"That won't happen," she replied.

"But what if they—"

"That won't happen," she said again more firmly.

Anton nodded and said nothing.

"So what should we do today?" Emma asked.

He had no idea.

CHAPTER 21
MONDAY, MAY 10

Anton swaggered down the hallway holding Emma's hand. He nodded politely to students at their lockers and asked them how they were doing. Most stared at him blankly. A few told him where to shove it. But some actually smiled and answered him.

"Stop being so goofy," Emma said.

"I can't help it," he replied. "You know how happy I am? I can't even believe yo' parents okay with us bein' together. I feel like I been reborn or somethin'."

She smiled remembering her phone conversation with him the previous night. She had gone home that evening to face the wrath of her parents. She knew they would object, demand she stay away from him, argue that he was no good for her and would never be. She prepared herself for the fight, but the fight never came.

They asked her a few specific questions about him and then asked her if she was happy. Her parents asked her if she was happy, Emma thought in disbelief. She never thought that was a concern of theirs, but when they voiced it, she could do nothing but run into her mother's arms and hug her tightly. Then she ran to her father and did the same.

She told Anton over the phone and he nearly rendered her deaf by his reaction. Then he insisted she was lying, but she promised him she was not. It was all too real, but she felt like she was living in a fantasy. The world around her was getting bigger as she let the ones she loved in on her secret. She liked feeling utterly exposed. Now no one was in the dark, and the hope grew inside of her that she and Anton could be happy. Possibly forever.

"Now you officially my shorty," he said.

"Oh jeez," Emma replied.

He scrutinized her. "Hmm, you really short. Maybe I'm'll have to call you my shorty shorty."

"You're silly," she said laughing and nudging him.

"Say, what the world look like down there?" He squatted until he was eye level with her. Then he looked around him, down at his feet and up above.

Emma stood staring at him, hands on her hips.

"Man, it feel weird down here," he said. "Like I could walk right into a mouse hole no problem."

She smacked his arm. He shoved his face into hers, their eyes dead even.

"Gimme a kiss," he ordered, and she had to obey.

He stood up and stretched his back.

"What does the world look like up there?" Emma asked after a moment.

"Well, climb on and I'll show you." He squatted again and let her climb onto his back. He latched his arms under her knees and stood straight up.

"Wow. So this is what you get to see every day," Emma said looking around.

She noticed that she looked down at most people as they walked by. A few were eye level, but no one passed by her who was taller.

"Not too bad, huh? And I can tell you when it's gonna rain," he said

She laughed brightly. Anton walked her down the hallway and back before putting her down. The bell was going to ring, she reminded him, and she couldn't be late. He didn't care if he was. She kissed him on the cheek before heading for the stairwell. He wanted to go with her. Could he sit with her in class without the teacher knowing? He knew that wouldn't work.

"Go to class," he heard her call from afar. He sighed and obeyed.

She started the climb up the stairwell unaware of Nate who was headed down. The stairwell was so packed with students that she only felt his presence after he passed by her. When she approached the landing, she turned and looked down. He was looking up at her.

He stood there staring at her as if considering something. He didn't look menacing; he looked sad and defeated. She had never seen him look that way. She had only ever seen indifference or anger. She raised her hand to wave at him, thinking absurdly that perhaps he wouldn't look so sad if she acknowledged him. It was as though her wave jolted him back to reality. His face flushed with resentment, and he turned to leave.

―

Anton found Nate outside hanging with some friends after school. New friends, Anton thought bitterly. He approached Nate with resolve. They were going to cut the shit, he thought decidedly. He knew what Nate was up to. He knew that he was falling deep into bad drugs, hanging with the really dangerous crowd. Anton was scared for his friend, and he missed him. He couldn't stand not having Nate be a part of his life. They had too long a history for him to just let Nate walk away.

"Hey man," Anton said. "Gotta second?"

Nate looked at him confused. "What you want?" he

asked.

"Can I talk to you somewhere else?" Anton asked looking at Nate's friends. They were such punkass bitches, he thought.

"Whateva," Nate replied.

He took his time saying goodbye to his friends before walking with Anton towards the student parking lot.

"Why we goin' here?" Nate asked. "You get yo'self a car or somethin'?"

"Nah man. I ain't made that much money," Anton replied.

"Oh that's right. I forgot you got that job," Nate replied.

"Yeah. I'm tryin' to pick up as many shifts as they let me. I wanna car."

"What you need a car for? Yo' girl take you wherever you need," Nate said. His tone was sulky.

"She can't drive me around for the rest of my life," Anton pointed out.

Nate was quiet. He stood with Anton at the edge of the parking lot, hands shoved in his pockets trying to appear uncaring. Anton decided it was time to get to the point.

"What's goin' on with you lately, man?" he asked.

"What you mean?" Nate replied.

"I mean, who these jokers you hangin' with? We hate those guys, Nate."

"They cool," Nate said. He shrugged and kicked at a large rock on the pavement.

"Come on, Nate. Where you been? Kareem say you never hang out no more," Anton said.

"What the fuck you care?" Nate asked suddenly.

"I care 'cause you my friend," Anton said. "My best friend."

Nate shifted uneasily.

"And I'm worried about you," Anton added.

The look on Nate's face made Anton wish he hadn't added that last part.

"This some kinda intervention or somethin'? Yo' girl put you up to this, 'cause I know you wouldn't think of it?" Nate said.

"What are you talkin' about?" Anton asked.

"I don't need you comin' around tellin' me you worried about me, you condescendin' muthafucka."

Anton felt the anger rising.

"I ain't tryin' to be condescending, Nate. I just know you been doin' drugs you shouldn't."

Nate laughed derisively. "Man, she really cleaned up yo' ass fast! You used to smoke weed. What? You not do that no more?"

"Man, I ain't talkin' 'bout weed. I'm talkin' 'bout crack and shit like that. Why you doin' that, Nate?"

"It ain't yo' business what I do," Nate replied.

Anton felt frustrated, unable to find the words that would penetrate his friend's heart and soften him. Where was the kid who used to play with him on the scary metal slide and merry-go-round in their neighborhood? Where was the kid who used to smile?

"Nate, can't we just cut this shit out and be cool?" Anton asked.

"No."

"Why not?" Anton asked.

"Because you a traitor, man. And I don't hang with no traitors," Nate replied.

"Why can't you just let that go, man? Nobody else around here seem to have a problem with me and Emma except you," Anton said.

"That ain't true. I know lots of people who think it's bullshit. You just don't know 'cause you been in yo' white world lately."

"I'm still hangin' with all the guys we hung with,"

Anton argued.

"You talkin' about Kareem and Lamar?" Nate asked. "Shit, those muthafuckas be traitors, too. Hangin' with yo' girl's little white bitches. They nothin' but some sell-outs like you."

Anton felt exasperated. There was no way to break through the wall; Nate had sealed it up, fortified it with the impenetrable forces of hate. Anton could bang his fists against the wall with all of the might in his body and it would never move.

"So you tellin' me that after bein' friends for thirteen years, you gonna just drop me like that?" Anton asked.

Nate walked towards him, shoving his face into Anton's face and pointing a finger at his chest.

"No man, I didn't drop you. You walked away from me," he said heatedly. "And don't you fuckin' forget it."

He pushed past Anton toward the road. He had missed the bus and would have to walk home. Emma sat in her car watching from the other side of the parking lot. She sensed from the body language of both boys that their fight was not resolved, and her heart dropped. She saw Anton walk towards her and started the car.

He climbed in muttering to himself. She said nothing allowing him to work out his frustrated feelings. She did take his hand in hers while she drove, and he let her. She left it at that. If he wanted to talk about it, she would let him. But she wouldn't ask. She wouldn't push it.

She waited, hoping he would share with her and let her help him carry the burden of grief over the loss of his friend. But he remained quiet, cut off from her. She did not know what else she could do but take him home and love him and help him forget for awhile. She hoped that would be enough.

CHAPTER 22
THURSDAY, MAY 20

She felt him staring at her. She didn't see him, but she knew he was there. She felt nervous and wondered why Anton was taking so long to get to her locker. Where did he go? She could not remember. She tried to ignore the eyes she did not see. She tried to imagine that he wasn't there and that she was alone changing out her books. Where was Morgan? Aubrey? Where was Kareem? No one was around, and she felt the anxiety creep into her heart making it beat fast and irregular.

She closed her locker door and turned around. He was there just as she suspected, scowling as he looked her up and down. He let his eyes rove over her slowly, and he made sure that she could see him doing it. She shifted nervously and thought that maybe she should go to the bathroom. She could hide there, she thought, and then the anger rose. Why would she let him intimidate her that way? But she left for the bathroom anyhow.

He stayed close behind her, stalking her. She panicked and quickened her step. She rounded the hallway and was just there at the entrance to the women's restroom when he jumped in front of her blocking her way.

"Hey Emma," he said sneering.

She remained silent, her eyes darting all around.

"Lookin' for yo' boyfriend?" he asked.

"What do you want?" she replied shakily.

"I don't want nothin'," he said affecting puzzlement. "I was just comin' over to say hello."

She made a move to walk around him, but he blocked her way.

"You don't wanna be friendly with me?" he asked backing her against the wall.

She said nothing.

"That hurt my feelin's. You friendly with other niggas. Why you not wanna be friendly with me?"

He moved closer to her. Emma drew in her breath sharply as she felt his hand brush her hip. People were passing by in all directions. Did no one see what he was doing to her? She wanted to scream, but she was afraid of what he would do.

"You friendly with other niggas," he said sensuously, looking at her face. "Very friendly."

"Please go away," she whispered.

"You don't wanna be very friendly with me?"

He spoke so softly that his words were barely audible above the commotion in the hallway, but she heard them. She also felt his hand move from her hip to her backside, squeezing her, and she instinctively pushed him away. He laughed scornfully as she hurried into the bathroom.

"Fucking bitch," she heard him say as the door closed behind her.

—

Anton shoved another chip in his mouth and looked at her.

"Emma, what the hell is goin' on? I about ate yo' whole bag of chips and you just let me. You love yo' chips and you always givin' me hell about eatin' 'em. So what's goin' on?"

"I share with you," she replied distracted.

Anton looked at her unconvinced.

"I don't want to talk about it," she said quietly.

Aubrey and Sarah noticed it too, and they tried to draw it out of her delicately.

"Did something happen with your parents?" Aubrey asked.

"No."

"Did something happen in class today?" Sarah tried.

"No."

"Are you not feeling well?" Aubrey asked.

"Just drop it, okay?" Emma snapped. She got up from the table abruptly and went to the trash can to dispose of her uneaten lunch. Anton told the girls to stay, that he would go and talk to her.

"Baby, you gotta tell me what's wrong," Anton said when he reached her.

She looked up from the trash can, and he saw the tears swimming in her eyes.

"I just can't," she said.

"Yes you can," he replied. He put his arms around her, and she began crying in earnest.

"It's okay," he said, taking her hand and leading her to a more private area of the outside courtyard.

"He said things to me," Emma cried as they sat down on a low brick wall.

"Who said things to you?" Anton asked. He felt the bearlike protective nature take over. It pervaded his limbs instantly. He was ready for the attack; all he needed was a name.

"Nate," she said quietly.

Anton's heart sank. He felt his hands ball into fists.

"What did he say to you?" he asked, trying with difficulty to control his temper.

"I don't know. He said hello, but he wasn't being nice about it. He wanted to know why I wasn't friendly with him, that I was friendly with other black guys. Although he didn't say black guys. He said the "n" word. He was really nasty about the way he said it. And then he touched me."

Anton was already across the courtyard in search of Nate. Emma ran to him and grabbed his arm.

"Please don't, Anton. I'm begging," she pleaded, pulling on his arm.

"Emma, you lost yo' mind if you think I'm'll let that little bitch talk to you like that," Anton said, stopping his search to look at his girlfriend. "Where'd he touch you?"

"Nowhere," she said.

He bent low until his face was even with hers. He tried for patience.

"Emma, you just said he touched you. Now you gonna tell me he didn't?"

"Please Anton," Emma said.

"Where did he touch you?" Anton tried again, this time his temper getting the better of him.

"On my hip," she whispered.

"Anywhere else?" he asked. He thought it an absurd question. Nate touching his girlfriend's hip was enough to drive him insane. He would kill him. He knew he would.

"No," Emma replied.

Anton searched her face. He knew she was lying.

"Where else did he touch you, Emma?"

The tears were spilling over. She couldn't say it. She felt humiliated and afraid of what Anton would do.

"Where else, Emma?" he asked impatiently, and then the horrifying thought occurred to him. "Did he touch yo' ass?"

Emma nodded.

"Muthafuckin' bitch. I'm'll kill him," Anton said, and he proceeded with his ruthless search.

Emma followed behind him, pleading with him to stop, telling him that it would only make things worse. She told him she was fine, that it wasn't a big deal, that he should be the better man and let it go. Anton ignored her. The better man, he thought incredibly. The better man was going to beat the shit out of Nate.

He searched the entire school building until he spotted Nate at the end of a hallway on the upper level floor. Nate saw him and knew why he had come. He pushed past the people he was talking to and headed for the stairwell. Anton was gone in a flash, and Emma couldn't hope to keep up with him.

"Why you runnin', nigga?" Anton shouted at the top of the stairs. "You afraid of me?"

"I ain't afraid of yo' ass, muthafucka," Nate spat. He was at the bottom of the stairs looking up at Anton.

"Then get yo'self up here so we can have a little chat," Anton ordered.

"I got nothin' to say to you, you fuckin' sell-out," Nate replied.

"Well I got plenty to say to you. How the fuck you think you gonna treat my girl like that?" Anton asked. He felt as though he were spitting the words.

"So the bitch told you, huh?" Nate asked scathingly.

"Don't call her a bitch, you stupid muthafucka," Anton yelled.

"By the way, Anton, she gotta nice ass," Nate said. "Thanks for sharin'."

People were gathering in the stairwell, charged for a fight. Emma came in just as Anton was headed down the stairs. She watched from above as Nate stood his ground when Anton reached the landing.

"You wanna say that again?" Anton asked advancing on Nate.

Emma thought that he had grown another four feet. He looked frightening and menacing the way he towered over Nate, balled fists ready for the assault. His face portrayed pure hatred, and Emma was certain that he could kill Nate with his bare hands if he wanted.

"I said yo' little ho up there gotta nice ass. We should tag team sometime."

Anton's fist was swift and accurate. It crashed into Nate's jaw, sending him spiraling to the floor. He lay there for a moment, massaging his throbbing cheek, then jumped up from the floor and ran into Anton wrapping his arms around him in a bear hug and slamming him into the wall. He drew back his fist to hit Anton, but he was too slow. Anton punched him hard in the stomach making him stumble backwards then again to his face making him hit the concrete landing with a sickening smack. Nate tried once more to get up, but the pain in his stomach was too great. He lay breathing heavily, knowing he was badly beaten and humiliated for it.

"That's right, nigga," Anton taunted. "Don't you fuckin' talk to Emma ever again. Don't you fuckin' talk to me ever again. We through. I don't even know you."

He walked back up the steps avoiding the stares of the several students lining the walls of the stairwell. He took Emma's hand and led her out.

—

"You'll probably get suspended, you know," Emma said.

She was sitting at his desk that afternoon editing their paper. They were nearly through and had only a few pages left to write.

"No teachers were there," Anton pointed out. He was lying on his bed staring at the ceiling.

"There are cameras everywhere," Emma reminded him. She made a note in the margin of one of the pages as she spoke.

"So? Somebody in charge gotta see it in person," Anton argued.

"I'm not sure it works that way," Emma replied.

"What the hell, Emma? Do you want me to get suspended? I'm already in enough trouble as it is. Ain't no way my mama won't find out about this."

"How would your mother find out?" Emma asked.

"She just will. She got these magic ways of always knowing what's goin' on with me. She knew we was havin' sex long before that embarrassin' conversation. She knew when I took that kid's video game even though he never told a soul 'cause I told him I'd beat the shit outta him. I swore to her that he gave it to me. She knew I was lyin' right through my teeth. The woman knows."

Emma smirked. "You were such a bad kid."

"I know it. And I'm tryin' to be better. Look how good I am with you. You know I ain't even smoked up since we got together?"

"I didn't know you smoked weed to begin with," Emma said.

"Girl, you so naïve," Anton said. "You met my friends?"

Emma grunted.

"Anyway, I'm tryin' to be good but what choice did I have? That little muthafucka. I couldn't let him talk to you like that, do what he did to you. What kinda boyfriend would I be if I let little bitches like Nate talk to you like that?"

"I appreciate you wanting to protect me or fight for my honor or whatever, but I can handle my own," Emma said.

"Girl, please. You know you need me."

He didn't say it teasingly. He said it with all the seriousness of a black man who knows he's dating a white woman in the uncertain world of high school.

Emma sat quietly for a time. She pretended to edit

their paper when she was really running the words he just said over and over in her mind. Did she need him, she wondered? She wanted him; that she knew. But did she need him? And if she did, did that make her weak? Did that put her in a vulnerable position? What if one day he went away? Where would her need go? Would she transfer it to another boy, the next one to come along and tell her he loved her and would love her forever? An alarming feeling crept into her heart, and she tried hard to ignore it.

"I can't believe no one went to the administration. How did you make it the rest of the day without being called to the office?" she asked. "I mean, didn't somebody see Nate?"

"That little shit prolly left school. That's what I'd of done if I was humiliated like that," Anton replied.

"But still, no one went to the office?" Emma said.

"Jesus, Emma, can we talk about somethin' else?"

Emma bristled. Anton noticed and rolled his eyes.

"I'm just tired of talkin' about it. What's done is done. Monday mornin' come and I get in trouble, then I get in trouble. There ain't nothin' I can do about any of it right now, so I don't wanna worry about it," he said.

"I just don't want you to get suspended on account of me. I mean, finals start next week," she said. "And you should care about that."

"Baby, I do care. They not gonna say I can't graduate. I don't want you worryin' about me," Anton said holding his arms out for her.

She put down her pen and went to him. She let him snuggle her against his body, running his hands up and down her back.

"Now this make me feel better," he said contented.

Emma, however, did not feel better. She couldn't lie there with him silent when a million thoughts and questions were running through her mind. She sat up abruptly.

"He lives in this neighborhood, Anton," she said.

"Who live here?"

"Nate. Nate, Anton. You know who I'm talking about," she snapped.

"And?"

"I just think you went about it all the wrong way. You two were best friends. You should have tried to talk to him and—"

"Emma, you need to stop right there," Anton interrupted. "Did he not harass you at school? Did he not put his hands on you?"

"Well, yeah but—"

"Enough. Nobody gonna get a talkin' to about somethin' like that. They gonna get the shit beat out of 'em. I can't believe you sittin' here worryin' about my friendship with Nate. He killed that when he touched you."

"I just thought that—"

"Well, stop thinkin' then," Anton interrupted.

"Excuse me?" she asked.

"Emma, you was a victim and I stuck up for you," he said.

"Well, maybe I don't want to be a victim. Maybe I could have handled it myself. But I didn't get a chance to because you took care of it for me. You know, you can't do that all the time."

"I'm sorry. Did you say you was gonna handle it? Because I remember you cryin' yo' eyes out to me in the courtyard," Anton said. "And anyway, what's wrong with beatin' the shit outta some punk who's messin' with my girl?"

"What if you're not there one day? Huh? I have to be able to deal with things on my own," Emma said.

"You actin' like I'm goin' somewhere. I ain't goin' nowhere."

"I know that, Anton. I know. It just makes me feel

weak and helpless," Emma said quietly.

Anton thought for a moment.

"Emma, I don't mean to make you feel that way. But I'm yo' boyfriend and it's my job to protect you. And don't say it ain't 'cause it is. And I want to. And Nate? He just a mean guy. He losin' it, I really think he is. And I don't want you to feel like you gotta go up against him alone. He crazy. I don't know what he do. You understand I was just doin' what I thought was right?"

Emma nodded.

"I still think you scrappy," he said trying for lightness.

She smiled and bent to kiss his lips. He pulled her down on top of him and let her kiss him thoroughly.

"You so tiny," he said feeling the full weight of her body on his. She felt like a blanket to him, warm and light.

She smiled into his neck.

"I think I could put you in my pocket and carry you 'round all day," he said running his hands down her back and letting them rest on her bottom.

"I don't know how much I'd like that," she replied.

"Why? You could poke yo' head out and look around. And then if you see somethin' you don't like, you just tuck yo'self right back down in my pocket. I'll take care of you."

"Yeah, but what about when you have to go to the bathroom?" she asked.

Anton laughed. "I guess I didn't think about that."

He kissed her forehead and made her look up at him.

"We okay?" he asked.

"Yes," she said.

"Okay, 'cause I plan on keepin' you, so I wanna make sure everything's okay."

"Everything's okay," she said, and as she lay in his arms, she knew it was.

CHAPTER 23
SATURDAY, MAY 22

"I got somethin' for you," Anton said. He pulled out a small box from inside his pants pocket and gave it to her. He looked nervous and unsure.

"That better not be—"

"Relax, girl! I ain't even ready to get married yet. And anyway, how long we known each other? Five minutes?" he asked.

She smiled and took the box.

"I know it hasn't been long," she said. "But it feels like it, doesn't it?"

"Yeah," he said looking at his feet.

They were standing by the water's edge. They were about to take a walk when Anton remembered the gift he had for her. He thought it felt weird to be standing when she opened it, so he invited her to sit down with him.

They settled themselves on the soft ground side by side. Emma opened the box carefully and pulled out a thin silver bracelet. It had a single charm in the shape of a heart. She held it up to examine it, and Anton got worried.

"They said it was white gold, but I don't know. They prolly scammed me, but I thought it was pretty. I thought you'd like it." He searched her face for an answer.

"I love it," she said quietly. "It's beautiful. Thank you."

He breathed a sigh of relief then offered to put it on her. She let him fasten it to her wrist then studied it once more.

"I notice you ain't never wear bracelets. I hope it ain't 'cause you don't like 'em," he said, feeling the uncertainty come back.

"I love bracelets," she replied.

"So that can be the bracelet you was searchin' for in my room that one time," he said grinning.

"Huh?"

"Girl, you always forget that," he said. "When you came back to me. You pretended to look for yo' missin' bracelet."

"I remember," she said. Even now, after everything they shared, the thought of that evening still made her blush.

"Well, here it is," he said, fingering it carefully.

"I love it," she said again.

Anton felt giddy. He had never bought a gift for a girl before, and he was unsure what to get Emma. But he knew he wanted to get her something. He decided to spend his first paycheck on her, but he found the bracelet at a local pawn shop long before pay day and wanted to get it right away. He was afraid that someone would snatch it up. His mother offered him the money, and he promised to pay her back. He knew it was expensive, and he didn't care. He would give her everything he had, give her whatever she wanted because he loved her.

She continued to stare at it, how it lit up her wrist in the afternoon sun, and she decided something.

"I won't take it off," she said.

"Girl, you gotta take it off to shower and stuff," Anton pointed out.

"I won't take it off. Ever," she said fiercely.

He did not reply. He took her hand and led her back to the car. Suddenly he did not feel like going for a walk. He took her to his house instead.

"How you do this to me?" he asked, leading her down the small hallway to his bedroom and shutting the door behind him. "How you make me want you so much?"

She shrugged and he laughed. He walked towards her, and she let him wrap her up, kiss her long and slow until her lips tingled and ached. She sensed he wanted more, but she had something else in mind.

"Can we talk?" she asked.

"We can always talk," he responded looking down at her. "What you wanna talk about?"

"Sometimes I get scared," she admitted quietly, gently detaching herself from his embrace and sitting down on the bed. Anton followed suit. "What do we do when we graduate?"

"What you mean?" he asked. "The same thing we doin' now." He knew exactly what she meant. She was going away and it would be harder for them. Still, he was determined to keep her. He assumed her feelings were the same.

"I never expected to be with you," she said. She fingered her new bracelet. "I never expected to fall in love with you. Is it real? It hasn't been long. But it feels real to me. That has to be right, don't you think?"

"'Course it's right," Anton replied. "And it's real, Emma. Why you scared it's not? You love me, right?"

She nodded.

"And I love you," he said. "That's real."

She smiled.

"I never expected you'd fall in love with me, though," Anton admitted. "I knew I loved you from the moment I saw you last year."

"What?" Emma said. "Last year?"

"Girl, you so clueless," Anton answered lying back on his duvet cover. She did the same.

"You noticed me last year?"

"'Course I did," Anton replied looking up at the bedroom ceiling. "We had history together. Don't you remember?"

"I don't remember," Emma admitted. "I don't remember anything really until the day I met you in English class."

"Well, you was just as cute then as you are now. I thought I'd never get a chance to talk to you, so I tried to put you outta my mind," Anton replied. "But I knew I loved you anyway. I figured I'd just have to be with another girl but always love you. And that ain't fair to nobody."

"But you didn't even know me," Emma said.

"Yes I did," Anton replied.

"How?"

"Girl, you know I can't explain it. I just knew you, and I knew if I ever had the opportunity to be with you that I wasn't gonna mess that up."

"Do you think we had sex too early?" Emma asked abruptly. She saw him turn to face her in her peripheral vision and kept her eyes glued to the ceiling.

"No."

"Are you saying that because you're an eighteen-year-old boy?" she asked.

"Yes."

Emma laughed. "Seriously, Anton," she insisted, and looked at him.

"Emma, you are mine forever. Do you understand that? So it don't matter that I made love to you now or waited three months or ten years. You my girl and you always gonna be my girl," Anton said. He felt instantly possessive and pulled her on top of him. She didn't resist.

"I can't imagine ever being without you," she said. "I

don't care if that sounds melodramatic. I don't care that it's been a few weeks. I love you, Anton."

"I know that," he said. "I love you, too."

"Call me 'baby,'" she demanded.

"Baby, I love you," he said.

She bent down until her face was even with his and smiled. And then she kissed him and let him love her thoroughly all afternoon until she felt drunk and dizzy.

—

Anton knew his mother would yell at him if he didn't finish the two loads of laundry she told him to do before going to work. He would have rather stayed in bed with Emma, but then he didn't like the prospect of his mother screaming at him all night. And to be honest, he was exhausted and even sore, he noticed quite suddenly. He did not realize he could make love to her so much. And he wanted to force his body to keep going, but he could not. He was completely and deliciously spent, and he imagined she was too.

He watched her leave thinking he would be very tired at work that evening. And weak, too. How was he going to be able to load heavy boxes all night? All he wanted to do was crawl into bed and sleep for a few days, build up his strength once more so that he could love her all over again. The thought was so enticing. Perhaps he could grab a short nap, he thought, but just as he walked back to his bedroom, he spotted the laundry basket. He cursed softly and picked it up.

He made his way downstairs and across the complex to the community laundry room. He opened the door and was relieved to see no one inside. He wouldn't have to wait for a machine. He loaded two washers and was about to go back upstairs when he heard the door open. He turned around to see who it was.

Nate stood before him looking confused, slightly dazed. Anton tensed immediately, unsure what to say. He noticed the long bruise lining Nate's jaw and cringed at the memory of the fight between them. Nate approached him, and Anton could smell alcohol and the strong, acrid stench of marijuana.

It happened so fast that he had no time to react. Nate's arm shot up straight and stiff in front of Anton, his fingers wrapped tightly around a shiny metal object. He pointed it directly at Anton, moving forward with determination until the tip of the gun found Anton's eye. He pressed on the gun shoving it hard against Anton's face, and instinctively Anton threw up his hands in surrender.

"Yeah, that's right nigga. Throw them hands up," Nate taunted. He pushed on the gun forcing Anton's head back against the wall.

"What the fuck you doin' Nate?" Anton asked. The fear was palpable in his voice, on his face, throughout his body. "Where you get a gun, man?"

"Don't fuckin' talk to me!" Nate screamed pumping the gun for emphasis. "Muthafuckin' white pussy-lovin' piece of shit!"

Anton did not reply. Instead he prayed silently for a way out, but no opportunity presented itself, and he knew that he had to consider the likelihood of dying today. The absurdity of it, he thought, that he could go from making love all afternoon and feeling the world was a glorious place to dying in a grimy laundry room.

"We was like brothas, man!" Nate cried. Only then did Anton notice the streaks on his friend's face left by tears. "Then you fuckin' turn on me! You fuckin' do that to me in front of everyone!"

He pressed the gun even harder against Anton's eye, and Anton felt the dull ache of the muscles surrounding his eye socket.

"Man, what could I do? You said those things, Nate," Anton said trying to calm him down. "I'm sorry, man."

"Over some white pussy?!" Nate screamed. "You gonna turn yo' back on yo' brotha for some white pussy?!"

Anton didn't know what to say. But he knew he needed to keep talking, talking Nate down, talking the gun away.

He was shocked when Nate lowered the gun suddenly. He didn't move, however. He just watched as Nate seemed to battle the thoughts inside his head. It was then that Anton realized he was high on something in addition to the weed. Anton feared the hard drugs permeating Nate's body, wondering how he could possibly anticipate his friend's next move, knowing Nate was erratic and empowered by the gun. I'm going to die, he thought, breaking out in a cold sweat.

Nate's anger appeared to dissipate as he studied the gun in his hand. "Man, you remember Mrs. Wallace?" he asked suddenly.

"Yeah," Anton replied. His body was tense with uncertainty.

"You remember when we took her newspaper off her front stoop 'cause we wanted to check the movie times?" Nate continued.

"Yeah, man," Anton answered.

Nate suddenly laughed. "You remember her comin' over to my house and we was all alone and she come stormin' in cussin' and screamin'?"

"She beat the shit outta us," Anton said, shaking his head and smiling uneasily.

"Man, I ain't never cried so hard in my life!" Nate said. His laughter was pure. "We was only what? Eight? Nine years old? God, that bitch was crazy!"

Anton forced a laugh, but all the while he was

thinking of a way to get the gun from Nate's hand.

"Shit, we had us some crazy times," Nate said. The tears flowed freely then. He wiped at his face clumsily.

"Well, it ain't like they over," Anton pointed out.

"We was tight," Nate said, oblivious to his friend's words. He stumbled slightly. "You know I ain't even graduatin'?" he said. He looked at Anton with bloodshot eyes.

"What you talkin' about?" Anton said.

"You heard me. I ain't graduatin'. I'm'll be just like my moms, man. Workin' three piece of shit jobs so I can afford to live in this piece of shit dump." The tears were pouring forth, and he wiped at them carelessly.

Anton thought that perhaps this was his chance. He made a move towards Nate, but stopped short.

"You fucked it up, man," Nate said, raising the gun to Anton's chest.

"Tell me how to fix it," Anton said, his heart pounding in his ears. "I'll fix it."

"There ain't no fixin' that, man," Nate replied. "I seen yo' heart, man. I seen yo' true feelin's." He turned the gun to the side as though he were testing something. Testing which way to hold it for better control. Testing which way to best kill his friend.

"Jesus Christ, Nate," Anton said. The panic pervaded his voice.

"That bitch fucked everything up. We was fine. We was doin' our thing. She come in and I go out." Nate looked straight at Anton's face.

The vice on Anton's heart tightened. He wanted to reach out to his friend, to hug him and promise him that everything would be alright.

"It ain't like that," Anton pleaded.

"She come in, and I go out," Nate repeated. He lowered the gun again as though it was too heavy for him to hold up. He stumbled.

"You my best friend, Nate," Anton said softly.

"Am I?"

"Come on, man. You know you is. How you gonna not know that?"

"You said you didn't know me. That's what you said," Nate cried.

"I didn't mean it, man. I was angry. You know you my friend, Nate," Anton said.

Nate stood there staring at his friend. The tears continued to flow. It was agony watching him cry, Anton thought.

"I got nothin', man," Nate said.

"That ain't true, dog. You got lots of things," Anton said.

"I got no plans, no future. I lost everything, man. You walked away from me. Kareem, all them, they walked away from me," Nate cried. His cry came from the deepest parts. It sang a melody of utter hopelessness.

"Nobody walk away from you, Nate. We always yo' friends."

Nate looked at Anton as if he never knew him. "She come in. I go out," he said quietly.

There was a finality to the words that Anton understood. He closed his eyes and prayed for forgiveness. He readied himself for the bullet. There was a delay, and he opened his eyes to see Nate holding the weapon to his own head. Anton cried out and reached for the gun, but he was too late as the blast sounded in the empty room.

Anton watched in horror as his friend hit the floor with a loud thud, blood oozing hard and fast from the sides of his head. He screamed—a guttural cry from deep within—falling to his knees beside his friend.

"What the fuck, man!" he cried out, cradling Nate's head in his lap. "Jesus!"

The blood was everywhere, splattered on the walls

and washing machines, rushing steadily down Anton's arms and legs, pooling fast around him. He tried to stop it, pressing his hands firmly against the sides of Nate's head, ignoring the foreign and frightening feel of the asymmetrical holes on Nate's temples.

"Somebody fuckin' help me!" he screamed.

Someone must have heard the shot and called the police. Anton heard the sirens, still low and distant, but coming.

"They comin'," Anton whispered to Nate. "Hang in there, man. They comin'."

They were empty words, he knew, but he said them anyway. He sat on the hard concrete clutching his best friend, tears pouring over and falling to the ground to mix with the blood, lying to himself that the paramedics would be able to do something. They would work a miracle. They would bring Nate Dog back. He wasn't dead and gone. He couldn't be, because Anton would not imagine a world without his friend. That world did not exist.

The police and ambulance arrived shortly. Anton was whisked away, pushed to the side as the paramedics worked on his friend. They didn't appear to be moving fast, he thought. Why weren't they moving faster, with more urgency? When the sheet was pulled over Nate's face, Anton screamed—a raw, animal sound of the deepest anguish. He tried in desperation to push past the officers. He had to get to his friend. But they held him back, made him look from a distance as Nate's body was loaded into the ambulance.

CHAPTER 24
MONDAY, MAY 24

She could not reach him. She went to his house on Sunday, but he was not there. She called several times, but he did not answer. She texted him but received no replies. She was frantic, running through the events in her mind of the last time they were together. Did she do something wrong? Say something wrong? All she could remember was an afternoon of heaven. He had given her a bracelet, fastened it to her wrist, and then made love to her. How could any of that be wrong?

She walked down the hallway willing him to be at his locker. He was not, but she noticed several students gathered at the end of the corridor. They were hovering around someone's locker, their heads bent low, talking in whispers, and she needed to know why. She headed towards them, passing several girls who looked like they'd been crying. Her heart quickened. Something was amiss, and she tried hard to ignore the dread she felt snaking through her belly.

"What is it?" she demanded of the first person she saw. He was another senior she remembered seeing in her Calculus class. She did not know his name.

"Crazy shit, that's what. This dude shot himself in

the head over the weekend," the boy replied.

"Who? Who shot himself?" she asked with urgency.

"I don't know. I think his name is Nate or something."

She did not remember when she got in her car or drove to his house. She did not remember parking and going up the concrete steps. She remembered knocking, though. She wrapped her knuckles hard on the door, banging then hitting it. He didn't answer. But she was determined. She tested the doorknob, and it turned. She opened the door tentatively and called his name. There was no answer, but she heard the music coming from his bedroom.

She pushed his bedroom door open. He was sitting on the edge of his bed. He had been crying, she could tell; the streaks were still fresh on his face. He looked dazed and tired, staring blankly ahead. She walked towards him slowly, hearing the familiar voice of his favorite rapper blaring from the CD player.

Emma turned off the music and said his name softly. At first he appeared oblivious. It was not until she knelt in front of him and gently wiped under one of his eyes that he realized her presence. He jerked away looking at her as if she were a stranger.

"What you doin' here?" he asked.

How could she begin to tell him that she was sorry? She couldn't imagine losing a close friend so heinously, and the words that so often came easy to her were lost.

"Go back to school," he ordered and reached over to press PLAY on the stereo.

She moved to the bed and sat next to him. She thought that maybe she should be quiet for a time and let him listen to his song. She folded her hands on her lap and waited patiently, listening to words of a song she did not understand. She wished Anton did not understand them either. But he did, and she watched his great golden eyes well up with fresh tears that spilled over to the words of loss and despair.

Emma could bear it no more. She reached over and turned off the music. "Anton," she began. He looked at her waiting for her to continue. She closed her hands over his, looking up at him. "Tell me what I can do."

"I told you to go back to school," he said.

She didn't move. The heart charm on her bracelet brushed his wrist, and he yanked his hands away.

"There ain't nothin' you can do, okay?" he said harshly. "My friend is dead. Do you understand that? He ain't comin' back. You know how I know that? 'Cause I watched him blow his fuckin' brains out!"

Emma felt the tears running down her face. She could not comprehend what he said. He witnessed it. He witnessed the suicide.

"Why you cryin'?" he asked. "You didn't even like him."

"I'm crying because you're hurting and I don't know what to do. I want to be a good girlfriend to you, but I don't know how," she said sobbing.

He flinched at the word "girlfriend," and she saw.

"Emma, get outta my room. Go back to school. You don't need to be here," he said firmly.

"Please, Anton," she said.

He stood up suddenly and grabbed her upper arm. He dragged her from the bedroom to the front door where he released her. She would not give up. She wrapped her arms around his waist, holding him close, willing his anger to subside. But her forced embrace only fueled it, and he peeled her arms from around his body and held her at arm's length as though she were poisonous.

He looked her in the eyes, his voice low and controlled. "Get the fuck outta my house."

She ran out and slipped on the last stair, falling to the concrete pavement below. She cried out as she felt the instant burning on her knees. She looked down and saw the blood already oozing out of her, running down her legs in deep red ribbons. She had nothing to stop the blood and turned to his door. But he had already closed it, and she was not welcomed.

She carefully got into her car, grateful for the task of focusing on her knees so that she would not have to think about what he said to her. She tried to be careful, but she knew the blood was dripping onto her floor mats. She would have to clean them, she thought. How does one get blood out of carpet?

—

When she was freshly showered and bandaged, she sat down on her bed and cried. She cried for his hurtful words and the implications behind them. He blamed her. It was her fault that Nate was dead. She stole him away like a witch, cast a spell on him that made him abandon the life he knew with friends who cared about him. He left one friend utterly alone, and the result was a bullet to the head.

The tears poured over at the thought of her impending loneliness. He did not want her anymore. He hated her for the trouble she brought him, ravaging his world and making him forget who he was. It was her fault, and she could not undo it. She could not bring Nate back from the dead, or else she would. She would travel to the world beyond and search for him even if it took her years. She would find him and bring him back. And she would love him as the brother she never had.

She climbed into bed and pulled her knees to her chest. She rocked herself back and forth feeling the rising panic. She did not have the strength to fight it. She could only mutter useless words over and over to herself. "It'll be alright. It'll be alright. It'll be alright." But she knew that it would not. Nothing would be right again, and she thought of the three children playing Hide and Seek, wishing she could be with them now so that she could hide away forever and never be found.

Thursday, May 27

The week was a lonely one. He never came to school, and while her heart ached for him, she was glad for his absence. She would not know what to do if he were there. Her friends tried to comfort her. They hugged her and told her over and over that everything would be okay, that she would get over him and be happy again. She felt the bitterness creep in and curl around her heart. She hated the words they said to her. That's what everyone says when someone's heart gets broken, she thought. You'll move on. You'll get over it. But they did not feel her pain, could not hope to comprehend it. She could not even comprehend it.

She tried several times during the week to reach him. She called him and left him messages until his message box became full and she could no longer talk to him. He was like a ghost to her now, and she panicked at the thought that she may never see him again. Finals started today and would last through next week. Would he show up for those, she wondered? If not, then she would never see him again, at least not at school. She doubted that he would attend graduation.

She spotted Kareem during the middle of the day. She was hesitant at first to approach him; perhaps he shared Anton's feelings and was angry with her, but she was desperate for any news of her boyfriend. He was still her boyfriend, she thought resolutely. She walked swiftly towards Kareem before her courage failed her. She tapped on his shoulder, and he turned around.

His eyes were large and sad. He looked as tired as Anton had been the day she found him in his room.

"Hey Emma," he said softly.

"Kareem, I'm sorry," Emma said, tears running anew. She wondered how much she could cry before her body dried up and withered to nothing.

"I know," he said, the mist rising in his own eyes.

"I don't know what to do. Anton won't talk to me," Emma said.

"He a mess, Emma," Kareem replied, wiping carelessly at his chubby face.

"I feel like he hates me," she said quietly.

"He don't hate you. He don't know what he feel. He just know he hurtin'."

"But he won't even talk to me," Emma said.

"He won't talk to nobody. I had to force him to see me yesterday. His mama all concerned about him. She afraid he lost his mind. But who can blame him after what he saw."

Emma wiped her eyes.

"We was down at the store gettin' some snacks. We was all gonna play cards and get high. We didn't see nothin', but other people say he was holding Nate and there was blood everywhere. All over him. All over the floor." Kareem could not finish. He burst into tears, and Emma wrapped her arms around him, holding him to her because she didn't know what else to do.

"Nobody should see that, man. Nobody," he said after a time. She released him and he wiped at his face.

"Nate, he was so angry. I never understood that about him. Why he always so angry. I miss him, Emma, but maybe he at peace now, you know? I just hope he at peace."

Emma nodded but said nothing.

"I can't believe I'm here gonna take a test. My

teacher say she postpone it, but what's the point? I ain't gonna feel any better next week," he said.

Emma remembered the term paper in her bag. She forced herself to complete it this week without Anton. Nothing about it felt right because he was not with her to put the final pieces together, to make it theirs. She felt like it was her sorry attempt at writing for the both of them. They were her words at the end. She simply put his name on it.

"I gotta go," Kareem said, and Emma hugged him goodbye. She watched him lumber down the hallway, head down, until he disappeared around the corner.

She made her way to the bathroom before dropping off her term paper to Dr. Thompson. She walked slowly through the hallway, searching for Anton. Maybe he would show up at least for a moment so that she could tell him that she loved him. She forgot to tell him that when she last saw him.

She was unaware that she was being followed into the bathroom. She closed herself in the last stall and stood blowing her nose into some toilet tissue. She wiped at her eyes and took a deep breath. The bathroom was quiet, and she was glad for the temporary peace. She was tempted to hide in the stall for the rest of the afternoon, but she had a paper to turn in and a final to take.

She opened the door and walked out holding her term paper. She was greeted by three girls—friends of Nate's she recognized instantly. They were looking at her, heads cocked to the side, deciding what to do with her. The fear consumed her immediately, and she searched her mind for a way to escape.

"So you the white bitch thinkin' she can fuck a black guy," one of the girls said.

Emma said nothing. Her eyes darted wildly around. What could she do to get out of there, she thought? But the girls had her trapped against the far wall of the bathroom, and she only then noticed a fourth one standing guard by the door.

"You got some nerve, girl, thinkin' you can fuck one of ours," the girl continued. She appeared to be the leader of this very real, very scary gang.

Emma opened her mouth to say something. She always heard that talking helped. Maybe if she just said something, they would let her go. But the words stuck in her throat.

"You know you responsible for killin' him?" another one of the girls asked.

Emma shook her head.

"Oh you don't know? Well, you are. See, you get with a nigga and mess up his life and make him turn against his brotha. You make him humiliate his brotha in front of everyone. Yeah, I was there and saw the whole thing." It was the ring leader who spoke. "Then he go and kill hisself outta grief. And you responsible for that," she continued. "So the question is, what should happen to you?"

Emma felt the tears stinging her eyes, her face awash with them. Her body shook violently, the terror coursing throughout her making her feel like she would throw up or soil herself.

"I guess we gonna have to make you pay up," the ring leader continued, and she pulled a knife out of her purse.

"I'm begging," Emma whispered, feeling she would faint. "Please don't."

Her words went unheeded as the knife plunged into her stomach over and over again. It was an electric pain that rendered her speechless. She could do nothing but double over and try hard to protect herself, but the knife found its way between her arms, slicing her skin and battering her insides.

The girls ran out leaving her alone to watch the

blood seep into her shirtfront. She collapsed on the floor, blood smearing the term paper still clutched in her hand. She couldn't believe the amount of blood. She thought she could bath in it, swim in it, let it swallow her whole.

The electric pain subsided as she felt a new sensation. She didn't hurt anymore, and it made her giddy. She giggled as she clutched at the dirty floor. It was moving, she thought. The floor was moving, and her heartbeat quickened as she felt the lightheadedness that comes before a fainting spell. She thought that she might like to faint, and smiled dreamily as her eyelids closed.

CHAPTER 25
TUESDAY, JUNE 2

She woke from her dream. She felt a mask on her face and wanted to take it off. She willed her hands to move, but they remained frozen by her sides. She thought she would suffocate from the mask and felt desperate for someone to take it off. But then she realized it was pushing something into her body that she needed. She could almost hear it, a soothing song of life flowing into her, helping to make her strong again.

She thought she felt his hand in hers. His fingers were lightly stroking her palm. He was saying something to her. She thought she heard him crying, and she wanted to tell him that everything would be alright. That she was feeling better. She felt his lips on her forehead and his hand leave her hand. Don't go, she thought. Stay awhile. I'll take you to the movies. I'll take you to the park. We can sit and watch the ducks on the water and talk about our paper. You can say something funny and I'll laugh because I always laugh. We can do whatever you want, just please don't go.

Her head felt fuzzy and she slipped back into her dream.

Anton left her room unwillingly. His time was up—a short fifteen minutes—and he watched as her parents passed by him into the room. They acknowledged him but said nothing. He walked to the lobby and sunk deep into a chair. He would stay there and wait until he could see her again. He would sleep at the hospital every night until they released her.

He put his face in his hands and inhaled deeply. It was almost unbearable to see her for the first time. The respirator, the tubes everywhere, the thin hospital gown covering her grotesque wounds. He knew they were there, could imagine what they looked like, and he cried when he pictured what must have happened to her in that dirty, lonely bathroom. And he was not there to protect her. He had thrown her out of his house, his life, because he was consumed with his own grief. He never thought once how she must have felt.

Every day his mama urged him to go home. She worried constantly, he could tell, and he wished he could do something to ease her anxiety. She was there a lot, checking on Emma, giving him updates when he wasn't allowed to see her. He knew Emma wouldn't die because she was too young. She would fight it because he had to believe that she knew he still loved her. In spite of his anger and hurtful words, he loved her. And as soon as she opened her eyes he would tell her that. Tell her that he would never talk to her that way again, that he would cradle her against him forever whispering only the language of love into her ear, breathing the sweetness back into her. The pain would disappear as though it never existed, and they would find their way back to the time they first kissed.

He looked up when he heard someone clear his throat. It was Emma's father standing over him looking concerned. He sat down opposite Anton; his face looked haggard and as he began to talk, Anton heard the strain in his voice, like every word was a struggle.

"That's my baby girl in there," he said.

"I know," Anton replied.

"No, I don't think you do know," Mr. Chapman said. His tone was not accusatory. "See, I made her. And when I made that decision, I took on the responsibility of protecting her. Not until I thought she was old enough, but forever. Because she'll always be my baby girl, even when she's a hundred."

Anton was quiet, listening.

"I love her more than anything. I love her more than my own wife," Mr. Chapman said quietly.

Anton raised his eyebrows at that.

"And I get a sense that you love her too," he went on.

"I do," Anton said. His voice cracked, and he cleared it. "I do," he said more firmly.

"And what has your love done for her, son?" Mr. Chapman asked.

Anton had no reply.

"You see, my love heals and protects. That's a father's love. And no one in the world can match it. But your love? Your love has broken and scarred her. That's your love. Do you see the difference?"

Anton felt the tears sting his eyes. He wanted to say that her father was wrong, that his love could heal, too, but he couldn't.

"I can't tell you to stay away from my daughter," Mr. Chapman said. "You're going to do what you want based on what you feel is right. But Anton, you need to remember something. She will heal and come out of this place. She will resume her life as normal. But what has passed between the two of you is broken and can never be fixed. And if you try to hold onto her because of your own selfishness, you will destroy her."

Anton buried his face once more in his hands. He didn't want to believe it. They could get over this. They could both heal and move on. He knew he wanted that, and he knew she wanted that too.

Emma's father stood up slowly and placed his hand on Anton's shoulder. He stood there for a few moments then walked away.

—

It was late and Anton was allowed to see her for five minutes. The nurses were stubborn and wanted to keep him out completely, but his mother persuaded one of them to let him in. She was firm in her five-minute time limit, telling him he'd not see Emma again if he became difficult, and he nodded in understanding. She was disinclined to leave the room, and only did so when she was told to go and check on another patient. She closed the door quietly behind her.

He took Emma's hand immediately. He bent low to kiss it, thinking for a brief exhilarating moment that he felt her stir. But it was just his imagination. She lay motionless and very far away from him.

"Emma?" he said softly. "I don't know if you can hear me, but I'm'll say it anyway. I love you."

He waited, but she did not move.

"You gotta know that," he continued. "I can't believe the way I talked to you the other day. I was outta my mind, you've got to know that. I can't even imagine my life without you. And I know I'm only eighteen. I'm supposed to have the whole world opened to me, right? I don't want none of that. I just want you. You my world, Emma, and I just want you."

He wiped at his face and looked at her earnestly.

"Open your eyes, Emma," he demanded softly. She

stayed unmoving.

"Emma, do you hear me?" he asked. He was crying outright, the strain in his voice unbearable to his own ears. He did not recognize himself. "I love you," and he bent his head over her hand. "I love you. Do you hear me?"

I hear you, she thought. Don't you hear me saying that? Her mouth never moved, but she thought it did.

Thursday, July 16

They drove to the park in silence. It wasn't angry silence or scared silence. It was the silence that comes when two people have not seen each other for a long time. They were shy and tentative. Anton's heart hung low in his chest as though it were a battered star hanging on by a mere string. If the string broke, he knew the light would go out inside of him forever. Emma's heart was hopeful, like the brightness that follows a mighty storm. The clouds had cleared and now there was only the brilliance of the sun. She reached her hand over to his and gently took it.

He wanted to ask her if she liked the flowers he sent. He made sure they were waiting for her when she was released from the hospital. He had stopped going to see her after a week because it was too painful. Her parents became more and more uncomfortable with his presence, and he wanted to be respectful of them. Her condition was not improving either, and he could not bear to be so close to her while she was so clearly far away. In a dreamland, he thought, and wished he could go with her. When she woke up, he wanted to see her immediately. But there was already so much distance and so many other people who needed to see her. He didn't want to be in the way. And after all, what did he think he could possibly say to her?

Anton parked the car and told her to stay seated. He

walked around to her side and opened the door. He picked her up carefully, cradling her like a baby, and carried her to a park bench near a familiar spot they so often occupied in former days. He sat down, holding her on his lap, letting her head fall gently on his shoulder. He wasn't sure that he could speak right then. He didn't have the words, so he stroked her back instead and relished the feeling of her face nuzzling his neck.

"Do you want to see them?" she asked after a time.

He didn't know how to reply. Yes, he wanted to see her wounds. He didn't know why. He knew what they would do to him, how he would lose it completely when he saw the aftermath of his failure. He could not rid himself of the feeling that it was all of his fault that she got attacked. His mother told him time and again that he could not blame himself, that it wasn't his fault. And her words would soothe him and begin to change his mind. But then he would remember the words he said to Emma that day she came to his apartment and how he left her alone all week to believe that he hated her and didn't care what happened to her.

"I don't know," he said quietly.

"It's okay," she said. "They're not so bad."

His nod was almost imperceptible but she saw it and lifted her shirt to expose a heavily bandaged stomach. She peeled back one of the bandages, and Anton saw a small thin purplish wound stitched cleanly. He was tempted to run his finger over it, but thought better. He didn't want to get germs on it.

Emma placed the bandage back over the wound and pulled down her shirt.

"See? Not so bad," she said. "The doctor said they'll heal nicely. The scars won't be too noticeable."

Anton nodded but said nothing. He felt the lump in his throat and concentrated on pushing it down. Her beautiful stomach, he thought. The creamy whiteness forever scarred because of him.

"I've got battle scars," she said lightly. "Does that make me gangster?"

The tears that hovered on the edge of his eyes spilled over, and he cradled her head under his chin so that she would not see. He stroked her hair as he searched for his voice. It was failing him.

"Yeah," he croaked softly. "You gangsta."

"Good," she replied, pushing her body into him. He wanted to envelop her completely, shield her from everything on the outside. But he couldn't. It was impractical to hide her away forever. He knew he could not, and he suddenly remembered that she would be leaving soon for college.

It was over. He knew, but she did not. He could tell by the way she nuzzled him, how her body relaxed in his embrace, how she sighed when he kissed the top of her head. She was still hopeful, he thought, and that made her beautiful. Suddenly he could not bear to imagine a life without her.

He could try, he thought. He could try hard to make it work. In spite of all of the pain he felt, the hopelessness, he could not give her up. He knew he should, but he wasn't strong enough. He needed her and decided that he had to try. Perhaps they simply needed more time to heal.

"Tell me a story about when you were little," she said after awhile.

He thought he had exhausted them all. He was sure that she knew every detail about him by now, that even in the few short weeks of their relationship, he had given her everything, shown her everything about himself so that now he sat empty searching for a story she already knew.

"Well, let's see. Did I tell you 'bout the time I came home drunk? And mama whooped me so hard, I thought I was gonna die? Did I tell you that one?" he asked.

She laughed softly. "No," she replied, but he had.

"Okay then. So me and Kareem and Johnny D was goin' to Kareem's older brother's house one time. I think I was like twelve or somethin'. So anyways, we was gonna hang out and play video games, right? We wasn't lookin' for no trouble," he began, and she settled in for the story.

She listened while he stroked her hair and held her close.

EPILOGUE

"Baby, you know I hate bananas," Anton groaned as he examined the contents of his lunch bag.

"How many wives actually pack their husband's lunches?" Emma asked.

She was standing at the kitchen sink wearing a light cotton dress, her long hair pinned in a loose bun at the nape of her neck. She turned to face him, the question still on her face, and he smiled as he looked at her swollen belly.

"And anyway," she went on, "they're good for you."

"You right," he said walking towards her. He bent low and pressed his lips to her stomach.

"Your mama always right," he said into her belly. "Don't forget that."

He straightened up and kissed the top of her head.

A cry pierced the quiet moment, and Emma disappeared to the nursery. She came back holding a little girl who nuzzled her neck.

"Well, that was good," Emma said. "We made it a whole fifteen minutes."

"Baby girl, why you not sleep for yo' mama?" Anton asked the small child.

She had dark curly hair and light blue eyes. She

smiled at her daddy and reached for him. He took her and cradled her in his arms.

"You're going to be late, Anton," Emma warned.

"You say that every day, and every day I'm right on time," he said kissing his daughter on her cheeks and forehead and nose and chin. She giggled and grabbed at his lips.

Emma rolled her eyes and began emptying the dishwasher.

"Go to work," she ordered. "You're the only one with the paying job right now, remember?"

"You hear yo' mama talkin' to me like that?" he asked the little girl, and she squealed with delight.

He placed her on the kitchen floor and looked around for something to distract her. He pulled a wooden spoon out of the utensil holder beside the stove and gave it to her. He watched her briefly as she sat holding it poised over the floor before bringing it down on the tiles with a sudden smack. He smiled and walked over to his wife, taking the plate out of her hand and tossing it carelessly on the counter.

"Anton," Emma said exasperated.

"Mmm, say my name again," he cooed, pulling her into him.

She cocked her head in mild irritation, raising her eyebrows at him.

"Do you know you the prettiest thing on the planet? I wanna job where I can get paid to just sit around and watch you all day. How I get a job like that?" he asked her, placing a hand on her belly and rubbing it.

She laughed.

"You know I'm'll want another one after this," he said.

"You're insane!" she replied. "If you had it your way, I'd be pregnant for the rest of my life!"

"That's right," he agreed, moving his hand farther

down.

"Anton!" she squealed when his hand was in between her legs.

"Come on. Let's go practice," he said.

"You're impossible," she said, slapping his hand away. "Go to work."

"Fine, but I'm'll get me some of that when I get home," he said decidedly.

"I love you," she said, standing on her tiptoes to kiss his cheek. As usual, she couldn't reach and had to pull him down to her lips.

"I love you," he replied, kissing her forehead.

"I love you," she said as they walked together to the front door, and the familiar routine started.

"I love you," he said descending the front steps of their small blue house.

"I love you," she replied as he reached the driveway.

"I love you," he called from inside their car.

"I love you."

"I love you."

Emma woke with a start. She was shivering and sweating again, her side of the bed drenched with it. It was the third night. The same dream. She instinctively put her hands to her belly. It was flat. She lifted her shirt and fingered the lines of her scars. They were barely visible now, but she could still feel them, the healed skin thinner and papery. She turned to the man lying next to her. He was snoring soundly, reaching every now and then to scratch at his pale cheek. She looked at the clock. It was early, but not too early to get up. She knew she couldn't go back to sleep. She could not reenter the dream.

She took a shower and got dressed. She had an important meeting today and took special care to wear her most serious-looking business suit. She was going to make a lot of money, and the thought steadied her nerves.

Money. She made it her focus. And she was good at making it her focus. She was good at making it. She looked around her bathroom sink at the pricey creams, hair products and make-up, the expensive decorative marble. She looked at her image in the mirror and saw the silky expense of her designer suit. She blinked and her image changed. Now she was standing in front of the mirror wearing a tattered blue hoodie. She stared at herself for a moment thinking about the softness of the fleece lining. Then she remembered herself, blinking deliberately until her image returned to the present and she was again swathed in her fancy suit.

"Leave me alone," she said to her reflection, and she saw him in the distance, deep within the mirror, smiling at her.

She was ready to go hours before she needed to leave and sat at the kitchen counter staring at the clock. The time ticked slowly, and she could do nothing but wait. She played with her engagement ring, twisting the five-carat diamond out of sight, and then bringing it back around her finger. Mother would be so proud, she thought cynically. She checked the clock again. The hands hadn't moved. She looked back down at her ring and spun the diamond out of sight. That's better, she thought, and waited.

—

She walked right by him, consumed with her own thoughts. She was running the important points of her presentation through her head, making sure she had the language perfect. She heard him call.

"Emma? That you?"

She turned around, sure that she heard her name, sure she recognized that voice.

He stood feet away from her, holding a small brown bag, wearing a familiar hoodie—faded with time, she thought—but still the same.

"Oh my God, it *is* you!" he said.

"Anton?" She walked towards him, her heart beating wildly. It had been, what? Ten years?

Anton wanted to hug her, but he was uncertain. She hung back just out of reach, stiff and uneasy. She wore a tailored grey suit. Her hair was shorter now. It rested just above her shoulders. She had straightened it; it was smooth and glossy. Her heels gave her more height, but she was still the munchkin he remembered, he thought smiling. She looked powerful nevertheless, and he was afraid to touch her. He noticed a familiar necklace hidden beneath the collar of her shirt, a few pearls exposed.

"This is crazy," he said. "Ten years or somethin' like that. How you been?"

"I've been well," she replied. "Very busy."

"You look it. Where you off to now?" he asked.

"Oh, I have a meeting in a little while," she replied. Her eyes kept falling to the emblem on his chest—the familiar symbol on a familiar piece of clothing that long ago graced her body. She saw herself wearing it in a tiny room that housed the memories of a past love, and the sweat broke out on her hands.

"Yeah? What you doin' now?" he asked.

"I'm a pharmaceutical sales rep," she said, surreptitiously wiping her hands on her skirt.

He let out a low whistle. "That sound important."

She shrugged. "It's a job. I mean, don't get me wrong, I like it, but I'm busy all the time."

"Too busy for a personal life?" he asked.

"I don't know." She wanted to change the subject. "What do you have there?" she asked, pointing to the bag in his hand.

"Bagels. We love us some bagels at our house," he

said. "I'm just droppin' 'em off before I go to work. I'm still workin' at UPS after all these years. I love it. Full time now. Got great benefits. And I'm finishing up a certification to do taxes. You believe that? I'm'll be a CPA on the side."

"That's great," she said. She didn't know what else to say.

"You married?" he asked suddenly. He needed to know.

"Yes, three years," she replied. She did not want to ask it, but she knew she had to. "What about you?"

"Yeah. I been married almost eight years. You believe that?" he asked.

She managed a smile.

He searched her face. He could tell that she was uncomfortable, and it bothered him. He knew it was silly to expect to have an easy conversation, but this was Emma.

"You got kids?" he went on.

"No kids," she replied.

"I thought all women want babies," he said.

"Me too."

There was an uncomfortable silence. She passed a hand over her belly and thought about telling him. It would be the cruelest thing she could ever do, and wondered why she entertained the idea. It was only for a second. But she entertained it.

"What about you?" Emma finally asked. She knew it was the right thing to do to ask however much she didn't want to know. "Do you have kids?"

"I got one. A little boy. His name Jamal. He so funny, Emma. You should see him. That boy make me laugh all the time," Anton said, his face lighting up at the mention of his son. "He two now, and he talkin'. God, I thought I was gonna go to pieces when he said 'Daddy' for the first time. I know that make me sound like a big softie."

"That's sweet," Emma said quietly.

"Jordan say I'm a big cry baby all the time. She say every time he do somethin' new, I lose it," Anton said, chuckling.

Emma could not bear it. She did not want to hear about his wife or know anything about his son. She knew it was foolish and immature, but the pain. She could not comprehend the pain she felt, making her chest tight, making it hard to breathe. She was certain that if she stood there much longer, her heart would fail her. How, after so many years, could she still feel the ripeness of a past pain? Like it had only just happened yesterday and not ten years ago? She felt like an unfaithful wife, a cowardly woman who hid her weakness behind expensive things. As long as she kept thinking of money, she was safe. But she couldn't think of money right now, not with him standing there looking at her. What had she learned in ten years, she thought?

"Man, there just seem like so much to talk about," Anton continued. "But you gotta go to work. I gotta go to work."

She nodded but said nothing.

He pulled a cell phone out of his pants pocket. "What's yo' number?"

She rummaged around in her purse for her business cards. "Here," she said, handing him one.

He smiled at her.

"You always got it all together," he said amused. "Girl, you ain't change a bit."

She prayed he would never call her. She was certain he wouldn't. What could they really share with one another after ten years? How does one recount a decade? They didn't want to know the details of each other's lives. At least she didn't want to know. How could it mean anything to either of them? The stories wouldn't be theirs, not together. Just separate stories with a similar refrain playing in the background: what if. She was shocked by her reaction at seeing him—so changed by his circumstances, yet still the same boy she vowed to love forever. She was embarrassed.

"I better get going then," Emma said.

"A'ight. I call you sometime so we can sit down and really catch up," Anton said. He watched the uncertainty on her face.

"Okay," she replied.

She was visibly unsettled, and she was careful to make no move towards him, but he hugged her anyway. It was gentle and encouraging. And it lingered past the point of appropriateness. Her heart died then, she was sure, as she took in the familiar scent of him, the strong arms holding her. She was aware of nothing around her; the sounds of the city had stopped when he touched her. She felt herself falling into the memory of him, a dangerous place she buried long ago. He released her, and she breathed relief. He saw her exhale, knowing she was holding her breath the whole time he held her. He didn't know why she did that, and it made him sad.

She walked away not looking back.

Her destination was a few blocks ahead. She burst through the front door of the office building and headed straight for the ladies room. She willed herself to hold back the tears until she was in the safety of the bathroom. It was empty, and she quietly thanked God. She closed herself in the last stall, dropping her expensive bags on the floor, and sinking down on the toilet. She did not bother to look if it was clean.

She cried then, letting the raw emotions overtake her. She cried for the loss of her youth that bled out on a bathroom floor many years ago. She cried for the fairytale shattered by an exploding gun. She cried for all of the things she could not tell him, the regret, the fear of a future marked by desperation for things she could never have. She cried for the babies she would never bear.

She pleaded for God to take away her memories of him, but they came one by one, spilling into the forefront of her mind, vivid as the moment they had just happened. And she was seventeen all over again, lying beside him in his warm bed, and had just loved him, was drunk with the love he had poured into her.

"You gonna marry me?" he asked.

"What? Now?" she replied.

"No! Not now. In the future. You gonna marry me in the future?" he asked, absent-mindedly twirling a strand of her hair around his finger. He loved her hair, so soft and shiny.

"If you want," she said quietly.

"What kinda response is that? You know I want you to marry me. Don't even be tryin' to act all nonchalant about it."

She looked at him.

"Yeah, I know words like 'nonchalant'," he said, and she laughed.

"I want to marry you," she said, looking at his face in all seriousness.

"Good," he replied, and pulled her close to him wrapping his arms around her naked back. "You gonna give me babies?"

"What?"

"You heard me. You gonna have my babies? 'Cause I want babies. The world need more good things in it, don't you think?"

"I don't know if I want kids," she said honestly.

"Girl, you crazy. You havin' my babies and that's that," he said, squeezing her until she squealed. "Say you will," he demanded, not letting her go until she agreed.

"Okay, okay! I'll have your babies," she said.

"Good," he said, relaxing his grip and kissing the top of her head.

He rolled her over onto her back and she protested.

"I'm'll be gentle," he promised. "I know you tired and sore,

but I gotta have you again." He looked at her imploringly.

She nodded, and he took her, enveloped her in his arms, kissed her tenderly on the lips as he filled her completely. And he kept his promise. He was gentle.

Emma wiped at her face. She felt empty, drained of everything. Slowly she returned to the familiar shell—the shell of a woman who filled her life with unimportant things because she could not have the only thing that mattered to her. She was robbed of it a long time ago, learning in that moment that the world was nothing but an awful, scary place.

It felt good returning to her normalcy. It was what she became accustomed to. It was a safe feeling, a safe way to be. She drew in a long breath and exited the bathroom stall. She stood at the bathroom sink and began the task of fixing her make-up, making sure she got every detail perfect. She regained control of herself, straightening her suit jacket and smoothing her hair. She lingered in front of the mirror just a moment longer, checking that everything was in its right place. And she recognized herself again. Her face was blank, her blue eyes vacant as though she never had a struggle in her life. As though she never had a feeling. As though she never knew the pain of a broken heart. She liked what she saw and left the bathroom for her meeting.

Far away, on the other side of town, a young man walked through the front door of his house, picked up his little boy, cradled him closely, and wept.

ABOUT THE AUTHOR

S. Walden used to teach English before making the best decision of her life by becoming a full-time writer. She lives in Georgia with her very supportive husband who prefers physics textbooks over fiction and has a difficult time understanding why her characters must have personality flaws. She is wary of small children, so she has a Westie instead. Her dreams include raising chickens and owning and operating a beachside inn on the Gulf Coast (chickens included). When she's not writing, she's thinking about it.

She loves her fans and loves to hear from them. Email her at swaldenauthor@hotmail.com and follow her blog at http://swaldenauthor.blogspot.com where you can get up-to-date information on her current projects.

Other Titles by S. Walden:

Going Under
Honeysuckle Love

Made in the USA
Lexington, KY
29 April 2013